Samantha's Secret

A More Perfect Union Series Book 3

Betty Bolté

www.MysticOwlPublishing.com

Ebook ISBN-13: 978-1-7353748-8-8
Paperback ISBN-13: 978-1-7353748-7-1
Audiobook ISBN-13: 978-1-7353748-6-4

Also by Betty Bolté

Becoming Lady Washington: A Novel
Notes of Love and War

FURY FALLS INN
The Haunting of Fury Falls Inn
Under Lock and Key

A MORE PERFECT UNION SERIES
Elizabeth's Hope
Emily's Vow
Amy's Choice
Samantha's Secret
Evelyn's Promise

SECRETS OF ROSEVILLE SERIES
Undying Love
Haunted Melody
The Touchstone of Raven Hollow
Veiled Visions of Love
Charmed Against All Odds

Preface

Samantha's Secret is the third historical romance I ever published and as such it was written many years ago as I was a new author. It's amazing how much my storytelling skills have improved over the past five years since this book was originally published. The core of the story remains the same, but hopefully with more skilled telling. This edition is a revised version of the third book in the A More Perfect union historical romance series. I have corrected and revised the text throughout the story.

Thanks for reading!

The responsibility of inspiring the gathering had fallen on her. Locating a fitting passage to share with her friends and neighbors had taken several hours earlier in the afternoon. Her father's impressive library contained a wealth of material, but finding a quote worthy of the town's momentous events, indeed the future of the country, had proved a challenge. Eventually she'd uncovered a most fitting sentiment.

On a side path, her parents strolled toward her, arm in arm. They carried flutes of wine like candlesticks against a dark night. Aaron's burly frame dwarfed his petite wife, Cynthia. They each sported gray on their otherwise dark heads, brought on no doubt from the never ending tension and suspicion in town. With the Britons stripping everything of any value as they prepared to leave, her parents had become more and more withdrawn from her. What did they attempt to shield her from? Her biggest fear remained their intention to flee the town, forcing her to accompany them to some far off land, away from her beloved surroundings, her beloved country.

"My darling, you look beautiful this evening." Her father stopped before her and glanced at her mother. "Don't you agree?"

"Yes, of course." Cynthia sipped her wine, cutting off any further comment she may have made. She wore a gown of dark gray with pink insets and small lavender bows dotting its skirts. A white lace cap rested on her dark curls. Her appearance hid the worry she expressed about her reputation among the townspeople, a reputation based upon the frequent deaths of those under her care. Was it the result of bad fortune or bad choices? Samantha had started making notes on the cases she could, but most of the past cases would remain a mystery.

"Thank you for your kind words. I'm pleased the weather cooperated so we could enjoy the garden tonight." Samantha smiled and briefly inclined her head. The mingling crowd wore an array of somber colors mixed in with the occasional pastel gown or trousers. All wore some form of outer garment for warmth. "Another week and it will be too chilly to entertain out of doors. We'd miss a glorious night such as this to share with our friends."

"Indeed, indeed." Aaron's smile faded as he looked around the area, his gaze lighting on first one, then another, of the guests before finally focusing on the two-story home. "This house has served us well for many years. It will be hard to find another as fine."

Samantha heard a note of regret in his voice as her mother squeezed his arm. The sound of sadness raised tiny bumps along her flesh. She studied the shifting emotions playing across his features. "It is a good thing, then, that won't be necessary. The British will pull out ere long, and the town can return to normal."

"You speak the truth." Aaron patted his wife's hand gripping his arm but did not meet Samantha's eyes for a moment. Finally, he locked gazes with her. "The Britons will depart very soon."

Yet his tone—a quaver, a hesitation—suggested something amiss. Worry lines carved a valley between his brows, surrounded his tight lips. Her mother's usually expressive face held no hint as to her feelings other than boredom. Obviously, she must be agitated to have schooled her face into such a rigid mask. What had happened to provoke them so?

"How is Evelyn?" Cynthia changed the subject as she gave her attention to Samantha. "Pray tell me she is not still crying over that man."

"It is to be expected she'd grieve the death of the father of her child." Samantha slowly shook her head. "Even if he did treat her abysmally in the end. At one time, she must have been fond of him."

"So I'm told." Cynthia sighed and folded her hands. "I'll take some soothing tea up to her after everyone has eaten. Which reminds me, I had meant to inquire earlier. Did you have a plate sent up to her?"

"Amy carried a small plate up a while ago. Whether the poor woman ate it or not, I cannot say."

"She still must provide for her infant." Cynthia flexed her fingers and then studied the second floor window. "Evelyn's life has certainly been filled with sorrows and challenges."

"With luck, her fortunes will change for the better while she resides in town." Samantha's experiences would help her counsel the new widow on the hard decisions and unpleasant realities she'd face. In the distance, Amy waved at Samantha to hurry. "Tomorrow, I'll speak with Evelyn about her plans for the future."

"Very kind of you. Ah, I see you're being sought out." Aaron half bowed and then motioned for her to precede him down the path. "Time for the annual salute. Have you chosen a suitable sentiment to share with our guests?"

She nodded, aware of a sense of relief emanating from her parents, and made her way down the path, shells crunching with each step. She glanced back at her father's guarded expression and then drew in a breath, savoring the sweet aroma emanating from the massive rosemary bush huddled in the corner. Eager faces, alight with smiles, surrounded her. The string quartet finished playing Haydn in the background and fell silent.

Benjamin handed her a flute of sparkling wine when she reached the group of people gathered by the banquet table. She frowned, worry blooming inside. His lips pinched together as though he fought pain. His face appeared ashen in the flickering shadows of the lamplight. With surprise, she noticed when she accepted the flute from him that the touch of his hand left moisture on her fingers.

"Benjamin, are you feeling well?" Samantha studied his expression. The perspiration and tautness of his face sparked grave concern in her chest. "Tell me the truth."

"I'm fine, a touch tired." He wiped his hand down his dove gray evening coat and then smiled over Samantha's head. "Excellent. You made it!"

She turned to welcome the new arrival and froze, her flute trembling in tense fingers, the liquid sloshing within the fragile crystal. Dr. Trenton Cunningham. His sandy blond hair waved back from his open expression, crystal blue eyes echoing the wide smile revealing even white teeth. Broad shoulders filled the dark navy evening coat he wore, a canary yellow cravat neatly tied at his throat and tucked into an elaborately embroidered waistcoat. Creamy breeches hugged his strong thighs, and tall black boots completed his attire. Despite the formality of his clothes, Dr. Trent appeared as though he'd recently arrived on board a ship from some distant intriguing port. Fresh and windblown and ready for adventure.

"Benjamin, should you be out here?" Trent strode to stand by his friend, inspecting Benjamin with a sweeping glance. "You look terrible."

"I'll be fine. Besides, I wouldn't want to forego hearing Miss Samantha's toast, after all." Benjamin shook Trent's hand and then drew Amy up to his side.

Trent nodded at Amy, who smiled a greeting. "My heartfelt wishes to you both." He bowed at Samantha, his eyes sparkling as he gazed at her. "Miss Samantha, I'm honored to be included in your gathering this evening."

"I'm pleased your schedule permitted you to attend."

She dipped a curtsy, but her thigh underwent a spasm and jerked in protest. She lurched and flung her hands wide in an attempt to stay on her feet.

Trent grasped her arm as she found her balance, the contact of his hand jolting along every inch of her skin. *Gramercy*. Brows knitted, he gazed at her with concern evident in his countenance. She stepped away, out of his reach, and drew in a long breath. "Thank you."

He half bowed again, his arm sweeping in front of his waist, as he smiled at her. "My pleasure."

Although she'd been in his presence a handful of times—mainly when he challenged and decried her abilities as a healer—she couldn't deny the intense visceral impact she experienced each time. A purely physical effect, of course, one she would scrutinize and then ignore. After all, the combination of a tall gorgeous man who also proved strong and clever could not easily be dismissed. His mere presence was extraordinarily dangerous to her sense of well-being. She forced herself to remain still, appear calm, even while her heart raced. She'd never experienced such a combined sense of imbalance and headlong emotion. A definite curiosity, given her intended path forward.

The last time she'd seen him, Trent had been furious at what he'd called her ineptitude while treating Emily's young nephew the month before. He'd been wrong, of course, as little Tommy fully recovered from the snake bite without the doctor actually doing more than administering a small dose of emetic and then bathing the fever after her treatment. But she'd never had the opportunity to discuss the proper treatment, so he continued to act as though her skills proved inferior to his. After the fact, her mother relayed news of the latest snake bite remedy based on plantains, rum, and tobacco juice. If only she'd learned of the amazingly effective poultice sooner, little Tommy would have never suffered a prolonged ordeal. Next time, she'd know. Another chapter ended and book closed.

Though aware of the disquieting fact Benjamin summoned the young doctor, she'd hoped he'd wait to arrive after the party ended and the guests dispersed. Or at least he might have the courtesy to dawdle until after she'd made her short speech. But he'd shown up as eager and affecting as ever, unsettling her normally unflappable composure preceding her annual duty. Indeed, time had slipped away and the moment arrived. She turned back to face the guests, and raised her glass, the golden wine sloshing in the flute.

She waited for the conversations and laughter to die as one by one they noticed her. When all was quiet except for the call of night birds to one another, she lifted her glass a bit higher. "My friends, we gather this evening as in years past to rejoice in the bounty we've realized this year. As our country begins to define our government and create a new society, consider the wise words from the lauded Anna Bradstreet, who some have called the Tenth Muse, in her wonderfully inspiring *Meditations, Divine and Moral*."

Trent locked gazes with her, disconcerting her already churning thoughts. Strange how his presence caused such an extreme reaction. Was it the animosity she sensed flowing from him like sea foam after a storm? Or could it be more of an underlying awareness triggered by similar interests? He widened his eyes and then winked at her as a slow grin eased onto his lips. Startled, she blinked and then focused instead on the cluster of her closest friends and her parents. She took a breath, trying in vain to calm her agitation, and aimed a shaky smile at the gathering.

She must push through this disconcerting situation as swiftly as she dared. "Miss Bradstreet reminded us that, 'Authority without wisdom is like a heavy axe without an edge, fitter to bruise than polish.' Pray keep this thought in mind as the year draws to a close and we face new challenges. Our governor and other state leaders will need our support and God's guidance."

Glasses clinked all around her to the accompaniment of "Huzza! Huzza!" She let out a sigh masked as a laugh, raising her glass again to acknowledge the well wishes of the people before her.

She sipped the wine, the cheer of the moment echoing inside her heart. The sweet liquid slid down her throat, calming and buoying her at the same time. Looking over the crowd, she noted others mimicking her actions. All but two anyway. Her parents, grim faced and rigid, turned and stalked away. Their actions could only mean one thing. A chill born of dismay and fear froze her smile into place.

The expectant hush ended as the McAlesters' guests turned to each other and quiet conversations resumed. Couples drifted off, heads together, to meander through the winding paths of the herbal garden. An obligatory smile graced Samantha's lush lips. Trent tracked the direction of her gaze, following it to the elderly couple strolling away with unhurried steps but tense posture. He'd seen them earlier, learned the striking woman was the infamously suspect midwife Cynthia McAlester and her tall husband, Aaron, the sly loyalist merchant striving to keep his affairs out of the public eye. A couple meant for each other. Not that any one else characterized them as such, but the rumors moving through town must contain more than a hint of truth. Flicking a glance back to Samantha, he nodded to himself. Their daughter. He hadn't connected them as a family before. He remembered her fumbling attempts to heal the boy with the snake bite, an attempt that ended well only because he'd stepped in to help. She'd been out of her depth with such a delicate situation. No wonder she seemed familiar verging on dangerous. But then, with those lips enticing a man's kiss, her mere presence could become perilous to his equilibrium.

Samantha, although as beautiful as Cleopatra, embodied the outmoded medical approach he vowed to replace with current theories, techniques, and practices. The rise of trained doctors would ultimately force out the uneducated and ill-advised practices of the town's old midwives. While the conflict between the colonies and England raged, he'd been forced to attend university in Philadelphia rather than the prestigious University of Edinburgh in Scotland where he'd dreamed of studying. Still, the professors he studied under had been trained in Edinburgh, like his own father, so his education ranked with the best. On the other hand, women like Mrs. McAlester and Miss Samantha would have to come to grips with the cost of progress. He rather felt sorry for them, truth be told. In another life and circumstance, Samantha might be the type of woman who could prove a perfect companion and maybe even wife, with her understanding and knowledge of the life of one who cares for others. But with the times changing, moving to more modern ways and practices, well… He hoped she had another way to earn her keep after he convinced the town of his superior methods.

Her perplexed expression became a happy smile as she made her way to where Benjamin and Amy chatted with Frank and Emily beside a huge rosemary bush. The pungent aroma mingled with the seaside scents. The four friends greeted her with brief clasps, though Benjamin grimaced when he moved his arm to do so. Trent frowned, concern sweeping down his spine. Benjamin's rifle shot wound. The only reason Trent had been invited to this gathering. Even though they had no idea of his ultimate desire for the town, they treated him with caution even as they called him friend. He snorted. No surprise there.

Benjamin stepped away from the group and motioned Frank aside to have a conversation, handing off what looked like a small silver box with too casual movements. The way they subtly surveyed those around them, as if apprehensive, made Trent suspicious regarding the transaction. Frank slid the item into a pants pocket with a grim nod before the men rejoined the ladies. Mayhap Trent should investigate to satisfy his curiosity if for no other reason.

He strode over to stand by the group, and by extension Samantha, his black evening cloak bumping against his calves when he stopped. Samantha's stiff posture and composed countenance spoke volumes, revealing her level of concern with his company. She stood tense and ready, her arms crossed as if to ward off an attack, the soft fabric of her shawl quaking with her agitation. Although she wore a resolute smile, she kept a watchful eye on him as he joined the clutch of friends.

"Good evening." Benjamin nodded once. "Thanks for being here."

"My pleasure." Trent spread his cloak open enough to allow cooler air inside, then tugged the points of his waistcoat down into place. "How are you faring?"

"I'll tell you. He pretends nothing is wrong." Amy clasped a white gloved hand on Benjamin's good arm. "But I can tell he's in significant pain. More with each passing minute." She scrutinized Benjamin's face, frowned, glanced at Samantha and then back to meet Trent's eyes. "In fact, he's worse now than a few moments ago. Can either of you help him?"

"The poultice will take time to have full effect." Samantha stiffened at the inclusion of Trent so easily and moved closer to Benjamin. "Is it any better yet or would you prefer for me to redress the wound?"

"Come now, Miss McAlester." Trent stepped forward, drawing her attention. "Your particular skills are no longer needed as Benjamin has requested I attend to his injury henceforth."

Samantha blinked twice as she squared her shoulders, her chest thrusting forward to lend an intriguing view of creamy cleavage. Not that she seemed to notice, but the smoothness of her skin as it deepened into shadow between her breasts tempted him to explore. He inhaled sharply. An outrageous desire, one to set aside posthaste. She studied him when he met her gaze, her eyes narrowed and then focused on Benjamin. "Is that so?"

Benjamin shifted his weight to stand closer to Amy, one trouser leg half-disappearing into the voluminous folds of her long skirts. "Not exactly, Miss Samantha. Trent has been trained by the best minds in Philadelphia, so I asked him to assist you in my treatment."

Samantha lifted her chin and then turned to study Trent for several moments. "I really do not need your assistance, Dr. Trent. However, since Benjamin insists, I shall endeavor to consult you when any question arises. But pray stay out of my way as much as possible."

Damnation, he had thought her beautiful before. When her eyes sparked and her cheeks pinked with suppressed anger, he couldn't look away. "With all due respect, there is no call for you to trouble your pretty head with the matter."

Amy gasped, her brows arching. "Why would you say such a thing?"

"My apologies if I've offended you, Miss Amy." He shrugged but continued gazing upon Samantha's glowing features with admiration, including her dark pink lips. Invitingly ripe lips which, sadly, were definitely off limits to him.

"I merely believe Miss Samantha should concentrate on other areas more suited to her training. Assisting at child birth, for instance."

Samantha lifted one brow and drew in a long breath. Letting it out slowly, she moistened her lips with a flick of her tongue, stirring a reaction in Trent's groin. Damnation. He couldn't permit such a reaction. He cleared his throat as she clasped her gloved hands before her, searching his face until he grew uncomfortable and glanced away to compose himself.

"I can assure you, gentlemen," Samantha said, her words clipped and voice pulsating with suppressed emotions, "my talents and training enable me to treat any illness or complaint my patients may have."

"Any? My sweet woman, no doctor could hope to heal or cure every patient." Trent grinned at the naiveté of her statement. She may be beautiful but not necessarily as savvy as he'd been led to believe. "You're mistaken on the point."

"My mother has worked all her life to help those around her and she taught me everything she knows. I learned a great deal from her as well as a few other healers, as my friends can attest." She shot a look at Amy and Benjamin, one brow raised while she waited.

Trent frowned at the silent message passing between the friends. Exactly who were the others she trained under? Why not be forthright and state her credentials rather than resort to subterfuge and misdirection?

"Indeed, I can vouch for Samantha's abilities." Amy moved forward, her long skirts rustling, and reached out to grasp Samantha's arm to draw her closer. "For example, everyone knows how much she has helped the poor folk living up on The Neck, often for no compensation."

"On the mainland side of the peninsula? That's what's referred to as The Neck, right?" Trent allowed a short guffaw before the stern expression on Benjamin's face quelled the impulse to laugh outright. Working with the slaves and the free blacks did not recommend her efforts. They'd take whatever help they could find. "I suppose the amount of payment was commensurate to her abilities."

"You, sir, having only recently arrived in this city have no right to demean me with such a statement." Samantha bristled, unclasping her hands to brace them on her slim hips. Her green eyes glittered like bottle glass, cold and harsh. "How dare you?"

She glared at him but he couldn't stop looking at her. What was the question? He shook his head, her flaring nostrils and primly compressed lips entrancing. He really must pay attention and not let his physical response to her distract his objective. And yet… "Has any one ever told you how pretty you are when your eyes flash in anger? It takes my breath." Trent smiled, trying to divert the conversation to calmer seas. "You're a very handsome woman, Miss Samantha."

"Do not change the subject at hand." Samantha's tone held firm but her shoulders relaxed a small amount. "Pretty words will not sway me."

Trent considered the gorgeous woman before him. The softening of her posture implied she might be amenable to knowing him better despite her claim. He mentally shook his head as he perused the details of her face, the sprinkling of freckles across her pert nose, the crystalline nature of her emerald eyes, and the pure perfection of her skin. Unfortunately, the discord between them could only deepen as a result of their opposition on the matter of patient care.

"You two need to calm yourselves. Don't you agree, Ben?" Amy grinned and glanced up at Benjamin's white face. Her expression shifted to reflect her extreme disquiet at what she saw. "Ben, let me help you home. You need to rest."

Samantha edged closer to Benjamin, peering at him. "I do not understand why you have suddenly taken such a turn for the worse." Samantha examined Benjamin's face, a frown marring her classic features. "It's as if a shadow passed over your grave or a candle was snuffed."

Trent tore his gaze from Samantha to inspect Benjamin's aspect. He didn't like what he detected there. "The change in his countenance is indeed a pertinent fact which should inform our next decision regarding his care."

Benjamin nodded and then winced at the movement. "I believe Amy is right. Some rest may help alleviate my discomfort."

Trent cast a practiced eye over his new friend and patient, concerned at the pallor, the tension, and fatigue accompanying the trauma associated with the gunshot wound. He'd require assistance and observation. "I'll go with you."

Benjamin waved him off, then permitted Amy to take his arm as much needed support. "I'll be fine tonight. Just tired. But tomorrow, come tomorrow."

"I'll be there at first light." The combined effects of Benjamin's symptoms concerned him, but by delaying until the next day he had time to consult with his father and his extensive library of medical texts. "Go home and rest. Nothing else. I'll see you in the morning."

"We both will." Samantha patted Amy's shoulder before the couple slowly strolled down the winding path toward the arbor draped with dormant rose vines. They passed under the shadowy arch and disappeared into the waiting street beyond. "I do hope he's had a brief relapse which shall pass."

Emily shook her head. "I have a bad feeling about all of this, Samantha."

"As do I." Samantha folded her arms, her gaze lingering on the spot where Benjamin and Amy had disappeared.

"Em, I should see you home as the hour grows late, and I must be up early on the morrow." Frank crooked his arm to receive the weight of Emily's hand tucked around his elbow. "If you'll excuse us, Miss Samantha."

"Certainly." Samantha grinned after the couple strolling down the garden path. She turned back to Trent and sighed. "I suppose I should start winding up this affair. If you'll excuse me?" She tilted her head and then pivoted in preparation to move away.

Trent's heart raced as she turned to leave. He couldn't let her escape. Not yet. "Walk with me, Miss Samantha?" He didn't want to let her go even though she left him unsettled and defensive. For one thing, he wanted to understand her plan. For another, intriguingly, she enthralled him with her beauty, her voice, her smile, as fleeting as he'd seen it. "We should discuss our plans for Benjamin."

She paused to evaluate his request for a moment before nodding once, her black hair, pulled up in an intricate style with a cascade of curls, dancing about her shoulders. "Would you be so kind as to hand me a glass of wine from the tray? I'm parched."

"Very well, my fair queen." He made an elaborate bow, a brow lifted as he smiled at her, tempting her to play along with his charade. He wanted to win her over, to know her not on a professional level but on a personal one.

Startled, her eyes grew wide and then she blinked before raising the back of her hand to her brow and leaning as though about to fall. "Pray hurry, kind sir, before I faint away from lack of wine."

She had a sense of humor after all. Grinning, he clasped her hand and pulled her upright. "Indeed. Stay here while I search for a bolstering beverage for your enjoyment."

His smile spread as he turned to seek out the refreshment.

After a quick skim of the crowd, he spotted a young black woman slowly moving among the guests. Motioning to her, he waited for the girl to reach him, her long black gown relieved only by a white frilly apron and matching kerchief about her neck. As he watched her approach, sidling between a host of fellow residents as they laughed and chatted, it occurred to him every person in attendance at Samantha's party would need to be convinced his way of practicing the healing arts surpassed those of their friend and neighbor. Samantha had won the esteem of many, which also indicated their belief in her abilities. Changing their opinions of who to trust would prove a daunting task, but he'd had a great deal of practice at being persistent and even pigheaded if it came down to it. If he had any hope of seeing his ultimate goals come to pass, he needed a plan of his own.

Finally, the girl wended her way close enough and Trent snagged two flutes from the tray. He turned to offer one to Samantha, unsure of exactly what he wanted to relay to her. "M'lady."

"Thank you, kind sir." She lowered her hand to receive the glass and flashed a grin before sipping the garnet-colored wine. "I feel better already. Did you have something you wished to discuss?"

"Nothing specific." He motioned to the path leading away from the lamplight toward the shadows of the garden. As they walked, perhaps he'd fasten upon a proper starting point for their conversation. He simply had to stop staring at her so he could formulate a coherent thought not centered upon the complications resulting from his strong attraction to her. "Shall we?"

She stepped off and he matched her stride, surprised to note her limping ever so slightly as they strolled together. He considered offering his arm, but she stayed far enough apart to suggest she wouldn't welcome such an act. Although he no longer trusted the simples of a healer, the quantity and variety of plants they strolled past impressed even him. Indeed, the source of most medicines based on organic compounds could be readily produced using the plants in the extensive and inviting garden. The collection alone increased the value of the property despite its less than ideal location in town. So many of the buildings surrounding the house had burned in recent years, due to accidents and bombardments, until the area felt abandoned.

"Might I inquire as to the cause of your limp? How did you hurt yourself?" He held his breath. She might very well reveal a dark and questionable past with her explanation. Or the story might be related to a simple injury while working among her medicinal herbs. Regardless, would she entrust the details to him?

Her dark jade eyes flashed his direction then slid away. She lifted one shoulder and then let it settle back into place. Her gaze searched the black velvet heavens, a sliver of moon hanging over the party. "From behind the house, the stars are shining brighter, don't you think?"

He could take a hint. Her business, not his. He'd probably react the same way, assuming he had a secret regarding his past. Smiling to himself, he nodded. "Indeed."

She studied the sky for several strides. "This is not a good time for treating Benjamin's wound."

Frowning, Trent mulled over her words. What did she mean? He lifted his gaze to match the direction in which she looked. The cool evening air chilled around him as her meaning crystallized. "Please tell me you don't believe the stars' alignment has anything whatsoever to do with how well medicine works."

She tucked her shawl more tightly about her shoulders as she turned down a side path. "Absolutely. I'm surprised your fancy education didn't include an appreciation for the intricacies of nature's relationships."

"No, no, no." He shook his head for emphasis on his point. "I do not mean to offend, but this is one reason why I believe the old ways are based on fallacy and superstition."

"Yet they've proven successful for millennia."

"Success, like beauty, is in the eye of the beholder."

"Mayhap. How do you define it then?"

Trent examined the points of light in the sky, mulling her question and taking his time formulating a response. A whip-poor-will pierced the quiet surrounding them, the distant hum of the other guests creating a supportive consonance to their conversation. "Success means methodologies and practices which yield the same results each time they are employed. Despite which doctor uses them, the time of year, or what constellations are visible."

Samantha laughed out loud, a light trill of sound reminiscent of a warbler. "How do you expect every doctor to have the same results? Depending on not only the time of year but also on the options at hand, each will have different experience and capabilities. You said as much yourself, no doctor can cure everything."

"I intend to found a new hospital with trained doctors from around the globe." His pace quickened as he spoke of his dreams. He'd been working toward his goal since childhood when he comprehended not knowing the cause of an illness led to a person's death. He swallowed the emotion threatening to choke off his air. "After the fighting ends and Americans can begin to truly establish who we are as a country. Then my hospital will be among the leaders in medical advances, rivaling the hospital in Edinburgh itself."

Samantha halted abruptly, her skirts eddying about her ankles. She regarded him for two breaths, a frown forming.

"And as a result, you'll force healers such as myself out of business?"

Her fierce expression gave him pause. Made him reconsider blurting out the simple, "naturally," forming on his tongue. He'd learned at university he needed to work on diplomacy, improving his manners when working with patients. For that matter, people in general. But standing in front of this woman, he wanted her good opinion of him, and moreover he needed her to be in his life. He wouldn't make a stupid blunder which would jeopardize that possibility. He swallowed and hedged. "Not necessarily, no."

"But if it happens, so be it. Is that what you're saying?" She propped fists on hips, a scowl emphasizing her position on his plans. "You have no right to wipe away my practice in order for you to have one. The people will have a say in the matter."

"They will definitely have a say, and I'm afraid you'll find them flocking to the proven methods good doctors use. I'm sure they will see it's in their best interest." Trent studied the play of emotions competing in her expression. Perhaps she didn't realize the benefits she'd reap as his plan unfolded. Perhaps a gentle reminder would go a long way to smoothing out her ruffled feathers. "Don't worry. I'm sure you'll be happier tending your home without all the worry associated with caring for the ill and frail. You can still be a midwife, even if you're not a healer as you are now. After all, you'll want to find a good man to marry and bear his children."

"Do not presume to fathom what would make me happy. You do not have the right, Dr. Trent. We shall work together to please Benjamin, but nothing more. Now, if you're through deciding my life for me, I have ignored my real guests for far too long." With a curt nod, she spun and hurried back down the path.

What had he said wrong? He trailed after her, sauntering along the winding path as he considered the equally intriguing and infuriating woman. Reviewing their conversation, he found nothing unreasonable in his opinion. She must have simply misinterpreted his intent. *Women.* Leave it to the female of the species to take affront at common sense observations. Over time, she would come to appreciate the sensibility of his words.

Chapter Two

Soft sunlight washed across the street, urging the birds to awaken and serenade the day from their nests in the young trees planted along the thoroughfare. Low clouds hung to the west, the scent of rain heavy on the chill breeze. Samantha's dark blue skirts stirred up swirls of dust with each marching step. Deep concern for Benjamin's welfare had spurred her to rise extra early to finish preparing the stronger ointment she'd decided to try. She shifted the clay pot, wrapped in a red-and-white checkered cloth, to rest on one hip. The scent of ground cinnamon, mace, and cloves mixed with cow and hens dung lingered in the air as she hurried along Queen, past the burned out shells of houses intermixed with newly rebuilt homes, then turned right onto Bay. The stark memory of the terrifying fires of 1778 burning through nearly half of the town chilled her. Those buildings had stood so close to her parents' house that they'd nearly lost their home in the conflagration. She pulled her cloak tighter to ward off the cold inside as well as the wind whipping by. A large hunting dog loped across the street in front of her, disappearing down an alley. She calculated the time based on the sun's angle and then hastened her pace.

Perchance she'd arrive before the egotistical Dr. Trent interfered. Again.

His idea that she'd want to tend home and hearth instead of, not in addition to, caring for others galled until she quivered in outrage. Who did he think he was, taking such a high-handed view of her future? Speaking of which… Upon her return home, she'd sit down with Evelyn and help her plot out possible options, as well. The poor woman could not stay upstairs, cloistered in a room with her baby, forever. She must face her fate, as Samantha well understood. Her steps carried her swiftly down the street as her thoughts spun and dove in her mind like the river in the sky created by unending flocks of migrating starlings.

The slender woman, so beaten down by her husband's heavy handed ways, showed courage in the face of the previous threat. She'd been like a mother bear, protecting her young cub from the renegades only a day after bringing him into the world. That courage echoed the same kind of strength Samantha was known for, and would serve the young widow well as she gathered the pieces of her life and strode forward. With a flash of a smirk, Samantha realized she and Evelyn shared another status, though one few others knew about.

In due course, she arrived at Captain Sullivan's warehouse, which remained closed so early in the morning. The row of silent two-story buildings stood as a testament to the resiliency of the populace. Fire had destroyed half of the buildings, but they'd already been replaced with new brick and wood structures. Their freshly painted walls and shining windows fronted on the river and the harbor beyond. Hard to believe they'd only recently been built. She shook her head, recalling tales of the numerous out of control fires the town had battled over the years. Thoughts for another day. She slipped down the private alley and turned to hurry up the flight of wooden steps leading to the rooms above the shop, where Benjamin had taken up temporary quarters. She rapped on the door three times. While she waited, she surveyed the area stretching in either direction behind the row of businesses.

The rear of the store faced a narrow lane with white-washed clapboard houses on the other side. Down the way, she spotted the blacksmith opening the livery for business, carriages and various iron pieces visible as mute testimony of the man's skill. Beside the livery, a cabinetmaker's sign swung in the wind in front of a narrow single house, the entry door on the left side leading presumably into the dwelling's rooms as evidenced by the windows on the right. Next to that, a double house—one with rooms flanking a central hall rather than having the hall on one side and rooms along the other side as in a single house—boasted a sign advertising the tavern famous for its food and music performances. Indeed, taverns as a place of business and social activity constituted the most popular kind of business in Charles Town. Artisans followed close behind, providing bricklaying, glass making, leather tanning, and silversmithing. She loved the port city and its people, so varied and vibrant in times of peace. She wanted nothing more than to continue as healer and midwife, to give back to them after all they had done for her. Especially, after her disastrous adventure brought her home, reeling.

The door swung open behind her and she spun around, a smile in place at the hope Benjamin felt well enough to be on his feet. That the poultice she'd applied would yield the usual outcome, and he'd beam right back at her before long.

"Good morning." Trent angled his torso in a half bow and winked. "I'm glad you decided to join us, my lady."

She clutched the cloth-wrapped package closer. Her smile stretched into a nervous grin she feared revealed the depth of her unsettled emotions swirling through her in the man's company. What in the world was wrong with her? She wrestled her lips into a softer more normal line. Something about the handsome and exasperating man set her senses on fire, snatching her breath and leaving her legs trembling. And making her behave like a silly schoolgirl with an inappropriate crush on the teacher. But she'd come out to this part of town for Benjamin's benefit, not Trent's. She refused to appear any less confident than him.

"It's not as late as all that." She squared her shoulders before brushing past him when he stepped back. "What have you done with Benjamin? How does he fare?"

She paused inside the door to let her eyes adjust to the dim interior, finally spotting Benjamin sitting in a large cushioned chair by the crackling fire. His head rested on the back of the chair, eyes closed, apparently dozing. From where she stood across the room, a discernible tension pinched his pale features. Gramercy. Not better, then.

Early the afternoon previous, he'd seemed fine. A touch tired, mayhap. But last evening, he'd seemed almost normal and then without warning he appeared weaker. What had changed? She searched her memory of the previous night, without locating a reason for the change.

"Still in some distress, unfortunately." Trent nudged the door closed. He strode to stand with her as she continued observing Benjamin, trying to assure herself of his condition. After a moment, her attention was drawn by Trent shifting beside her, positioning himself closer at her side. Trent frowned as he blinked at her and then stared at the cloth-wrapped package in her hands. "What is that terrible smell?"

She stiffened at the derision laced through his words. "A green ointment I made to help heal the wound and lessen the amount of bruising."

He huffed at her description, nose wrinkling. "What's in it? Manure?"

"Yes, naturally, that is one of the ingredients. Mixed with many powerful herbs and spices. Oh, and black dew snails of course. It's one of the stronger poultices I have and will surely help him heal."

"If the stench doesn't kill us all first." He waved a hand in front of his face, his features screwed into a disgusted expression.

"Such is the petulant whine of a child, doctor." She turned and laid the package and her medicine bag on the square table situated under the single window with a lone ladder-back chair for company. Tugging off her gloves, she placed them on the wood surface, beside the lit oil lamp, and glanced over her shoulder at Trent. "The ointment has worked marvels for me over the years when the need arose."

"I hope the need never arises again." Trent grimaced, moving away from where she stood. "But when have you used it successfully in the past?"

She began unwrapping the cloth, revealing the gray clay pot with its red stopper. She turned to Benjamin, his countenance reflecting an unacceptable amount of pain. They must do something to make him comfortable. "For the injury to my thigh last year. Is Benjamin awake, do you think?"

"Yes, I am." Benjamin opened his eyes, his trademark grin fleeting as he shifted his position. "Wish I wasn't, though."

"We'll find a way to heal the wound and make you better." Samantha approached him and laid a hand on his forehead, feeling the heat before her fingers even touched the dry skin. She ignored Trent as he stepped closer, his proximity renewing the tremor in her hands. She busied them with checking the pulse in Benjamin's neck, praying Trent wouldn't notice. "Won't we?"

Trent nodded as he touched the back of his fingers to

Benjamin's brow. "I conferred with my father last evening about your condition. He agreed we need to bleed you to release the bad humors which will also help reduce the fever."

Samantha frowned, considering the suggestion. In her experience, the results of scarification varied in extremes. Either the patient got better or they died. "Where would you cut him, and how much blood would be required?"

Trent lifted a brow at her interrogation as he leaned toward Benjamin and motioned to his right forearm. "I believe below the wound is best. I'd make four small incisions and let them bleed until they fill the measured bowl I brought for the purpose. That should restore balance to his humors and allow him to rest comfortably."

Benjamin's ashen face paled even more as he gripped the arms of the chair. "I don't profess to tolerate the sight of my own blood. I can handle others, but not my own. Must you employ bloodletting?"

Trent regarded the man reclining on the chair. "It's that or rely on the old, unreliable ways like that putrid ointment Samantha concocted."

Putrid? Had he no sense? She straightened her spine and crossed her arms, literally holding herself together so she wouldn't lash out at the maddening man. The tremor disappeared with the rush of anger his statement evoked. She could temporarily disable him with one swift move. One swift kick in a sensitive place as a last effort to stop the flow of foolish commentary spewing from his mouth. "I told you, it's worked well for me, so you have no call in denouncing its effectiveness. Not to me."

"I see. That's why you still limp, because it proved such a great solution?" Trent turned back to their patient, effectively dismissing her complaint as he addressed Benjamin. "You don't need to watch if you don't care to, my friend, but we should do this as soon as possible."

"Why are you in such a hurry?" Samantha crossed her arms and regarded the two burly men. Surely they had time to give her simple the chance to work. She didn't cotton to releasing blood on a whim. "He's obviously against the idea. You should listen to your patient's desires."

"The longer we wait the more out of balance his humors will become." Trent paused in his preparations to peer at Benjamin. "We can do the wait-and-see method and hope you improve. Or we can employ my method, which has a better success rate. What do you wish me to do?"

"Very well." Benjamin released a bone-weary sigh and struggled to his feet with Trent's help. "Where do you wish for me to be? On the bed?"

"That is best. Here, lean on me." Trent braced an arm around Benjamin's waist, supporting him as they slowly walked out of the common room.

Yes, it was best for Benjamin to be on the bed so that when he fainted they wouldn't have to catch him. Benjamin had made his choice, so she'd abide by it. Samantha bit her lip as the two men disappeared into the bedroom ignoring her presence as if she were nothing more than a fly on the wall. Trent's treatment of her efforts made her seethe. Before she confronted Trent again, she must compose herself. Her entire life's work centered on seeking out effective ways to treat illness and injury. She'd read every book her father owned on topics ranging from politics to geography to medicine. Shadowed her mother on countless visits to the sick and hurt and dying, observing everything, assisting when asked, and comforting when needed. Sat patiently under the tutelage of the Cherokee and Creek shamans in order to fathom the intricate ways and intera-ctions of various aspects of nature. Combined and tested a multitude of herbs with different types of dirt and ingredients such as chicken manure, animal hair, and spider webs.

Learned about using unusual ingredients, such as ground quartz and even human urine, to effect a cure. Not every attempt succeeded, of course, but such was reality. Trent's disregard of her experience and abilities left an unpleasant taste of dismissal on her tongue.

She trailed after them, pleased to find the tiny bedroom clean and boasting two windows permitting light and air into the small space. Trent eased Benjamin down to sit on the side of the bed. Then he strode back into the main room, brushing past her with a quick grin, and returned in a moment or two with his medicine bag. Agitation over his dismissal of her swirled with the jolt of lightning shooting through her as a result of that little boy smile. The leather bag he carried in one hand likely proved necessary in order to convey all of the tools of his profession. Some of which, she was sure, resembled butchering implements. Samantha disliked the idea of bloodletting, but she had witnessed its effectiveness several times. It failed nearly as often, however. Why did it work on some occasions but not others? The question plagued her thoughts. Similar to the ointment, it seemed no one treatment proved useful in all situations. Would it work for Benjamin? There was so much mystery surrounding the causes of illnesses. Maybe one day answers would come to light, but for the time being all healers worked blind.

"After you finish, Trent, I'll apply my ointment." She smiled when he tensed but continued laying out his instruments. She would not let him ignore her or set aside what she could contribute. Her reputation as well as her friend's life were at stake. "The combination of our experience to determine the treatments will have the best chance of success. Agreed?"

Trent busily removed a dry bowl from his bag to catch the blood, followed by a scalpel with its handle at a sharp angle to position the cutting blade more comfortably for the doctor to hold. Which of course did nothing to make the patient more comfortable with the idea of being sliced open while they watched. She suppressed a shiver. If only they could numb the area before cutting. The thought sent a shudder rocking across her shoulders and she folded her arms to quell the motion. She wouldn't have permitted him to perform such an act on her person, preferring the traditional ways of healers, whether white or Indian. The newer approaches left much to be desired in patient care and comfort, to her mind.

She cleared her throat to draw Trent's attention. "I do wish we could wait a few days—"

Trent frowned at her from where he kneeled in front of Benjamin, a look demanding for her silence, and then focused on Benjamin's arm. "Please, do not babble on about the alignment of the stars again."

"Stars?" Benjamin raised both brows and peered at her. "What do the stars have to do with anything?"

"Everything." Samantha moved so she could supervise Trent as he prepared to make the incisions. She had no time to inform Benjamin or Trent of the strong reasoning behind her beliefs or the history of its effectiveness. Still, they needed to understand why she persisted with her opinion. "Astrology is very important when it comes to knowing the best time for certain activities. Healing among them."

"So you think we should delay the bloodletting?" Benjamin focused on her rather than Trent's hands. "Because the stars are not aligned properly?"

Trent had strong, capable hands, with long fingers tapering to narrow tips making it easier to perform delicate tasks such as slicing and stitching. Or soothing a frightened child. Or even calming a distraught woman as her husband lay ill. Or dying from an enemy musket ball. *Stop. Focus.* She returned her consideration to Trent's quickly moving hands.

"Exactly. The stars and planets impact life forms on Earth and in the ocean. Connections reach between the many elements of our world, engaging with each other in ways we do not fully comprehend. Unfortunately, we cannot risk delaying." Samantha smiled to reassure her friend. "It's best we proceed posthaste to make you well so your loving woman does not wring my neck."

Benjamin rewarded her with a weak smile. Samantha prevented a sad sigh from escaping when she considered the difference between his normal brazen grin and his current state. A flash of silver drew her attention to the scalpel in Trent's hand descending toward its questionable mission. Benjamin's eyes widened and then screwed shut as he clenched his jaw against the new pain in his arm. With a prolonged moan, Benjamin slumped onto his side, his right arm stretched out where Trent gripped it.

Samantha peered at the man and then up at Trent. "He passed out."

"Good." Trent slit the skin three more times, the blood beading and then rushing upon its release into the wide, deep, pewter vessel resting on the floor beneath Benjamin's arm.

"We'll leave them open until the bowl is full." Trent rose to his feet and wiped off the scalpel before wrapping it in a clean cloth and placing it back into the bag. "I suppose it's only right to allow you to try the ointment you brought."

"Thank you. As long as we maintain respect for each other, partnering to aid Benjamin need not be uncomfortable for either of us." The moment had arrived when she could demonstrate the traditional methods remained as good as or better than the new practices Trent preferred. She would not permit him to impair her reputation in town, nor be pushed aside as inconsequential. A frisson of concern wiggled down her back at the half-grin he aimed her direction. He expected her attempt would prove the opposite. Steeling her resolve, she nodded. "I'll only be a moment."

She hurried to retrieve the small jar. Snatching it off the table, she turned to go back to Benjamin's side, only to remember the clean cloth. Quickly grabbing it, she rushed into the chilly front bedroom. A glance at the bowl filling with blood revealed she had a few minutes before she could apply the aromatic mixture. She placed the items on the floor by the bed, arranging them within easy reach. What to do next? Her mother preached to her endlessly about idle hands being the devil's playthings. The scent of the ointment reached her nose.

"Perhaps some fresh air will help revive him." She caught Trent's attention by folding her hands before her skirts. "Do you agree?"

"Opening the windows may help, and it will reduce the odor of the ointment." He waved her toward the windows. "Please. While you do, I'll put pressure on the incisions so they stop bleeding."

Crossing the small room in three strides, she pushed the windows open enough to allow the frosty morning air to rush inside. Sounds of the town coming to life on the street below filtered into the room. Drawing a deep breath, she relished the refreshing breeze. Soon, based on the fragrance filling the room, a cold rain would arrive and settle the dust on the street. She leaned out the window and watched a carriage pulled by two horses move past the many gentlemen and ladies walking on the road. Horses waited at hitching rails. Sandpipers and terns flitted, hopped, and flew up and down the thoroughfare. Rain clouds continued to darken and build to the west.

"Miss Samantha, if you will, it's time to work your magic on him." Trent closed his bag with a sharp snap.

"It is not witchcraft." She pulled back inside the room and then strode to the sleeping man's side. She opened the pot where she'd left it on the floor and then addressed Trent standing at the foot of the bed. "My way may seem like magic to the uninformed, but I'd think you would have a better appreciation since the traditional approach forms the basis for your practices."

"Yet there'd be no need for improvements on something that worked without fail." Trent moved to stand behind her as she bent over Benjamin. "Let me see what you're doing."

The combination of his nearness coupled with his distrust accelerated her pulse. She took a deep breath to steady her nerves as well as her hands. *Ignore him. Concentrate.* Using one corner of the soft linen cloth, she scooped the green ointment from the container and onto the wound, and then also on the four incisions. The salve should help them heal with as little scarring as possible. Satisfied, she straightened and wiped her hands on a clean corner of the rag. Then she froze when Trent's hands landed on either side of her waist, squeezing gently as he indicated with a gentle tug for her to step aside. Her pulse echoed in her ears at his touch. Gramercy, what next?

"If you're finished, I'll bandage the wounds to keep them clean." His deep voice vibrated down her flesh, thrilling and daring. He seemed in no hurry to release her, but suddenly the aim behind his words sank in.

Bandages? "No, do not." She spun around to keep him from following through on his intent. He stood too close. Her breasts brushed his chest and erupted in fiery tingles, which ignited a pulsing response between her legs. The backs of her knees struck the bedframe. Her eyes widened and she gasped before placing both hands on his arms and pushing him back a step. "They… The wounds must be left open." Her voice emerged weak and uncertain.

"I—" Trent's gaze flicked to her mouth then back to meet hers. He closed the distance between them again but left a polite, if too small, gap between their bodies. He reached to grasp her arms. "I think…"

"Wh-what happened?" Benjamin's gravelly voice sounded behind her, filling the pause left by Trent's sudden silence.

Samantha pushed Trent away again with both hands, her nerves humming from the intensity of the unexpected emotion when they'd faced each other, chest to chest. She struggled to restore some shred of composure as she turned to smile at Benjamin, who sat rubbing his forehead with one hand. "You fainted, but it's over. Now you should rest."

"We've done all we can for the moment." Trent stepped around Samantha to talk to their patient, one hand resting in the small of her back. "I'll come by later to check on you."

"As will I." The audacity of the man. Samantha stepped to the side and shot a glare in Trent's direction as his hand fell away. "We're in this together."

"Thank you for your concern and care." Benjamin raised a brow as he smirked first at Trent, then Samantha, and back again to Trent. "I'm glad you've worked out a way to join forces on my behalf."

"Between us, we'll ensure you're fit as a fiddle long before your wedding day." Trent shook hands with Benjamin and then stepped away to pick up his bag. "Shall I walk you home, Samantha?"

Gramercy, not if she could prevent it. "No, thank you. I have other patients to see." Besides, she needed to put distance between the two of them before she caught fire. Lifting her chin, she acknowledged first Benjamin and then Trent with a confidence she didn't feel. "With both of us caring for our friend, he'll be well in no time."

"Yes, we shall make sure of it." Trent bade farewell to Benjamin and then ushered her outside. He slipped his hat on and then touched the brim before clattering down the long flight of steps to the ground below.

Only after he'd turned the corner did she release the breath she'd held and then started to descend the stairs. She placed each foot carefully on a tread, slowly making her way to the ground. She fought the urge to run, hide, leave.

The depth of awareness of Trent's every look, every movement, every word spoken, even the subtle scent clinging to him, set her on edge. Made her long to flee. Of course, she couldn't act on such tempting desires. Not with a patient needing her ministrations. What if her ointment failed? What if Benjamin died? She caught her breath at the memory of Trent's hands on her waist and then her body's visceral response to him. What if she fell in love with the one man who could ruin her?

The Neck never failed to depress Samantha. She should be used to it after the numerous visits she'd made. Yet something in the very air filtering into her lungs via quick shallow breaths conveyed a sense of hope held down by helplessness. Clapboard one-room houses desperate for a coating of whitewash flanked the rutted dirt road she traversed in a light carriage. The earlier rain shower had created a muddy mess of the street and left the afternoon cold and damp. Over the bobbing head of the chestnut horse pulling the conveyance, she nodded to several dark skinned women wearing somber gray dresses with white caps on their heads ambling toward her. The maids likely were on their way back to their small homes, such as they were, returning from working at the manor house farther up the road, out of sight of the slaves' quarters. Samantha pulled on the reins and halted her horse in front of a house distinguished by the swept front yard, a child-sized hoop and stick leaning against the step, and a smattering of weary rose bushes guarding the front door. A wooden barrel sat half under the eaves of the low pitched roof, positioned to catch rain to provide fresh water for the occupants. The area in front of the house featured shimmering puddles from the recent showers scattered among the patches of grass and sand. Relief, sweet and sharp, flooded through her when Lydia greeted her from the open door.

Great with child, Lydia moved with the cumbersome grace of a woman who had birthed five children. Her four sturdy boys had grown old enough to work out in the fields like their father, leaving the tired yet determined mother alone with her three-year-old daughter who ran past her and into the street. Lydia laughed, a deep chuckle rich with love, and eased down the one step to follow her daughter over to the carriage. The plantation owner had grudgingly released Lydia from her strenuous duties after Samantha intervened on her behalf as the time drew near for the baby to arrive. The only argument that had worked on the man ended up being based on money. She'd finally convinced him it was in his best interest to take the necessary precautions to avoid the potential loss of a valuable slave if the woman were to die in childbirth. Instead, Lydia worked on mending the other slaves' clothing. Even though she continued to contribute to the never-ending work of a plantation, the plantation owner had been terribly ugly about it. He'd pushed to the point of threatening to seek payment from her father should she fail to keep the woman healthy, but she'd pressed the matter until he relented. Observing her patient's deliberate movements, Samantha's relief grew. She'd done the right thing for her after all.

"Miss Samantha! Miss Samantha!" The child's high-pitched voice sang out her greeting as she danced in front of the house, the hem of her brown dress jumping about dirty knees.

"Good day, Angel." Samantha wrapped the reins around the brake and stepped quickly from the carriage in time to scoop the little one into her arms. "I've missed your smile."

Angel giggled when Samantha tickled her side and then sobered. "I missed you. You've been away a long time."

"Too long. I agree." Samantha kissed the child's cheek before lowering her to the ground, ruffling her dark hair. One day maybe she'd have her own child. A bitter pang swept her heart. Not too long ago, the hope of becoming a mother had seemed within her grasp. Before the bloody battle at Cowpens. "You've grown too big for me to hold for long."

"That's what my momma say too." Angel hopped up and down as though she wore springs upon her bare feet and pointed at Lydia. "She can't carry me because she's holding another baby."

"Angel, you hush now. That's enough." Lydia tugged on a threadbare cotton shawl wrapped around her thin shoulders, then rested her arms on her distended belly while the little girl dug her toes in the mud. "I's pleased you came today, Miss Samantha. My baby be due soon, but I can't say I feel right."

A wave of unease crashed into Samantha's core, inundating her earlier relief. Not another patient with issues. For so long, she'd managed to cure or relieve the pains of each of her patients. Until recent months, she'd even started to consider ways of furthering her education to expand her abilities and skills. The sudden change in her patients' health and recovery made her queasy, accompanied by a bitter burn at the back of her throat. This time would be different. She wouldn't let Lydia down after all she'd survived in her life. "Let's go inside, out of the chill."

At her mother's insistence, Angel hunkered by the fireplace on a blanket to play with a cornhusk doll while the women talked. They settled on rough wooden benches across from each other at the small trestle table shoved against one wall. Samantha quickly scrutinized the single room's condition, ensuring her patient's surroundings posed no threat to her health. The wooden floor showed signs of a recent sweeping. Bare wood shutters covered the windows, attempting to keep out the cold but failing to do more than dim the light inside. A cooking fire provided the mere illusion of warmth, a black cast iron tea kettle sending steam up the chimney. Small bunches of dried herbs hung from a rafter near the chimney. Two small shelves holding an assortment of dishes hung on the wall. The narrow cot Samantha had brought from her parents' house on her last visit for Lydia's comfort hugged the wall to the left of the fireplace. A makeshift pillow and thin blanket comprised the meager linens for the bed. A work table sat to the right of the fireplace, a bucket of water and a small remnant of soap waiting on its scarred surface. Against the far wall, a stacked pair of bunk beds provided a place to sleep off the drafty floor. No wonder sadness pervaded the entire area if everyone lived in similar circumstances.

The whole house could easily fit inside the guest parlor at the Sullivans' town house. Samantha tried to imagine the family sleeping on the thin mattresses or, worse, on a pile of straw on the wooden floor. Eating at the small table. Even dressing to meet the demands of a new day. All within the four brick walls. But she failed.

Instead, she leaned forward as she peered at Lydia's face, resting her hands on the table. "What seems to be the problem?"

"Nothing specific, just a sense of change." Lydia shrugged, dark eyes worried. "Somethin' different this time."

Samantha rose and moved to stand beside her patient, one hand resting on her shoulder. "Do you mind if I examine you?"

"Course not." Lydia pushed up to her feet and ambled over to the cot. Her threadbare dress brushed her ankles with each step. She laid down on top of the blanket, her head of curls on the wad of cloth with straw poking through the weave.

Silently, Samantha ran her hands over the woman's belly, checking for any signs of the baby in distress. Trent probably had some new tool he could use to tell what occurred inside Lydia. She sure wished she had something, some instrument or insight to inform her next steps. She must rely on her senses and experience to care for her patients. Not metal tools. *Stop. Trent's doctoring ways are not my ways.* Irritated with herself for allowing the temptation of newer methods to interfere with her concentration, she bent closer to Lydia. With a nod indicating the little girl, she fingered the edge of Lydia's dress hem. "Do you mind if I check below?"

"If'n you have to, then so be it." Lydia moved her hands to rest higher on her belly, lips pressed into a firm line. "Angel won't pay us no mind while she got that doll in her hands."

"Very well." Samantha lifted the dress, reaching under with practiced hands to probe and press the taut flesh, and finished her examination as quickly as possible. She'd examined many women about to bring a child into the world. At least she could perform the inspection visually as well as using her hands, unlike so many male doctors who resorted to feeling around under the woman's skirts without looking at what they probed out of a desire to maintain the mother's modesty. Yet too many times she'd discovered a condition visible but not palpable. What else might those same doctors have missed in their examinations? For herself, the combination of both techniques worked together to yield the most complete picture of the patient's situation. She considered Lydia's condition, her age, the probing's results, and then smiled at her patient. "I expect you'll be glad to know everything appears normal."

"Like I say, it's more a feeling than a pain." Lydia smoothed her dress back down into place and accepted Samantha's hand to help her rise from the bed. "I'll make us some tea if you'd like."

"Thank you, it would take the chill from my bones." She refreshed her hands from the bucket of water, drying them on the apron protecting her navy day dress, and then returned to the bench to sink onto the hard surface. "Your husband and the boys working?"

"Yes'm. They're cutting firewood today, last I heard." Within a few minutes, Lydia placed two chipped porcelain cups on the table then lowered herself onto the opposite bench. "Sorry I have no sugar or milk to offer."

Skimming the room, Samantha realized how little she did have in the way of victuals. Times such as those during an occupation proved difficult for everyone with the prices of everything so high as a result of the embargoes on staples. Even if the manor house had sufficient provisions, the slaves did not necessarily benefit, dependent on the largesse of their master and mistress. Far be it for her to add to their burden. "I prefer it plain."

Lydia smiled and sipped from the cup. "What should I do about this feeling?"

"I'll visit again in a few days to see how you fare." Samantha laid a hand on top of the other woman's. "If you need me sooner, please do not hesitate to send word. I won't let anything bad happen, you hear me?"

"Yes'm. I don't want nothing bad to happen to any of my family." Lydia made one slow dip of her head and then glanced at Angel playing quietly nearby. The girl made the cornhusk doll dance across the blanket, bobbing in a similar manner to Angel's earlier play outside. Clasping her hands together on the little table, Lydia regarded Samantha with grim determination apparent in her entire mien. "Between you and me, I'll tell you true that if this babe is born before them British pull out, we'll be on the boat with them."

"Oh, Lydia." Samantha worried her lower lip with her teeth. She'd miss her friend if they made the scary choice to leave, but she couldn't begrudge their desire for a life of their own, either. Even if it did mean leaving everything they knew for a distant land. Of course, the plantation owner would do everything in his power to have them returned if they made the attempt to flee to freedom. If returned, they'd be punished. "I don't know whether to applaud your courage or fear for you."

"We'd rather take our chances on a freedom we'd never know by staying." She smacked the wood table once with her palm, the cups jumping. "It's that simple."

And that dangerous. "I wish I could change things for you here, so you could stay and be free both." Samantha let out a sigh.

The laws put in place to prevent the threat of a slave uprising made it nearly impossible for any one to manumit a slave. Manumission, the freeing of slaves, required approval from the state, something not easy to obtain even if the slave had proven trustworthy and the owner desired to release the person. Most often those released from slavery were mulattos, the children of a black female slave and white male father. Even those occurrences remained infrequent.

Samantha squeezed the woman's hand, trying to convey her sympathy for her family's situation. "Unfortunately, such an act is not within my power."

Lydia stared at her for the span of three shaky breaths. "What would you do in our place, Miss Samantha? Stay and serve others, under their rule and at their mercy, or take the dreadful chance to run for a freedom of your own?"

Lydia asked a very good question. In fact, the very query she pondered about her parents subsequent to the harvest feast. After all, they'd turned away from joining in her toast to the leaders of America faced with establishing a new form of government. Turned their back on what the future might bring to Charles Town, too. Turned their backs on her?

The thought chilled her. Her father never openly discussed his political dealings, but from his actions and scattered comments he obviously leaned to the loyalist side. If so, what choice would he, and thus her mother, make as the Britons packed their bags for the journey home?

Her heart ached at the very real possibility of them leaving. She loved her parents and always would no matter what they chose to do next. They had educated her and provided for her all of her twenty-five years. Despite their past disagreements with her wishes, she'd back them to the hilt. But, honestly, she had no desire to leave South Carolina to live elsewhere with them. To start over in a new place would be a daunting undertaking at best. But could she stay if they bolted before the patriots exacted their revenge for her father's loyalties? What would become of her in the event?

Put simply, she'd end up at her parents' mercy if she went with them. Or on her own if she stayed. Either way, she'd be confronted with difficult choices only she could make. Much like the woman sitting with her, waiting for her response. "I understand what a difficult choice you face, Lydia."

"One thing." Lydia leaned forward, grabbing hold of both of Samantha's hands in an iron grip. "You's got to promise to keep mum. Don't want the massa to find out and try to stop us."

Samantha nodded, searching Lydia's serious expression. Is that why her parents walked away from the celebration? To not tip their hand? "Your secret is safe with me."

"George and the boys are ready to run any time we have the chance." Lydia folded her hands around the cup. "But I ain't going nowhere until this baby comes. I don't trust any one but you to bring the little one into this harsh world."

"Your belief in me is a high compliment." Samantha sipped her tea and then set the cup down on the table. The woman's faith in her skill brought hope to her heart. "I appreciate your kind words."

Lydia tilted her head as she studied Samantha's face for a moment. "Did somethin' happen?"

Samantha sighed and shook her head, dangling curls tickling her cheeks. How could she ever explain when she couldn't understand exactly what had occurred to turn Benjamin's recovery into a relapse? All under the chary regard of Trent Cunningham. She pulled her shoulders back and winked at Lydia. "Nothing I cannot handle."

When her patient and friend continued to wait expectantly, Samantha shrugged. "A young doctor seems to feel my ways are outdated and based on superstitions."

"I knows you too well, Miss Samantha." Lydia's chuckle rolled from deep in her chest. "What you aiming to do about such nonsense?"

"The only thing I can. I aim to prove him wrong." Samantha grinned and touched cups with Lydia. "He just doesn't know it yet."

Chapter Three

McCrady's tavern brimmed with customers that evening when Trent squealed open the door and stepped inside from the blustery rain. He paused to shake the drops from his overcoat while he searched for a vacant seat. Wandering among the townspeople, he made his way to the back of the room. He spotted a lone table in the far corner and hurried to it before someone else did. Two chairs meant he probably would not be eating alone. The next desperate soul who crossed the threshold would be forced to sit with him, and he with them. He sighed. Nevertheless, a hot meal and a pint would help him shed the chill clinging like a second skin and give him time to think.

The tavern exuded a friendly welcome with its cheery oil lamps hung about the rafters. Candles in silver holders sat on each wooden table. In the front corner, a young man played ballads on a flute. A young couple performed a lively dance to the tune. Trent enjoyed their energetic display. He hadn't danced for several years, because he'd dedicated most of his free time to further studies. The results would be worth his effort. He had to believe that much.

When he first arrived back in Charles Town a few months ago, his path stretched clear and straight before him. He'd graduated from the University of Pennsylvania, earned some money on the side toward a place to call his own, and committed to bettering this bustling port city by establishing a hospital. The trip from Philadelphia to his father's house had taken longer than during peace times, spanning four weeks instead of the normal two. Between the enemy encampments he'd had to skirt and bad weather which led to worse roads, he'd begun to think he'd never safely return to his home in Charles Town. He'd had plenty of time along the way to plan his next steps, carefully considered steps in danger of being overturned like the baggage wagon on his journey home.

The barkeeper placed a bowl of hot beef stew and a tankard of ale on the scarred wood table. Trent reached into his vest pocket, fishing for a few coins to cover the price of the meal. "Thank you."

The barkeeper waggled a hand in front of his well-used apron. "No need for that. Pay me before you leave, sir."

Frank nodded as the man turned away and then lifted his spoon to stir the steaming concoction. The hearty combination of simmered beef, carrots, and potatoes in a thick gravy made his mouth water. If only the elements of his life would come together as seamlessly as the ingredients of the stew. With the war ending and his livelihood on course, he'd decided during the arduous journey home that the next order of business would be finding a wife to manage his home and bear his children. A companion to share the events of his day. But the lady most attractive to his plan held herself apart from him even when they stood side by side. He grinned to himself. Or chest to chest. The memory of her startled expression made him chuckle. The moment their gazes had met, he knew she was the woman he wanted at his side. But then there was the tension surrounding treatment of Benjamin's fever and infection. Such a tangled mess. How would he ever convince beautiful, courageous, caring Samantha to take a chance on him when his goal was diametrically opposed to hers?

He blew on a spoonful to cool it before taking it into his mouth. The front door swung open, drawing his attention and permitting Samantha to enter the crowded, boisterous room. He could barely see her for all of the people between them. Her black curls had been captured on top of her head and flowed down her back. Her gaze swept the room, finally stopping when she caught him watching her. She'd never find another seat in the noisy, crowded establishment. He beckoned for her to join him. She shrugged, a light lift and fall of her shoulders, and started toward him. The crowd parted for her as though sensing she meant business. The set of her jaw as she drew closer warned him of her mood. Perhaps if they avoided speaking about Benjamin or medicine, they'd get along.

"Hello, Miss Samantha. How fare you this rainy evening?" He rose to help her remove her cloak and to pull the other chair out for her. She sank gracefully onto the seat. He hung the sodden garment within easy reach on a wood peg on the wall.

"I am well, thank you." She slipped her black gloves from her hands, laying them across her lap. "Oh, the stew looks divine. I didn't realize how hungry I am."

"I can do something about that." Trent signaled the barkeeper, who nodded his understanding of Trent's order. "What brings you out on a night so wet and dreary?"

Samantha chuckled, a rich sound that made him smile. "My parents elected to stay at home to avoid potential confrontation and to keep poor Evelyn company. I felt trapped within the house and chose to find my entertainment in town. The smell of beef stew drew me inside."

"It is well for your parents to keep to themselves. They should be more discreet about their political leanings." Trent fiddled with the spoon handle as he studied her relaxed expression. "If they're not more circumspect, their loyalties may cause no end of trouble for them."

The barkeeper returned with Samantha's stew and a small beer. The aroma of apples and spice evoked fond childhood memories. Samantha carefully placed a linen napkin in her lap to protect her brown dress, a color reminiscent of the thousands of walnuts he'd shelled for his mother when he was a boy. Thinking of her, long dead, made his eyes smart and he blinked to force the tears back.

"Father is aware of how the town feels about loyalists." She lifted a spoonful of stew and held it aloft over the bowl. "I can only hope he doesn't force the town's hand by flaunting his feelings on the topic of independence."

Trent stared at her, entranced by the precise movement as Samantha slipped the spoon into and out of her mouth. As she chewed, her gaze met his. How could a simple, straightforward look evoke such a stirring beneath his belt?

"I agree with you. No good will come of it." Her lips pressed together and then parted to allow another bite inside. He should focus on his point, and not his body's reaction to the temptress before him. Maybe a change of subject would help. "Benjamin told me you're a fine seamstress and have helped make shirts and pants for our troops."

Samantha rested her spoon in the bowl. Taking a long sip from her mug, she regarded him over the rim until she set the vessel on the table. "It was quite nice of Benjamin to compliment my efforts. I find practicing my technique while sewing helps me with stitches when a patient's wound calls for them. I've settled on using catgut, like when I stitched together a man's thigh after the wheel broke on his wagon and a flying spoke managed to slice it open. What do you use to close up a wound?"

Damnation. They were back to discussing medicine again. He detected a stiffening of her shoulders along with an erratic pulse at the base of her throat. Had she steered the conversation back to medicine because it was a safer topic? Was she unsure of herself around him? What a compliment, as he had wondered if she felt anything for him. Keeping a straight face in light of her nervous reaction proved challenging. "Silk is my current preference. However, one of my professors, Dr. Philip Physick, has been experimenting with leather sutures that actually dissolve in the body. That would be something to see. But enough shop talk, my dear. Let's enjoy our dinners, shall we?"

"Dissolving sutures?" Samantha gaped at him. "I've never heard of such a wonder."

"I learned so much at college, but I wish this war hadn't prevented me from studying in Edinburgh. That's where the real advancements are being made."

"What of fevers? Is there progress on the best way to banish the heat from the body?

"I did hear of a pair of doctors who cured a man of his fever using a series of treatments." Trent sipped his ale, contemplating the interest shining from her eyes. "As I recall, it was up in North Carolina."

"What did they do?" She spooned a bite of stew between her perfect teeth and he briefly wished he could be the spoon.

Focusing his attention with no little difficulty, he shrugged. "I do not know for certain everything they might have tried. All I heard was they applied a blister between his shoulders, gave him medicine to open his pores and bowels, and fed him wine and other stimulating drinks."

"To what aim?" Samantha leaned forward, a slight frown clouding her eyes. "Their method contradicts all my training. What happened?"

"They induced a sweat, and within a couple of days he was improving." Trent took a bite of stew, chewing slowly while Samantha regarded him in silence.

"So we should blister Benjamin and force wine down his throat and then make him sweat in order to reduce the fever?" She shook her head. "That combination makes no sense."

"You might be correct in your appraisal, because two weeks later the man died." Trent lifted a spoonful, ready to eat it. "But without the trial and error of knowledgeable doctors, it would be impossible to narrow the possibilities down to only those that work."

She pursed her lips and nodded. "Perhaps I was hasty to dismiss your education and experience." She stirred her stew, slipping another spoonful into her mouth as she studied him. She dabbed her mouth with the napkin and replaced it in her lap. "We could learn from each other's experiences."

"Maybe." Trent leaned back on his chair. "You do have quite a bit to catch up on."

Damnation. He'd said the wrong thing. Yet again, his propensity to blurt out whatever popped into his brain put him at odds with a beautiful woman. He could tell from the way she regarded him, eyes glittering, brows pulled down, and lips pressed into a line.

Samantha placed her spoon in the bowl with care, pulled the napkin from her lap, and put it beside the bowl. She met his gaze, silently perusing his face. "I've enjoyed our talk, Dr. Trent, but I'm afraid I must be on my way."

Back to the formal address again. He sighed. It was his own fault. "Please, you've barely touched your dinner. If I have offended you, I apologize." He rose as Samantha stood. They were of nearly equal height, but he gazed down at her for a long moment. "It was not my intent. Won't you stay?"

She held still as a marble statue for several seconds, then

shook her head. "My cloak, if you please." She tugged her gloves on and waited for him to retrieve the garment and ease it onto her shoulders. Tying it closed, she paused to meet his gaze. "Thank you for dinner. It was enlightening."

"My pleasure. I hope we can do it again sometime." Soon, too. If he hadn't blurted out that comment, perhaps she'd have stayed long enough to really become acquainted. Instead, she turned to make her way through the crowded tavern. "Miss Samantha, let me walk you home, please?"

She looked over her shoulder at him, frowning. "Mayhap I'll see you at Benjamin's. Good-night."

"Fare well." Without another word, she wove a path through the other customers. Away from him. Away from them. If only the elements of his life would come together, maybe he could find peace and contentment. But as long as Samantha resisted being with him, he had a nearly insurmountable feat to perform. How does a man make a woman fall in love with him?

Samantha strolled toward home along Bay, leaving behind the bustling McCrady's Tavern. Why had Trent spoiled the evening by denigrating her education just as she had started to like the man? Friendship with the enticing doctor might be the most she could expect from him, especially if he continued to dismiss her abilities. Catherine Manning nodded in greeting as she hurried by, the empty basket dangling on her arm an indicator she aimed to visit the public market over at the corner of Church and Cumberland. If so, Caroline best hurry before they packed up their wares for the day. The sun hung low in the sky, emphasizing the contours of houses and trees as well as the lateness of the hour. A cool cat's paw breeze caressed Samantha's cheeks, prompting her to snug her cloak closer. She turned onto Queen, recalling the harsh expulsion of Mr. William Johnson and his family during the Briton's capture of the town. Mr. Johnson had been overtly critical of the British and an ardent patriot, and thus they'd thrown him in the prison at St. Augustine and his entire family was banished. With good fortune, they'd be able to return to their home soon, the one that stood right down the alley she glanced at as she lengthened her stride. For the moment, she must reach her own house as soon as possible. Quickening her pace, she soon strode up the front steps of her home and pushed inside.

She hung her cloak on a peg by the door before making her way into the parlor, following the sound of voices in serious conversation. Her mother sat relaxed by a cheery fire, while her father stood with one foot balanced on the andirons and an arm resting on the mantel. Evelyn looked up from where she sat on the settee facing her parents, her infant son cradled in her arms, and smiled at Samantha.

Relief flowed through Samantha at how well and content Evelyn appeared. Clear gray-green eyes regarded Samantha before blinking twice. Since losing her husband, the stoop to the woman's shoulders had eased, allowing her to sit straight and proper, hinting at a tall, elegant posture. Dressed in one of Samantha's day dresses, Evelyn presented a tidy and graceful young mother. Given enough time, the woman would surely recover from the oppression her husband had bestowed upon her. Samantha returned her smile as she entered the cozy room.

"I'm happy to see you. Your mother told me all about poor Benjamin. After all he did for us, I detest he's enduring such hardship." Evelyn patted the empty seat beside her and then jostled her baby to quiet his murmurings. "Come sit with me. How does Benjamin fare?"

Samantha crossed to sink gratefully on the deep cushion, the plush pad welcome after spending the afternoon on the hard carriage seat and then the hard wood chair at the tavern. "He's not well, but Trent and I shall do everything in our power to help him improve."

"Should you need my advice, I shall be pleased to confer with you." Cynthia sipped sherry from a small crystal glass, her gaze fixed on Samantha. "I do have some experience in such matters."

"Thank you, Mother." Despite the offer of assistance, Samantha couldn't rely upon her mother if she were to effectively and decisively demonstrate her skills to Trent. She had to do this on her own or not at all, but her mother simply wouldn't understand her reasoning. In fact, she'd most likely take it personally. Best to change the subject and not delve into the matter. "Evelyn, how is little Jim faring this evening?"

"He's doing well." Evelyn smiled down on her son who lay snuggled in her arms. His dark hair covered his tiny head while his fingers clutched the edge of the soft blanket swaddling his body. She raised her gaze to contemplate Samantha, a smile sliding into place. "Thanks to you."

Samantha nodded in acknowledgement, grateful beyond words for the kindness in the sentiment. "And what about you?"

"I am well, but I fear I must not wear out my welcome with you gracious people." She glanced at Samantha's parents and back again. "My gratitude knows no bounds for your welcome. However, my parents sent word this afternoon that they insist, despite my initial misgivings, their house has room for me and my son as well as my maid, Belinda. So we shall move into my parents' town house and relieve your family of having us as a burden to your fine household."

Aaron strode to the sidebar in five long steps. He poured his nightly brandy and a glass of sherry, then approached Samantha to hand her the crystal glass half-full of garnet-colored wine before crossing to a chair near his wife. He sank onto the cushioned seat, sipping his brandy from the elegant crystal glass reserved for the purpose. "A wise move, to be with your family in times such as these."

"Indeed." Cynthia nodded, her gaze sliding from Evelyn to rest on Samantha. "Family always takes care of their own. Don't you agree, Aaron?"

"One way or another, yes, family cares for family." Aaron rested his glass on a crossed knee as he let his words linger in the air. He regarded Samantha until she squirmed and looked away. "And Evelyn, my dear, you must think of us as your extended family from here on."

Evelyn as family? A superb idea. She'd always wanted a sibling, and now perhaps she'd have one. "Then it is settled. We will be sisters from this moment." Samantha smiled at Evelyn as she clasped her hands together and laid them in her lap. "I will help you move to your home in the morning. But what will you do then?"

Evelyn lifted her shoulders and let them slide back into place. "That is a query which must wait for another day. My entire future changed with the death of my husband and the destruction of his family home."

"Most assuredly." Samantha glanced at her parents, silently pondering the emotions flickering in their expressions. Family needs remained her first priority. She raised her glass of sherry, the others slowly mirroring her actions. "To my new sister, new beginnings, and to families sticking together no matter what." She sipped, hoping against hope for her wishes to come to pass.

Over the next three days, Samantha trudged down Queen and turned onto Bay to visit Benjamin each morning and reapply the ointment, but hoping for a change in his condition for the better. Trent also tended to him, had even bled their patient twice more, though the second time he had done so with reluctant skill and Benjamin's even more reluctant agreement. Nothing they had tried seemed to turn the tide in Benjamin's favor. Surely something had changed to cause his sudden weakness, but what? The mystery surrounding the precipitous debility plagued her thoughts. The story of the feverish man being sweated to break the fever haunted her thoughts as well. Why had the blister and other efforts succeeded in ending the fever but not in curing the man? Yawning, she mounted the stairs to his apartment and rapped on the door three times before pushing inside.

The common room greeted her with cold silence and a suspicious smell. She inhaled deeply and then coughed at the pungent scent. Clearing her throat, she waited for her thoughts to clear. Too many late nights poring over her herbals and simples left her brain muzzy. She sniffed, recognizing the worrisome odor of dying flesh. *Gramercy.* First task of the morning, arrest the advance of her worst fear, the devilish gangrene.

She marched across the empty room and into the stuffy bedroom. Benjamin sprawled on the bed, covers twisted about as though he'd tossed and turned for hours. His hair lay matted to his head, fine lines carved between his drawn brows. Gripping the tiny pot of the strongest ointment she'd ever mixed, one concocted by drawing upon both her father's extensive resources and her own knowledge of medicinal interactions, she rushed to his side.

"Benjamin, are you awake?" She pressed a hand to his hot forehead, his fever warming her flesh. She jostled him. "Ben?"

He blinked open bloodshot eyes. "Is it morning? I feel awful."

He looked awful. She perused his features and shook her head.

The mystery had only deepened since the last time she'd seen him. "I brought another, stronger medicine. Can you sit up?"

"If I must." He moaned and closed his eyes for a moment, opening them to fix bleary eyes on her worried face. Concentrating, he pushed one-handed against the mattress, attempting to shift into a sitting position, only to collapse. He shook his head, flopped back on the bed. "Sorry."

"It's all right." Every day he grew weaker, more ill. The debility seemed to have begun at the harvest dinner, but somehow she must find a way to halt its progress. Fear for his life swelled inside her heart, impeding her ability to draw a steady breath. "Stay where you are."

"What is wrong with me?" Benjamin shook his head again, a slow movement from side to side. "Why won't it heal?"

"I do not know, my friend." She gripped his good hand and then opened her red bag. "But I will find the answer. You have my word."

With efficient movements, she cleaned the boundaries of the seeping wound, inspecting its condition carefully. She detected the earliest signs of gangrene threatening the lower edge of the gaping hole the bullet had torn in his right shoulder. Quickly, she wiggled and then popped the cork on the clay pot, the strong scent of cloves and cinnamon filling her nostrils, and applied the odiferous concoction until the reddish ointment completely covered the wound.

Wiping her hands on a clean rag, she judged his condition. Pale, sweaty, sunken cheeks. So frail and weak. Nothing at all like the robust man who'd saved her and Amy a few weeks ago in the forest. Nor the man who'd fought off the renegades surrounding the manor house. The fever must break. Although, other patients had survived recurring ailments, like dysentery or malaria, with the intermittent or even continual low fever associated with the illnesses. As long as the temperature didn't climb too high, he stood a chance of recovering. But the gangrene was a different matter entirely. If it spread, grew out of control, the only recourse remained amputation. What else could she try if the ointment failed to halt the progression of dying skin?

"Benjamin, can you hear me?" She squeezed his hand to rouse him. "I'm going to make a pot of tea for you to sip. Can you drink it?"

He stirred, nodded. "If you'll help."

"Of course. I'll be back in a moment." At least he could still speak and comprehend his situation. "Rest until I return."

She grabbed her bag, hurried into the common room, and crossed to the fireplace. A pile of ashes sat in the center of the brick hearth. *Gramercy.* Somebody had not tended it properly, a situation she'd make sure to correct. It was a good thing she didn't rely upon slave labor to keep house, or she wouldn't have the necessary skills to remedy the lack of a fire. She quickly cleaned out the ashes using a small shovel to transfer them into the wooden bucket reserved for such use. Then she laid some tinder in the center of the brick hearth and added a few twigs of varying size to the pile. Snatching the metal fire striker and piece of flint from the small tinder box, she struck them together, pleased to finally see a few small sparks with each strike. After several attempts, she managed to relight the fire, a low flame licking the twigs as she added a few larger sticks and then several logs from the rack to one side. When the fire blazed hot enough, she wiped her hands and turned to make the special tea she'd brought to try to help Benjamin combat the fever.

She poured water from the urn into a black pot and hung it on a hook, before swinging the pot over the licking flames. While she waited for the water to heat, she straightened up the room from their earlier visits. She spied a silver tea service and set of porcelain cups resting on a shelf beside the chimney. Although the silver could use a good polishing, it would suffice for the occasion. The cups rattled on their saucers as she hurried to move the set to the table. Propping fists on hips, she contemplated her next move. With so few items contained in the room, her options for keeping busy were limited. The place needed a woman's touch to make it more comfortable and useful. Mayhap Amy could help in that regard. For now, there was little to be done except for the tidying she'd already accomplished. All she had left was waiting for the water to boil. Finally, after long minutes, she spotted steam rising from the kettle. She slipped a packet and a small container of honey from her bag and brewed the tea using special fever-reducing herbs she'd gathered from the garden earlier in the season, and then dried and blended them for greatest potency. Stirring a spoonful of honey into the pot, she sniffed. Perfect.

She carried the tray into the bedroom and set it on the night table before pouring the fragrant brew into a cup. "Benjamin, let me help you sit up."

He grunted and shoved at the covers. She gently slipped an arm under his shoulders and lifted. Together, they wrestled him upward, moaning and breathing hard, into position against the headboard. She wiped a hand over her own brow to dry the perspiration gathered there. Resting his head against the wooden board, he panted until his breathing calmed. He squinted at her, the extent of his weariness evident. "I'm tired of feeling this way. I have important duties to perform."

Samantha retrieved a cup and held it to Benjamin's lips. "I'm afraid your duties must wait until you've recovered your strength."

"The Governor may disagree with you." He sipped, focusing on the cup clashing with his chattering teeth. A few more swallows and Benjamin drained the remainder of tea from the vessel. He flopped his head back with a thump against the headboard. "I'm cold and so tired. Please, Samantha, help me."

"I'm doing my best." Which may not be good enough, but she wouldn't stop trying until she'd exhausted every possibility. Cold resolve fought with the uncertainty in her heart. "Do not fear."

He huffed a chuckle which set him into a fit of coughing. After he'd finished, he shook his head at her, the glimmer of his trademark grin flitting across his lips. "Too late for that."

The front door clicked open in the other room and banged closed. Footsteps followed, heralding Trent's arrival in the bedroom. Samantha sensed his concern before she turned to greet him, a concern she shared. At the same time, another worry invaded her heart. Trent's presence focused her awareness on the attraction she couldn't deny she felt for the frowning man staring at Benjamin. Did he not feel the draw, the pull to move closer? She chided herself for her foolish response and forced her attention on what Trent was saying rather than the impressive physical attributes of the man.

"Benjamin, how fare you this morning?" Trent strode closer to Benjamin, his black leather bag in hand. He pressed his lips together, as though to prevent himself from letting slip his true opinion.

"I'm feeling no better than yesterday or the day before." Benjamin pulled the light quilt up, clenching it with both hands. "How fare you?"

"I am fine, thanks for asking. However, I'm deeply concerned for your welfare." Trent dropped his bag to the wood floor and regarded Samantha. "Your estimation of his condition?"

His attention weighed on her, sparked a visceral response in her chest that spread throughout her body. A response she would ignore. "Weaker, still a touch feverish. The skin appeared to be resisting my ointments, so I've applied a stronger one."

Lines appeared between his eyes at her words. "Resisting? How so?"

"Possibly the first signs of gangrene on the lower edge of the wound." The spark of fear in his expression mirrored her own. She paused, considering her next words with care. "We may want to remove the dead flesh."

Trent drew a breath and let it out in a rush. "My father recommends amputation when gangrene sets in. The sooner it is accomplished the better the prognosis for the patient."

"Amputate?" Benjamin inhaled sharply and frowned. "No."

Trent nodded, a grim expression blanketing his features. "I'm afraid we have no means with which to stop the progression of the disease other than cut it out, or off."

Benjamin without an arm? Granted the wound was in the shoulder, but the closest location for the cut to be made would be at the joint. What if it spread in the opposite direction? Toward his head rather than down his arm? She'd assisted at amputations, and hoped to never witness one again. Most patients fainted with the first few strokes of the saw, but only after the agony rendered them senseless. Samantha shivered, imagining the trauma and pain followed by the horrendous recovery. What would he do after such a dangerous and life-changing surgery?

"I shall not permit such an act." Samantha marched to face Trent. "You cannot do such a terrible thing to my friend."

"Not even to save his life?" Trent bent to search in his bag, rummaging among metallic and leather items hidden from view. He withdrew a thin bladed hand saw, checked its sharpness, and then peered at Samantha. "Do not allow emotion to guide your decision."

The points of the saw glinted in the morning light. Samantha swallowed the cry of dismay that the sight of the tool speared through her very soul. More appropriate for butchering than saving a man's life.

"Trent, you must hear me." Benjamin shook his head, his lank, sweaty, black hair slapping his pallid cheeks. His eyes remained on the blade Trent held in the air. "No amputation. Not even to save my life. What kind of life would I have left without my arm?"

"Miss Amy may well disagree, preferring you alive." Trent considered Benjamin's set jaw. "What would you have me do? I must proceed."

"Nay, I say." Benjamin swallowed hard and clutched the quilt until he fairly mangled the colorful spread. "I'd rather die than be a partial man, handicapped for the remainder of my days. What kind of provider would I be in that state?" He glared at Trent, holding him still with the intensity of his expression.

Trent grunted and shook his head slowly as he wrapped the blade in an oiled cloth and slipped the saw back into the confines of the leather bag. "Very well, but do not say I didn't warn you. I consulted my father, as he knows best in these matters with all his doctoring experience."

"No, he does not." Samantha confronted Trent, standing too close for her peace of mind, but close enough to ensure he fully comprehended her position on the subject. "Gangrene is not always fatal. Not if it's caught early. I've turned it before."

"See, she's had a different result than your father." Benjamin sank against the headboard again, hope flaring in his bloodshot eyes. "Listen to her. For now, I am exhausted. Help me recline so I may sleep."

Trent stepped closer and helped ease Benjamin down into a more comfortable position. "Rest easy, friend. We shall resolve your condition soon."

Samantha dragged the covers over him with a final reminder to drink all of the tea. "I shall return tomorrow to check on you."

When she turned to gather her belongings, Trent stopped her with a hand on her arm. The depth of his concern shook her almost as much as the sensations flooding her brain. "Come talk with me."

She nodded, desperate for him to release her arm so her thoughts would untangle. After his hand fell away, she dragged in a silent breath and slowly exhaled. Calm eased through her, replacing the turmoil. She strolled after him into the common room where the cheery fire had burned away the earlier chill.

He paused by the table, placing his black bag on the wood surface. He considered her for a moment. "You do know we may have no choice but to cut off his arm should the decay spread."

The shock of his words made her mouth fall open. Anger mixed with a sense of betrayal flared fast and hot, searing her chest, at the implication of his statement. "You promised to not do so. More to the point, I promised to not allow you to do so."

"Do not think for one moment I would allow my friend to die over his pride." Trent's brows drew down, a flash of pain dimming the vibrancy of his crystal blue eyes. "I may not have known him as long as you and your friends, but his friendship means a great deal to me."

"Your friendship may be tested." She studied him, noted the tension in his shoulders, the grief hinted at in his eyes. Sensing his anguish, she relaxed her defensive posture. He surely wouldn't perform the surgery against his friend's wishes. As a doctor, he must honor his patient's desires, even if he did not agree. "Let us leave him to rest and the ointment to do its job."

Trent raked a hand through shoulder-length sandy hair—why on Earth didn't he keep it tied up so it wouldn't tempt her?—and picked up his bag. "Very well. But know this, my dear…"

She raised a brow at the daring endearment falling easily from his lips. "Yes?"

"I have only his best interests in mind. Not yours."

"As do I." What did he think, mayhap she cared more about herself than for her patient? Sure, her reputation stood to be helped or hindered by the outcome, judged on the success or failure of her ways, but Benjamin's health remained her primary concern. If need be, she'd bow to Trent's methods in order to best serve Benjamin. Of course, that wouldn't be necessary. "I shall do all in my power to ensure a full recovery."

Trent motioned to the door with a swipe of his free hand. "Shall we?"

Samantha headed toward the exit at the same time Trent moved to grasp the latch. She collided with him, bumping off his tall solid frame much like a billiard ball striking the padded edge of the table. His hand steadied her until she'd recovered her balance, but her senses reeled at the onslaught of sensation his light touch ignited. She really must rein in the errant response. Swallowing, she stepped sideways, breaking the contact.

"My apologies, Miss Samantha." He bowed and straightened, eyes twinkling with mirth.

She chuckled nervously and smoothed her skirt with one hand, gripping her bag in the other. Something devilish and unnerving lurked in his gaze and she looked away. "I should have waited for you to open the door. It is my fault."

"I believe we were in too big a hurry. Shall we try again?" He strode over to the door, pulling it open and then ushering her through without further incident.

They descended the flight of stairs and then made their way to Bay Street and its flurry of midmorning activity passing by. Several carriages and a host of people flowed before them. The increased pace of the town reflected the hope and relief of the people as true freedom from oppression loomed on the horizon like the sun rising to greet the dawn.

"Good day, Miss Samantha. Until tomorrow." He tipped his hat and sauntered away in the general direction of the Exchange, his wide smile lingering in her mind's eye.

With each step he took, she breathed easier and her senses returned to normal. At the same time, her heart sank when she realized normal no longer appealed when compared to the heady heights his touch evoked. *Gramercy*.

Chapter Four

"Milk or sugar?" Emily waited for Samantha's response, the silver spoon hovering over the steaming tea cup.

The Sullivans' parlor had become a second home to Samantha over the past year. She perused the familiar opulent furnishings surrounding her. A floor-to-ceiling bookcase lined the far wall, the shelves fairly groaning under the weight of the many books and decorative objects they held. Heavy drapes covered the two front windows flanking a stack of ornate trunks. After the Britons left, taking their suspicious, prying eyes with them, perhaps the drapes would be opened more often. Oriental carpets lay beneath the cherry and mahogany chairs and settee. A merry blaze filled the fireplace, its pops and hisses comforting in the lulls of their conversation. Amber and garnet port filled cut glass decanters on the small table between the chairs.

The same port used to make their vow to remain unmarried back in October. Of course, her friends made the promise to protect their broken hearts, but those vows had been destined to be dashed against the rocks. Both Emily and Amy cared too much and too deeply for their men to remain spinsters. Samantha's vow, however, held firm. It must.

She'd loved with all she had once, and would never subject her heart to such a grievous pain again. On the low table in front of her, a matching pair of silver plates holding biscuits and dried fruit reflected the flickering firelight along with her frown. She cleared her expression and regarded her friend. Emily served in the role of hostess with easy grace, her countenance curious at the prolonged delay before Samantha answered her question.

"A little of each, please." Samantha took the proffered cup and saucer, anxious for the tea's calming influence. She sniffed the pleasing aroma and sipped, the hot sweet liquid settling her frayed emotions. So many questions and worries floated in her mind, both puzzling and disturbing. She decided to ask the most benign question haunting her thoughts. "How does Frank feel about the controversy sparked by the mysterious Penny Marsh's essays? Why does he dare print them?"

Emily's cup wobbled in the saucer as she gripped it with both hands. The liquid sloshed out, casting drops of tea onto her nut brown dress. She set the saucer on the table and then dabbed the damp spots with a lace-edged linen napkin. Satisfied, she gracefully lifted the saucer again before slowly focusing on Samantha. "I assume he would not publish them if he did not feel they have merit. Why do you ask?"

"I suspect I know the author's true identity." Samantha sipped her tea, detecting a nervous edge to her friend's actions. "She lives here in town, unless I am mistaken."

Emily's eyes looked everywhere but at Samantha while the cup clinked against the saucer. Her lips parted, to say something or in surprise. Her gaze slid to Samantha, eyes wide. "You think so?"

"I've suspected for some time you are Penny Marsh." Samantha lifted her cup in salute. "I applaud your talents as much as your views and audacity."

"Thank you." Pink appeared on Emily's cheeks. "How did you guess?"

Samantha chuckled and shook her head, long black curls brushing her shoulders. "Little slips of the tongue and pieces of paper exchanging hands. The number of nights you've had little sleep."

"So obvious?" Emily flinched, though a sly smile eased onto her lips. "Surely Father does not know."

"As far as I am aware, he does not." Samantha sipped her tea, grateful for the revival of her spirits. "Will you tell him?"

Emily gaped, panic etched in her expression. "No. Never. He'd forbid me to lower myself to publish anything. Then he'd remove my quill and paper. Please, do not breathe a word to him."

"Do not fret. I won't say a word. When does the next one appear?"

"In tomorrow's paper." Emily relaxed from her panicked posture. "It's a demand for equal opportunities for all children. Frank thought it rather fine."

"Anything you do, Emily, I'm sure he approves. He's besotted."

Emily's blush deepened. "And I with him."

With their marriage only a month away, their feelings for each other should only grow stronger. "Have you and Amy decided where to hold the joint ceremony?"

Emily poured more tea into her cup, stirred in a half spoon of sugar, and then laid the tiny spoon on the saucer with a delicate *tink*. "Frank graciously offered his entire house for the event. The redecorating will be completed before Christmas. The parlor is going to be entirely rearranged to allow for the mass of guests and flowers I anticipate."

"At least the Britons relinquished the property back into his hands. It's better than losing everything to their avarice." Samantha lowered the saucer to rest on one knee.

"Although they stripped out everything of value, he retained ownership."

"I certainly agree with you." Emily set her saucer on the table and folded her hands in her lap. "When the Britons eventually evacuate the town—as soon as there is adequate fair weather I understand—we can relax a bit on that particular score."

Their departure could not occur soon enough. Samantha took a long drink and then placed her empty cup and saucer alongside Emily's. "So many changes loom before us. Each family will be faced with challenging and difficult choices. One of my patients is even considering leaving town along with the British."

"I'm not surprised. Many loyalists will flee from the anticipated persecution by the patriots." Emily relaxed against the back of the settee and leveled a cool stare at Samantha. "You have a loyalist for a patient? Are you not worried about payment and perhaps even treachery?"

"Political leanings do not enter into the conversation when someone is in need of my talents." At least, not that she'd witnessed. Emily's point may prove a valuable insight, however. She'd be on her guard for such retaliations. "Besides, I did not say they are loyalists."

Emily inclined her head in apology. "Granted. At least we have nothing to fear with regard to retribution, being patriots, I mean."

Unease flowed into Samantha's heart. The image of her parents turning away from her toast to the country's future, followed by the tense exchange in the parlor regarding the role of family in times of crisis, flashed in her memory. "Indeed."

The back door banged shut, interrupting their conversation. Heavy footsteps pounded down the hall. Samantha raised a brow and angled her head as she regarded Emily. "Your father?"

Emily's quick besotted grin and head bob suggested Frank most likely had arrived as well. Samantha returned the smile, happy Emily had found her heart's desire. She didn't begrudge her friends falling in love and marrying, but she would never again permit herself to succumb to a man's affections. Even if she imprudently reacted to his company.

"Emily? Where are you?" Joshua Sullivan filled the door with his broad shoulders and imposing height. "Ah, there you are, my dear."

Frank followed Captain Sullivan into the parlor. "Good day, Miss Samantha."

"Frank. Captain." Samantha nodded to each in greeting.

Frank sought out Emily, striding quickly to her side to kiss her hand. "Good afternoon, Em. How fare you?"

"I'm well, thank you." Emily blushed and lowered her hand to motion to the tea service. "Would you care for a cup of Samantha's fine blend of tea?" At his nod, she addressed the captain. "Father?"

"Of course." Captain Sullivan dropped onto one of the imported cherry wood chairs, stretching his booted feet before him. "I'm pleased to see you, Miss Samantha."

"Likewise, Captain." Samantha smoothed her skirts with both hands and then rested one on her injured thigh. She longed to massage where it ached but did not want to draw attention to her ongoing recovery. Trent's earlier comment regarding the failure of her ointment to heal her own wound still rankled, and worse made her wonder if he were correct in his judgment.

Frank occupied the other chair closest to Emily as she poured and served their tea, adding the preferred amounts of sugar and milk for her companions from long experience.

"I'm sure we didn't mean to interrupt your conversation, ladies." Frank lifted the cup, wrapping his long fingers around the porcelain. "What were you discussing when we arrived?"

Samantha shifted to ease the throbbing in her leg. "How loyalists will be treated after the Britons leave."

"The list continues to grow of the British sympathizers' real and personal property in town which will be subject to confiscation the day the patriots retake control of Charles Town." Captain Sullivan raised his cup and drank the steaming liquid before pinning his steady gaze on Samantha. "I'm sorry to say your father's property was added to the list as of this morning."

"Excuse me?" She couldn't possibly have heard him correctly. Dismay clogged her throat. "Father's property is to be auctioned along with the rest? That cannot possibly be correct."

"My deepest regrets, Miss Samantha, but your father openly declared himself a loyalist." The captain shrugged one shoulder. "I cannot fathom his logic, but the result of his decision means he'll lose everything he worked for over the last decade. The state passed the Act of Confiscation unanimously, and that means they will claim his house and his business, as well as all its contents at the time of their appropriation by the state. I'm afraid you will all need to find another place to live."

"But Samantha?" Emily leaned forward in her angst. "Where will you go? Please do not tell me you'd leave. You cannot. Not now."

"This is such a surprise I do not know what to think or how to react." Samantha had never considered the possibility of being forced from her home. Sure, her folks may leave her in town alone, but to have all of the property taken from her by the state she loved? The very idea sparked outrage simmering in her stomach. "I won't move. I can't. My garden forms the basis of my practice."

Captain Sullivan set his tea cup on the saucer and plunked it on the table. "You have no choice. Maidens cannot own property."

Agitation forced her to rise and pace, her long, dark blue skirts battering the furniture with each sharp turn. She was not a maiden, but nobody knew that. Nor would she reveal the truth of her situation. Her thoughts whirled. She must concentrate. Sort out her options. Would her parents leave, dragging her with them or would they go without her? *Should* she go with them? The only options for loyalists remained to flee the country or to melt back into the general populace in another state where nobody would know their former political position. No, she had no desire to travel to another country nor to flee the state. Her life was in South Carolina. Halting, she faced Captain Sullivan. "I shall fight this action. From whom should I beg assistance?"

"You have no recourse." He fluttered a hand and then gulped his tea. "It's futile to argue the matter."

Frank rose and crossed the room, looming over her slender frame. "I agree with the captain. You have no hope of retaining your father's property as your own."

She snorted with annoyance. "I must try. Surely the good people of Charles Town will not punish me for my father's position."

"They are punishing your father, not you. It's his property at risk." Frank gripped her upper arms to ensure she listened to him. "Keep in mind the coverture laws do not permit unmarried women to own property."

"Damn stupid law…" Samantha dragged in a breath, attempting to calm the hurt and anger swirling in her stomach like a cyclone. Her attempt failed. Summoning as much self-control as she could muster, she composed herself. "Please, Frank. Tell me who I can speak with about the matter."

He regarded her for the span of two agitated breaths before shrugging. "George Manning has been tasked with overseeing the confiscation and subsequent auction."

"Thank you." Having a plan helped settle her chaotic emotions. "I'll seek him out when the appropriate time arrives."

Emily cleared her throat, drawing all eyes in the room to her. "Father, perhaps Mr. Manning could assist with acquiring a piece of vacant property as well, namely the old widow Murray's bake shop. Would you ask him, please?"

Emily's forced innocent expression, the wide eyes blinking slowly beneath arched brows, brought a grin to Samantha's mouth. Added to the effect was the small smile that made a bow out of Emily's lips. Perhaps not the best time to raise her shocking idea, but the horse had escaped the barn.

Captain Sullivan smirked at his daughter with questioning eyes. "Why, pray tell, would I want a bake shop?"

Emily gave her father a slow, secretive smile. "So I may convert it into a lovely accessories boutique to showcase my sewing."

Samantha gaped at her friend and waited for the explosion from her father. While Samantha understood the original reason for Emily's desire to provide for herself, that reason no longer existed. After she and Frank wed, her energies would be consumed with running their household, not running a shop.

"A what? Did I hear you correctly?" Captain Sullivan shot from his chair, fists clenched at his side, his anger and surprise stiffening his entire frame. "My daughter wishes to be a common seamstress?"

Emily flowed to her feet, calm and serene in the face of her father's outrage. "No, sir. I wish to become a merchant, like you. I wish to support myself with my own talents."

"I cannot allow you to do this." The captain's fists moved to his hips as he slowly shook his head. "You're to be married in the New Year. You have no need to support yourself, to impugn your future husband's standing in town by suggesting he cannot provide adequately for your needs."

Emily's calm ruffled as she lifted her chin. "Surely my actions would not be misconstrued in such a fashion. I shall make my reasons clear to any one who asks."

Samantha observed the exchange with a mix of horror and pride. Emily had determined to be in control of her destiny. Her writing and desire to operate a business both pointed to a need to live on her own terms. Her own form of independence, as it were. Yet she flouted the propriety expected of young women in proper society.

"Do you suppose our neighbors condone your aim?" Samantha sank back onto the settee, the fight in her dissipating as reason flowed into her mind. She'd have to wait until the government actually claimed her father's property. Until then, there was nothing to fight for. In the interim, she'd plan her approach, work out her arguments, so she'd be prepared when the time arrived.

Emily pivoted and crossed her arms. "In time, they will adjust to the reality."

Captain Sullivan dropped his hands to his sides. "Frank, talk to your betrothed. Mayhap she'll listen to your counsel. Lord knows she doesn't listen to mine."

Frank strode over to Emily, took both her hands in his, and kissed each in turn. "Em, if you love me, if you love your father, trust me to look into if and when your request might be granted at a later time." He pressed his lips briefly to hers. "You have my word."

Emily nodded but her expression turned mutinous. "Only if later means within the next year, not ten years from now. Do you promise?"

"I promise." He kissed her again, shaking with suppressed laughter. "One thing is for certain. Life with you will most definitely be an adventure."

"Of that you may be assured." Samantha pressed a hand to her aching thigh before standing. "I believe I'll excuse myself as I have much work ahead of me this evening."

After saying her farewells to the group, Samantha let herself out of the house. As she strolled home along the busy afternoon thoroughfare, her thoughts turned to Benjamin and his perplexing wound which refused to heal. To the fever which refused to relent. So many times an injury or ailment returned without any explanation she could fathom. She'd even heard that the seemingly indomitable George Washington suffered from repeated fevers and illness. But did any one question his doctor's ministrations? No, of course not. Likewise, had any one denigrated Mrs. Elizabeth Jackson's efforts to treat the poor patriots imprisoned on the British ships last year? Even though she'd eventually contracted the dreaded cholera herself and left her young fourteen-year-old son Andrew an orphan, nobody had spoken ill of her. Trent's attitude and insistence on his method being superior rankled in her chest almost as much as her physical reaction to him confused and intrigued her. But gramercy, he couldn't claim she'd not done her part to assist Benjamin. She'd give the ointment another few days to do its job before she'd even consider the possibility that Trent may be right. Her ways had worked countless times before. A niggle of doubt crept into her mind. What would she do if she were wrong and he turned out to be correct?

Samantha strolled through the garden, inspecting its condition, stopping to pick out a weed here and there. Sunshine touched the tops of the trees, leaving the shrubs and bushes in shadow. A light morning breeze tugged at her ebony hair, indulgently left hanging long and loose about her shoulders. Before long, she'd have to go back inside to break the fast with her parents and Evelyn. Afterward, she'd help

Evelyn move to her parents' house. Truth be told, it would be easy to accomplish the move, given the poor woman had no worldly goods. Only her son and her slave and the clothes on their backs.

She stared at the house for several minutes, fascinated by the way the panes of glass in the windows reflected the growing sunlight, and reluctant to enter its confines again. The cool breeze stirred her long hair and made her shiver. Or was it the house itself? *Do not be silly.* The house was her home. At least for the moment. Yet the atmosphere inside sizzled with tension and the portent of change. Her mother and father withheld a momentous decision from her. She could feel it lingering in the air, waiting to spring upon her like a mountain lion attacking a fawn. The suspicion that they contemplated leaving, whether they spoke on the subject or not, unsettled her. After they revealed their intent, she'd be faced with her own decision. In the event, her duty warred with her desires.

If she had a choice, she'd stay with her parents, supporting them in their decisions and with their activities. However, her duty called her to stay and care for her patients, her friends. Her obligations to the town, and more to the country, outweighed those to her parents, especially when she considered her father's political position. She blinked and turned away from her perusal of the back of the house. It had never occurred to her she might find herself at such a crossroad.

Looping around the back of the garden, she made her way slowly toward the house. Mentally, she noted a long list of tasks the garden demanded. Pruning the rose bushes. Thinning the abundance of honeysuckle to increase the number of flowers in the spring. Nipping the dead blossoms from the chrysanthemums. Cleaning up the snakeroot and chamomile beds. Cutting the low new branches from the dogwood tree trunks. So much to do, but every moment in the garden helped to calm her anxieties over her future.

The back door creaked open, drawing her attention. Belinda, in a light blue dress with a navy apron, appeared on the step and raised a hand to shade her dark eyes. Her ebony curls glinted in the sunlight, topped with a white cap. Anticipating the reason for the maid's presence, Samantha quickened her pace.

"There you are, Miss." Belinda held the door open as Samantha drew closer. "Miss Cynthia asked me to fetch you for breakfast."

"Thank you. Sorry to make you come search for me." Samantha climbed the steps to follow Belinda inside.

She hurried through the cozy kitchen, past the happy fire warming the kettle and heating the oven to bake the sweet breads, and into the hall. Her mother's high-pitched voice carried to her from the dining room. She should have returned much sooner, but she'd been distracted and upset by the looming changes. Guilt washed over her as she strode along the hardwood floor. Everyone else must already be seated, waiting on her. She paused in the open door, barely noticing the fine damask cloth draped over the table, platters of sliced meats and yellow cheeses interspersed with bowls of boiled eggs, red apples, and golden pears. A tureen of porridge stood in the center, steam escaping from under its lid. She knew not where the bounty of food came from, how many favors, or threats, her father had employed to provide such an abundant repast. Aaron sat at the head of the table, with her mother to his right. Her parents acknowledged her arrival with silence. Evelyn occupied the seat on the far side, gazing at her with a bemused smile. Samantha quickly took her place on the closest side of the long table.

"Please forgive me for being tardy." Samantha tucked her napkin into the bodice of her gown, spreading the cloth to protect her yellow day dress. "I'm relieved you did not wait for me."

"We waited until the hour arrived. What detained you?" Aaron peered at her over his coffee. "A patient, perhaps?"

"No. I needed to inspect the state of the garden." Selecting a slice of cold duck and a rasher of bacon, she replaced the platter on the table. "I warrant it will take quite some time to put it to rights for the winter."

Cynthia regarded her for several moments, until Samantha met her troubled gaze. Then she glanced at Aaron before resuming picking at her bowl of porridge liberally sprinkled with currants. A frown pulled at Samantha's brows as she watched her mother's slow movements with her spoon. Cynthia raised her eyes to meet Samantha's. There it was again, the worry on her mother's visage. Samantha observed the same anxiety on Aaron's face.

Eventually, they'd be forced to share whatever concerned them both so. In the meantime, Samantha had worries of her own. She caught Evelyn's attention. "Will you be ready to go to your parents' house after breakfast?"

"Indeed." Evelyn placed her cup on its saucer and considered each person at the table. "I wish to thank you all again for sheltering me in my immediate distress. You've been very kind. But I've been a burden long enough and am anxious to return to my family."

"Family is so important to cling to in these uncertain and dynamic times." Cynthia dipped into the hot cereal and then held the spoonful poised over her bowl to allow it to cool. "We are pleased to help you return to the comfort and safety of yours."

Samantha blinked at her mother's words. What prompted another discussion about family? Another tremor inched down her spine as the possible meanings flitted through her mind.

Samantha snared her mother's attention with the tilt of her head. "It is a good thing we have one another to rely upon. I cannot imagine forging ahead after the war without my parents to guide me."

Cynthia laid her spoon down, dabbed at her lips with her linen napkin. "We would never do anything that might endanger your welfare, my dear. But you must consider what you'd do should something happen to us."

Ah, here it comes. Samantha fiddled with her fork as she stared at her mother. "What do you think might happen?"

Aaron cleared his throat, drawing Samantha's gaze from her mother to rest upon his serious visage. "We may not have a choice but to consider leaving. If we are forced out, you are welcome to go with us. If you do not wish to leave, then I'll make appropriate arrangements for your shelter until a suitable husband can be identified. I've been remiss in not attending to the matter sooner."

"Leave?" Samantha dropped her fork with a clatter onto her plate. "Or marry? Surely you jest. You know I will not marry a—" She glanced at Evelyn, reluctant even now to reveal her secret in front of her parents.

Evelyn cocked her head, curiosity plain on her features. Samantha shook her head, letting Evelyn know she had misspoken.

"Like us, you may not have any choice in the matter." Cynthia stirred her porridge, lowering her eyes to focus on the movement of the spoon. "Some events are beyond our control."

"Enough of the serious talk for now. Much is to be thrashed out before we can make a knowledgeable choice." Aaron speared a bite of roast duck and placed it in his mouth, chewing the meat with the same concentration as he'd use mulling over a serious decision. "We can speak more on the subject later, after certain discussions take place."

Samantha gaped at her father, full understanding dawning. Ultimately, she'd have to choose to either leave with them or be left behind to fend for herself. Or foisted upon another man as a wife or left with family as a supposed spinster fit only to supervise the children. She couldn't reveal her secret to any one without courting their reprobation of her past. None of the possibilities appealed, each weighed and found wanting before being discarded. Whatever would become of her? Her appetite fled, so she arranged her fork on her plate, removed her napkin, and laid it on the table.

"When you're ready, Evelyn, I'll escort you home." Samantha scooted her chair away from the table and stood. "If you'll excuse me?"

"You've barely touched your food. Are you feeling well?" Evelyn's shocked frown mirrored the surprise on Cynthia and Aaron's faces.

Samantha was sick with dread, but she couldn't say as much. "I'm fine. I merely wish to tend to a few things before we go." Samantha looked to her father, silently asking for his permission to leave the room. Upon his nod, she dipped a quick curtsy to her mother and then strode away from the simmering tension surrounding her parents.

Her father's library, a place of restorative calm, beckoned her. The many volumes of literature and references helped to soothe her agitation. Books did not care about the upsets of her life. They provided a constant in an ever-changing world. Her father had collected many famous works, several from William Shakespeare, a translation of Ovid's *Metamorphosis*, and her favorite, *Meditations, Divine and Moral*, by Anne Dudley Bradstreet. His library held both interesting and amusing books, from Oliver Goldsmith's eight volume treatise *An History of the Earth, and Animated Nature*, to the often read Jonathan Swift's *The Beauties of Swift: or, the Favorite Offspring of Wit and Genius*. She trailed a finger along the leather bindings, lingering when she reached the most used books on medical practices. Buchan's *Domestic Medicine* and Bell's *System of Operative Surgery* displayed worn covers from the many hours she and her mother had pored over the details of their contents, certain pages dog-eared to make the information quickly attainable. Those books in conjunction with her own commonplace book filled with numerous recipes for simples and cures from many sources comprised the basis of her knowledge.

Several of the recipes she'd carefully recorded in her commonplace came directly from a Cherokee shaman she'd spent weeks with as he helped her heal the wound in her thigh. If Little Running Bear had not stumbled upon her, lying wounded and bleeding profusely behind an immense oak tree after the battle at Cowpens, she would have died like her sweet Edward. The terrible event played in her mind, a horrible tragedy performed on stage in her memory.

They were prepared for the fight, ready to confront and eliminate the British threat on the rolling hills of the area normally used to contain the cattle prior to slaughter. The Cowpens area, during the course of the war, had become a gathering place for the militia, and thus was familiar ground for the Americans. That chilly winter morning when they met the infamous Lieutenant Colonel Banastre Tarleton and his men, Brigadier General Daniel Morgan had prepared and readied his troops to defeat the bloody British officer. The morning fog had burned off in time to reveal the enemy had move closer than anticipated, apparently marching overnight while leaving untended campfires as decoys. The fighting started abruptly with shots and shouts as the two sides clashed.

Intense fighting claimed lives on both sides, men falling to the ground all around where Samantha, known as Sam Mason to her compatriots, fought beside her husband

Edward Mason. But the depth of defense General Morgan had put into place worked as he had intended. He'd instructed his infantrymen to fire three well aimed shots, then fall back for the next line of Americans to take up the battle. After they'd deployed their shots, they too fell back in orderly fashion to expose the Continentals, the core of the defense resting upon the veteran light infantrymen of the Maryland Line. Those men were led by Colonel John Eager Howard and knew their roles well. Tarleton suffered the loss of more than one hundred men killed and two hundred more wounded. Morgan's forces ruled the day with only a dozen men killed and fifty wounded. But the battle, though ultimately won by the Americans, proved to be a different kind of slaughter for Samantha.

As the redcoats had charged, firing volley after volley into the American line, cheering and huzzahing their way up the low rise, a shot pierced Edward's heart. Before Samantha could even cry out at the blood spreading across the front of his shirt, a British bayonet stabbed through her leg. The sound of Edward's lifeless body hitting the ground was obliterated by her scream of pain combined with grief, and then sweet oblivion swept over her as she fainted. She had never fainted before, for any reason. But she remained glad she had that day. Simply put, if she hadn't, she'd be dead. When she awoke, only bodies surrounded her. She dragged herself behind the nearby tree, knowing she must not be discovered dressed as a man fighting or face reprimand and then sent home in disgrace. Better to hide and tend to her wounds, both the physical gash in her upper thigh and the rent in her heart at the death of her husband.

She'd spent several weeks with Little Running Bear, observing and absorbing his techniques and methods. She'd scrutinized the way he interacted with his patients, employing both physical and mystical means to accomplish the healing of wounds and diseases. He had many astonishing ways she'd noted in her book. She gasped when a sudden thought popped into her head. Little Running Bear had his own rather unorthodox process for ridding a patient of a fever.

A tap on the library door startled her. She spun to find Evelyn poised on the lintel, her homespun gown clean but showing signs of wear from the forced evacuation of her home. That morning had been nearly as scary as the day Samantha became a widow. The worst aspect of her loss remained the secrecy surrounding her marriage which led to her inability to mourn in public. Her grief continued to regularly depress her spirits, but it also helped her to commiserate with her patients when they lost a loved one.

"We are ready to go." Evelyn motioned to her slave, Belinda, standing behind her, holding the squirming swaddled infant. "I'm sure Amy will enjoy a visit with you upon our arrival."

Shaking off her morbid thoughts, Samantha forced a smile. "Let me retrieve my cloak and we shall be off."

Minutes later the threesome strolled along the unusually busy streets toward the Abernathy home. The rumors of an imminent embarkation by the British onto the hundreds of waiting ships tugging at their anchors in the harbor set off a frenzy of activity in town. Any day, the blasted Britons would set sail for other lands, taking with them the acts of violence against the Americans as well as any free blacks who wished to take a chance on their personal freedom elsewhere. The problem, of course, came from the fact that no guarantees had been issued of their freedom and no assurance given that those blacks who took the opportunity were indeed free to take such a chance.

They turned down Church Street and made their way past the impressive French Huguenot Church, with its soaring spires and arched windows. The original immigrants had arrived in Charles Town in 1680, as a result of King Louis XIV revoking the Edict of Nantes which forced Protestants out of France. Over the ensuing century, many of the Huguenots had become wealthy plantation owners and merchants. Though despite their riches, they likely struggled along with the rest of the citizens of South Carolina in the grips of the soaring inflation the war had caused.

"Dr. Chalmers' theory that these filthy streets are the source for diseases hasn't gained much traction with the state government." Samantha shook her head as the doctor's residence came into view. The dirt and sand street they traversed, like all of the city's thoroughfares, ran with emptied chamber pots and refuse from the homes and businesses along the road.

"I do not find it surprising his concept should meet with resistance." Evelyn gripped a large covered basket containing victuals from the McAlester larder with both hands. "Precocious ideas such as his are always met with caution."

"Still, he suggested the connection nearly twelve years ago and has yet to provide evidence to support his claim," Samantha said. "I wonder if he ever will find a way to do so."

"I hear he partnered with Dr. Lining to better understand the dreaded yellow fever." Evelyn shifted the heft of the basket as they turned onto Broad, heading west and away from the rising sun. "Let's hope he has more success with that endeavor."

"I do hope they can locate the source of the illness and then a way to prevent its spread. So many have died from the contagion."

As they strolled past the many buildings and houses along Broad, Samantha pondered when she might have chance to visit the Apothecary farther along, a block or two past the Abernathy home. Her supplies of certain hard to find ingredients, such as syrup of white poppies, copperas, and dittany, had dwindled to an alarmingly low amount. Additionally, she loved venturing inside the shop, particularly since it was one of the oldest houses in the city. Its high pitched gable roof and dormer windows complemented the cypress walls to perfection.

When they approached the two-story Abernathy home off of Broad, the front door flung open. Amy, attired in a blue-gray day dress with a wide white collar and lacy kerchief tucked into the bodice, rushed down the steps and threw her arms around Evelyn.

"Welcome home, my dear sister!" Amy kissed both of Evelyn's cheeks amidst laughter and tears. "I've prepared your room for you and your little one. Let me see the sweet child."

"I'm glad to be home, so thank you." Evelyn returned Amy's long embrace.

Finally, Amy broke free and then took little Jim from Belinda, gushing over her nephew for several minutes, while Samantha, Evelyn, and Belinda stood by, chuckling at her enthusiasm. After several minutes, Amy ushered everyone into the house. Amy's mother, Lucille Abernathy, met them in the front hall, her hazelnut gown brushing the wood floor with each stride.

"Evelyn, my dear, I'm so glad you've come home." Lucille hugged her daughter before transferring the wriggling and cooing baby from Amy's grasp into her own capable arms. "We'll take good care of you both."

"Thank you, Mother." Evelyn grinned as her mother rocked Jim side to side.

No doubt existed in Samantha's mind that Evelyn and Jim would fine succor and support in the family home. The Abernathy home exuded love and contentment. A sense of security pervaded the house, stemming directly from the devotion shared among the inhabitants.

"Come have some of Samantha's fine herbal tea and cakes to celebrate." Amy led the way into the formal parlor at the front of the house. "I do not know what we'd have done without your teas, Samantha."

"I'm sure you'd find another beverage." Samantha chose an elegant Queen Anne chair with an intricately embroidered cushion. "If nothing else, you'd likely would have settled for chocolate or even coffee."

She fancied the fine furniture of the parlor, the place for receiving guests. Mayhap one day she might afford such beautiful furnishings. From the furniture to the oriental carpets to the display of crystal bottles filled with colorful liquors, the parlor intimated the refinement and success of the Abernathy household. Amy settled beside Evelyn on a high-backed settee, their skirts smashed together from their close proximity. Lucille occupied a matching chair flanking the fireplace where she could reach the tea service on the low table. She began pouring the fragrant tea and handing around the cups.

"I'm so excited to have you here." Amy squeezed Evelyn's hand. She accepted the cup and saucer from her mother and then looked at Evelyn. "Though I despise the reasons for the necessity, of course."

Evelyn smiled wistfully at her sister. "Walter, may he rest in peace, died defending his home and his family. I'll never forget his actions."

Nor would Samantha. Including his abusive treatment of his wife, and possibly poisoning her as well. She had no proof of the latter, but she'd always wonder. With a nod of thanks, she took the tea cup and saucer from Lucille.

"Samantha, how is Benjamin faring?" Lucille peered at her. "Better, I trust."

"Unfortunately, no. Which reminds me of a favor I wish to beg of you." Samantha sipped her tea, the hot liquid warming her. "I cannot stay by his side as I have other patients I must see to as well. Amy, I wonder if I might trouble you to keep a close eye on his condition, and inform me of any change?"

"Of course. What shall I do, though?" Amy placed her cup and saucer on the low table. "Sit by his side and read to him?"

"He may enjoy your efforts if you elect to do so. However, his quarters reek of masculine neglect." Samantha lifted a brow, looking in Amy's direction. "I believe some feminine touches are in order to soften the harsh environment and make him more comfortable."

Amy chuckled as a sly smile spread across her lips. "Indeed. I believe I can assist in making his abode helpful to his recovery."

"Very good." Samantha sipped her tea and then smiled at Amy. "I believe Benjamin will be the better for your attention."

"You must make him well soon." Amy's expression sobered, the sparkle in her eyes dimming. "After all, Emily and I are planning quite a wonderful marriage ceremony at Frank's lovely house. We wouldn't want Benjamin to not be in attendance for his own wedding."

"Of course." The wedding. She'd nearly forgotten. Or rather, more pressing concerns had shoved the thought far beneath other priorities. She inwardly groaned. Now she must show the requisite interest. "How are your plans progressing?"

"We've begun making over our best gowns for the occasion." Amy patted her lap with both hands. "Emily is such a wonder with her embroidery. She'll make both of our gowns the talk of the season. Which is her intent so that her deuced shop might be a success despite her father's objections."

Samantha recalled her own parents' objections to her

marriage to Edward. Their protests led to the need for the secret ceremony by the frontier minister rather than by the rector in Charles Town for everyone to witness. She'd never told any one about the marriage. Not her parents nor her friends. She and Edward had promised to keep the event between them until they found an appropriate time to share the news with friends and family. Before only God and the officiator, they had joined their lives as one, standing in a secluded glade bathed in dappled sunshine. She'd thought it the most perfect setting, but now as she contemplated the ceremony ahead for her friends, she rather envied them the public celebration. How wonderful it would be to share the happiness surrounding the blessed event.

"Is she still going on about her accessories shop?" Lucille shook her head. "I shall have to speak to her about such foolishness."

"I don't believe it foolish for a woman to look out for herself." Samantha studied Lucille, her head tilted to one side. Did the woman really have so little faith in her niece's talents and capabilities? "We should be able to provide for ourselves in the event no man is willing or able to do so."

"I dare say Emily shall not find herself in such a position, as long as Frank is alive and well." A tight smile eased onto Lucille's lips as she glanced at Amy and then met Samantha's eyes once more.

"That is my exact point." Samantha leaned forward, clasping her hands together in her lap. "What would become of her if, God forbid, something befell Frank so he could not provide for her welfare? Would she be forced to rely upon family in order to survive?"

"Are you demeaning my need to move home?" Evelyn asked quietly.

Abashed, Samantha sat back and gazed at Evelyn. "My sincere apology to you. I meant no offense. Of course you should seek assistance after the birth of your baby and then losing your husband all in a few days span. But in the long run, after the period of mourning is completed, what will you do?"

Evelyn sat rigidly on the settee, pulling slightly away from her sister. "I cannot answer your query at this moment, as the wounds are too fresh upon my heart. But believe me when I tell you that I shall not sit by and languish."

Samantha bowed her head, chagrined at the idea she'd injured her newly adopted sister in any way, and then glanced at Amy. "I fear my blunt words have offended, so I will beg you to excuse me."

"You do not need to leave, my friend." Amy reached out a hand to grip Samantha's forearm. "I wish to tell you more about the upcoming nuptials. We have some fine ideas for the feast and the entertainment for the Twelfth Night festivities."

The idea of delving deeper into the particulars for the happy occasion made Samantha's stomach turn over in a most unpleasant manner. She should have shared her past wedding and widowhood with Emily and Amy. For some inexplicable reason, revealing the event had no longer seemed important after Edward died. Essentially, as far as any other person knew, she was unmarried. Hiding her grief did not lessen its impact upon her, but it did prevent others from chastising her for ignoring her parents' wishes. Perhaps if she'd listened to their preferences she would not be a widow, but she also would not have known the love of her husband. Amy's elated expression as she held fast to Samantha's arm made her feel all the more guilt at not revealing the entire truth. Chagrined at the secret between them, one which close friends normally would share in, Samantha clasped her hands and pressed the palms tight together in a futile attempt to calm her agitation. Amy released her arm and sat back, a frown settled on her face.

"I'm certain your plans will yield a beautiful event." Samantha stood and smoothed her gown into place. "I would cherish hearing more about them, but please keep the pleasure of the conversation for another visit. I'll see myself out, if you'll allow me."

Moments later, after more remonstrations to stay followed by quick hugs and Amy's repeated promises to visit Benjamin, Samantha stood on the street, trying to catch her breath and decide which direction to turn. Home or to visit Benjamin? Drawn in both directions, she looked first one way and then the other. She sighed as she admitted to herself which destination beckoned more urgently. Knowing Amy planned to see Benjamin posthaste, she sauntered toward home to face the pending decisions lurking in the shadows there, awaiting her return.

Chapter Five

Samantha rushed into Benjamin's apartment the next morning, not bothering to pause and knock. The door banged closed behind her. A fire burned in the fireplace, the black kettle steaming on the hook. She sniffed. Soup most likely. The rest of the room showed marks of a woman's touch. Amy must have taken her advice. Nothing looked amiss. Why had Amy summoned her? She strode toward the bedroom. "Amy? Where are you?"

"Oh, thank God, Samantha." Amy ran through the door to grab hold of Samantha's arm and drag her back toward the bedroom. "His skin is red, and there's a strong smelling pus oozing from his wound. Hurry!"

Samantha went to Benjamin where he rested on the bed. His black hair lay plastered against his scalp. Dark circles emphasized his eyelids, closed to block out the early morning daylight streaming through the windows. A quick inspection of the wound site confirmed Amy's description.

"Get me some hot water and a clean rag, and hurry." Samantha checked his temperature, worried when he felt even warmer than her last visit. "Benjamin?"

He blinked awake, and she nearly gasped at how faded his vibrant blue eyes had become. How distant and unfocused they seemed. She simply had to figure out a means to make this man well or he'd die. She wouldn't be able to face Amy if her methods failed to save him.

"How do you feel?" She smoothed his damp hair back from his face. The contrast from how he looked a few weeks before to the man lying weak and sweaty on the mussed bed shocked her. Only a few times in her life had she seen the threat of a grim death so plainly evident in a person's features. No, she wouldn't permit him to die. She'd do all in her power to prevent such an end to his brave life after he'd risked all for his country.

Amy arrived carrying a bowl with steaming water and a clean cloth. Samantha indicated for her to place them on the little table. She did as directed and then stepped to the end of the bed, worry creasing her face.

"Worse." Benjamin stretched his head and neck from side to side. The lone word came out with pain lingering on the edges.

"Did you drink the tea?" The pot rested on the night table. She hefted it, relieved to find it empty. "Let me make more after I clean your wound."

"Trent?" Benjamin grimaced and shifted on the bed. "Is he…coming?"

"I sent for him," Amy said, gripping the footboard. "He should arrive momentarily."

Samantha stiffened at the name, as though he could be conjured by merely saying the word. Even without his physical presence, she detected her own pulse increase. She quashed the response with a silent rebuke to herself. "I'm sure he'll visit soon. Now hold still."

Efficiently, she cleaned away the drying paste with firm but gentle strokes of the rag. Stifling her reaction to the quantity of pus, she was relieved when she did not see any more dying skin. While the oozing created concern in her breast, the pus was better than gangrene any day.

The outer door opened and then closed. Footsteps sounded on the wood floor, drawing closer with each beat. Anticipation increased her pulse rate and made her breath hitch. Samantha concentrated on her task though entirely aware of the man drawing closer with each racing beat of her heart.

"Thank goodness. Trent is here." Amy released the wood footboard and strode from the room.

Did he have to show up at that precise moment, when she had exposed the wound to the air and his scrutiny? Her fingers shook as she dipped the cloth into the bowl.

"Wait, let me see the injury." Trent appeared at the open door and moved quickly toward the bed.

Samantha's senses tingled when he stopped beside her to examine Benjamin. "He's a bit warmer than yesterday, which worries me, but the edge of the wound appears healthy."

"Yes, but his health has not improved." Trent regarded her silently before shaking his head. "You do see that he is extremely ill and the wound is resisting that foul unguent you've been applying so religiously."

"I know he's ill, but I believe my salve is reversing the gangrene's hold. It's his fever that worries me even more. I have some ideas on that, but for now step back so I can tend to him."

He studied her for several long moments before slowly nodding. "Only because you have already begun to clean the wound will I agree for you to continue. But I'm watching to make sure you do not hurt him further." Trent reluctantly shifted to stand closer to Amy, though he leaned forward so he could do as he had warned.

Nothing like a distrustful audience. She carefully washed the wound with the warm water, but her ministrations still caused Benjamin to moan and grunt with each dab and swipe of the cloth. When she'd finished, Trent motioned for her to move away. Biting her lip so as to not say the retort threatening to rush from her mouth, she retreated several steps.

"I'm going to bleed you, Benjamin." Trent retrieved his measured bowl and scalpel from his ever-present black bag. "But this should be the last time. Then I'm going to give you a purge to help balance your humors. If your temperature is not better by tomorrow, we'll need to reconsider amputation before the sickness spreads."

Amy gasped beside her. Samantha put an arm around her shoulders and squeezed hard. Amy had not been privy to the earlier discussion related to the drastic measure. Despite Trent's eagerness, Samantha had made Benjamin a promise. He would not lose his arm. *Would not.*

Benjamin shook his head vehemently. "No. You won't cut my arm off." He aimed determined eyes at Samantha. "Don't let him."

"I promise." Samantha nodded and then addressed Trent. "You must respect your patient's request, doctor."

"Why won't you acknowledge the wisdom of the procedure?" Trent glared at her and then glanced at Benjamin, his expression softening at the determination evident in his patient's eyes.

"I'd rather die." Benjamin's resolve pushed through tense lips. "Upon my word, do not cut off my arm."

"Ben…" Amy's voice trailed off, a tear sliding down her cheek. She sniffed and turned away.

Samantha glanced between the two men, saw a silent exchange pass from determined to accepting. She folded her arms and stared at the doctor. "Trent, you made a promise to Benjamin."

"Against my better judgment." Trent fingered the handle of the scalpel as he considered Benjamin's words. "Very well, my friend, as you wish. I won't resort to amputation unless you permit me to do so. But will you allow me to bleed you?"

"Last time?" Benjamin waited for Trent's response.

"If it doesn't work, I'll consult with my father to determine another course of action. One that doesn't involve salves and ointments."

"You said you'd consult with me." Samantha dropped her hands to her sides and stepped closer to the bed. "Unlike the fools in North Carolina, I have an idea for employing a simple sweating technique I picked up from a Cherokee medicine man. I think—"

"You cannot seriously expect me to agree to use anything savages on the frontier use." Trent gaped at her with arched brows. Slowly, he shook his head and then turned back to Benjamin. "What do you think?"

Benjamin considered each of them and settled back. He drew in a long breath and pushed up his sleeve. "Anything to try to make me better. I ache all over."

"I've witnessed the technique I'm considering work many times." Samantha grabbed hold of Trent's arm to secure his full attention. That was a huge mistake. She let go just as quickly and drew in a steadying breath. "Trust me on this."

Trent glanced over his shoulder at her with a serious expression. "If my hospital existed, we wouldn't be having this argument as only trained doctors would have a say in the patient's treatment."

"Remind me to never step foot in such a place." Samantha surveyed Benjamin's condition, her practiced eye noting fine details. Eyes squinting slightly against the brightness of the light flooding the room. Tiny lines radiating from his drawn mouth, indicating the level of pain he endured. Fingers gripping the quilt draped over his supine form. After all she'd witnessed of the supposedly better ways of doctors, she'd stick to the old ways, thank you very much. "I'd not hand over control of my care to a stranger."

While Trent prepared to reopen the incisions, Samantha checked Benjamin's temperature with a hand on his forehead. Poor thing really did have a fever. Not enough to really alarm her, but worrisome. Everyone had to ward off a temperature now and again. It was the ones that persisted that concerned more than those which came and went. She snatched up the tea pot and hurried to the common room where she quickly brewed a fresh pot.

As she carried the tea into the bedroom, Benjamin cried out and then collapsed onto the mattress. She bit her lip to stifle a grin. Apparently he'd still not become accustomed to seeing his own blood. She quickly set the items on the table and then turned to inspect her patient.

Trent continued making the incisions wide enough to drain into the bowl beneath Benjamin's limp arm. She pressed a hand to Benjamin's forehead. He lay still, unmoving, not reacting to her touch. "I do believe he has swooned yet again."

"He'll come round in time." Trent inserted the tip of the scalpel and sliced steadily across Benjamin's skin. "Miss Amy, would you be so kind as to open the windows? The fresh air seems to help revive him."

"Certainly." A look of relief on her face, Amy turned away from the sight of the oozing blood running down Benjamin's arm into the bowl, and hurried to open the windows.

"While he's relaxed, I'll reapply the salve." After receiving Trent's reluctant permission, Samantha slathered on more of the reddish ointment, covering the infected area in a thick layer. With good fortune, the concoction would yield the hoped for results within the next few days. If the fever didn't break in that time, then she'd use Little Running Bear's method. It would do no harm and may even benefit Benjamin.

"Miss Samantha, I believe we should discontinue the application of odiferous ointments given the lack of progress our patient is making." Trent wiped the blade on a clean corner of the bloody cloth in his hand, then wrapped it in another cloth and stowed it in his bag. "Don't you agree?"

"I believe you should speak to George Manning, the lawyer in charge of transferring loyalist property into patriot hands." Trent's constant lack of faith in her methods irked her to the bone. She rubbed her hands clean and tucked the rag into her bag before addressing him. "Then you'll have your hospital and may do as you wish. In the meantime, we stick to our plan."

He grabbed her arms and pulled her close, eyes flashing, jaw set as he gently shook her. "Face facts, Samantha. Your ways have been disproven. Your mysterious combinations of plants and spices and manure do not heal so much as delay healing."

She gasped from the impact of his words, the fierceness of his expression, the grip on her arms, and the electric pulses shimmying through her at his touch. Coherent thought fled with the cool breeze drifting across her too warm cheeks. She desperately moistened dry lips and swallowed. What was the matter with her? Trent wanted to take away everything she'd worked for, and she behaved like some wanton maid. *Gramercy*. Mentally shaking herself, she straightened her spine and then drew a calming breath.

"Release me." Samantha attempted to step back, increase the distance between them. "Now." She waited for him to let her go, but he held firm.

"You must agree he's not improving using this course of action." He examined her expression with serious eyes. "Do you not?"

She shook her head, lifting her chin. Hoping he'd let go so she could more readily focus on the topic at hand. "The gangrenous tissue has healed."

He frowned. "Yet the fever remains, the skin is not mending." He gently shook her again, freezing her in place with his intensity. "We must change direction of the treatment in order to save his life. Such is common sense when one method fails to produce the intended results."

"Then why do you cling to the hope that bleeding him will help when it has not? We should consider following Little Running Bear's technique. I know it will help." She detected a steely resolve in his posture, understood his meaning. He implied another approach which they'd already discussed and dismissed. *No. Not amputation.* "You must adhere to our patient's wishes. You promised him. Now promise me."

He clenched his jaw, his usually friendly eyes hard and serious. "You cannot dictate to me how I should treat my patient."

"No, but *our* patient can." She indicated his hands grasping her arms. Met his eyes again. "You're hurting me."

His grip relaxed but didn't release. His expression changed from determined to something softer, more intimate. "My apologies for your discomfort."

"Promise me you'll adhere to his wishes." *And let go of me, before the desire to taste your lips proves too great.* She chewed her lower lip to keep herself from following her wayward musings. Honestly, she must wrestle her errant thoughts back to ladylike channels.

He studied her for an extended moment, then nodded once. "Very well, I shall promise. But you must promise me something in exchange."

"Seeing as you have me held captive, I doubt I can refuse. What is your demand?"

"If there is no improvement in his condition over the

next fortnight, I shall take full command of his treatment. Agreed?"

His suggestion that he could better treat the man made her bristle. Then she relaxed after some consideration. She had nothing to lose given her treatment would prevail in less time than a fortnight. She smiled at him and his grip tightened. "Agreed. Now will you release me?"

Amy sauntered back to stand at the foot of the bed, amusement on her face. "Honestly, Trent, the poor woman shouldn't have to endure being handled roughly as well as tongue lashed."

Trent opened his hands as though he realized he still held her arms and stepped back. "My apologies for abusing you in such a manner, Miss Samantha." He inclined his head in a brief nod. "I'm afraid I could not help myself as we held such an intense conversation."

"Forgiven."

"I do not believe Benjamin should be left alone, as weak as he is." Amy folded her hands before her skirts. "I've decided I shall stay with Benjamin until he's well."

"I had hoped you'd come to that conclusion. Thank you." Samantha rubbed her arms where Trent had held fast only moments before, relieving the tingling his touch left behind.

It was Trent's turn to gasp as he realized what Amy intimated with her decision. "Miss Amy, a young woman such as yourself should not even consider staying with a single man, no matter how ill he might be. It simply is not proper. You should have a chaperone at a minimum."

"How quaint. He's my betrothed and thus my responsibility." Amy chuckled as she laid a hand on Trent's rigid arm. "Do not fret. I shall request assistance from my mother and Evelyn when needed. Mayhap Emily will pop in to assist from time to time, as wedding plans and renovations allow."

"As you wish." Trent shook his head, a rueful smile flickering on his lips. "You ladies appear to have things well in hand."

"Yes, we do." Samantha slipped the wrapped pot into her medicine bag. "Benjamin is in excellent hands."

"Go with you?" Samantha sat back against the hard chair, gaping at her father as if he'd lost his sense. The surreal conversation over a late lunch with her parents the next afternoon quaked every semblance of stability within her. "Where would we go?"

"Canada. I hear it's beautiful and remains faithful to the King." Her father poked his three-tined fork into the fried pastry stuffed with lamb kidneys and onions on his plate. A pile of fresh greens drizzled with olive oil waited alongside. "We'd be welcome there."

Leave her patients and friends? Charles Town? South Carolina? *America*? Her very being rebelled at the prospect. "I cannot."

"Be sensible, child." Her mother sliced into the delicate pastry and then fixed her sad eyes upon Samantha. "You have no future here. Come with us, keep the family together."

"I cannot bear the thought of leaving the country I love, to remain under the thumb of King George. Surely you don't have to evacuate along with the British." Tears closed her throat. Her parents calmly discussed fleeing town, having no idea the depth of pain slicing through her at the thought of abandoning the house, the extensive library in the parlor, and most of all the beautiful garden. Her *home*. She'd fight for it with every breath in her body. "There must be a way."

"I feared you'd say as much. I cannot leave without ensuring your safety and shelter. I hate it has come to this point, as I fear it means I may never see my only child again."

Aaron placed a bite into his mouth and chewed, silently studying her for several moments. "That is why I've made the necessary arrangements."

Samantha had made her specialty, little fried birds, at her parents' request. She'd happily agreed to make them not realizing the meal may well be her parents' last one in Charles Town.

"What do you mean?" She contemplated her own little bird and elected to eat the greens instead. Her appetite had flown away yet again.

"The moment we leave, they will confiscate all of my property. Every piece of land, building, and warehouse, and all they contain. You won't be able to stay here when they do." He dabbed his mouth with a napkin. "I hate to leave you behind, especially when I have no idea what may happen. But I know you, my darling daughter. Given your anticipated desire to remain in town, I have arranged for my partner to house you until you find a better situation. He has already begun searching for a fitting husband for you."

With each word from his mouth, her spirits sank and her determination deepened. "Thank you, Father, but your partner's assistance will not be necessary." So casual, so accepting of the circumstances. She couldn't tolerate his belief that she needed a husband to survive. She'd find her own way if they had so little care for her future. She'd forge her own path forward. "I shall fight for my home. Please thank your partner for his proffered generosity but I shall not need it."

Her father huffed and shook his head. "You will not win, daughter. The law is on their side, not ours, nor yours."

"I must try. You must see why I am compelled to attempt to retain my home. If you'll excuse me." She folded her napkin and rose to her feet.

"Where are you going?" Her father dropped his fork with a clank onto his plate.

She turned and regarded him, counting to five before trusting herself to respond. "To see Mr. Manning and find out what I must do to keep our home."

Aaron stood and placed both hands on the table. "We shall leave shortly. Do not tarry should you wish to kiss your mother good-bye."

"Please, Samantha, come with us." Tears stood in her mother's eyes. "We don't want you to stay here and face the uncertain future of this poor country. Nor the wrath of the fools who think they've won something grand by defeating our king." She brushed away the tears leaking down her cheeks. "What will become of you?"

Samantha looked at Cynthia and then Aaron. "I love you both, but I sincerely believe in the future of America and of Charles Town. Leaving my home and country is entirely out of the question. I shall return posthaste after speaking with Mr. Manning. Please, do not leave before my return."

Draping her heavy shawl about her shoulders, she hurried from the house and strode down Queen toward King. All along the street, burned out hulls of houses stood as silent testimony of the 1778 conflagration. With the end of the war in sight, hope for rebuilding the town swept through Samantha as she strode past house after house. She turned onto King and walked on for several minutes before marveling at the increased activity in the beef market on the corner of King and Broad. The poor statue of William Pitt, which faced east on Broad, looking straight at the Exchange at the bottom of the street, still had no right arm thanks to the shelling by the British over the past years. She continued on her way, aware of the distance she had to traverse and the time slipping away when her parents would board their waiting wagon. They'd probably find some ship to carry them north along the Atlantic coast and into Canada. The trip would surely take months. Months during which she would rarely if ever receive a letter or message from them while they located a place to settle. She would have no way of knowing if they even survived the passage on the ship. The immensity of the choice her parents had made overwhelmed her. The hot prickle of tears smarted her eyes.

She absently greeted folks as they strolled by, her thoughts in turmoil. Her home and garden meant more to her than she could adequately commit to words. The recently planted snakeroot would not reach useful size and maturity for years. The lush rosemary bush took five years to reach its current dimensions. So many necessary plants both for medicinal and victual purposes resided within the elaborate garden. How would she continue her practice without access to the very tools of her trade?

Stalking up the front walk to the imposing brick house on King, she rapped on the door.

The door swung open and George Manning himself greeted her. His height and breadth coupled with agreeable features made her feel safe in his presence. Although he had not resided in town for very long, he and his wife merged with the other residents with surprising speed and ease. Hope swelled in her chest as she smiled at him.

"Miss McAlester, what a pleasant surprise. Come in." He ushered her inside with a swoop of a hand.

"Thank you." She took several steps into the softly lit interior.

Clutching her shawl to bolster her confidence, she noted the gleaming stone floors and whitewashed walls. Oil portraits of finely attired men with their hunting dogs hung on the far wall. A pianoforte stood in the center of the parlor to their left. The opulence of the Manning home reminded her of the vast gap in status between her father and the man closing the door behind her. Not that her parents wanted for much, her father's dealings having provided well for them even during the lean years. But compared to George Manning's status, her father's ventures did not measure up. What was she doing in this luxurious place? The laws were clear. She had no chance. She had no choice.

Swallowing the dismay rising in her throat, she turned to face the handsome lawyer. "My father prepares to abandon his property and leave me homeless. More to the point, my midwife and healing practice relies upon the garden behind the house. I cannot survive without my plants. Please, sir. I beg of you. Do not take my home from me."

His happy smile sobered. "My sorrow for your situation is boundless, but I fear my hands are tied in this matter. The governor has declared by the Act of Confiscation that all loyalist properties are to be secured and returned to patriotic hands as quickly as possible."

"But sir, where am I to go? Has the governor no regard for my fate?" Despite the heavy knitted wrap, she shivered.

George splayed his hands, palm up. "Your father's declarations and actions leave no doubt as to his political leanings, which of course means when he leaves town, as I understand he intends to do this very day, my job is clear. I shall begin the process to transfer legal ownership to the town for auction at a later time."

Samantha held out a hand as if she could halt the hated words from emerging from his mouth. If only she could ward off the dreadful reality. "But I am a patriotic woman. Why cannot I keep the house?"

He started shaking his head before she'd asked her question. "Impossible, simply impossible. Women are not legally competent to sign contracts."

"But sir…" What more could she say in her defense? The law was clear. Her shoulders drooped. "Is there no recourse?"

"No, my dear." He slowly shook his head and then ushered her to the door. Opening it, he paused. "I strongly recommend you find another place to live within the next few weeks. If I can assist you in any way, naturally, I am at your service."

Back on the street, both familiar and foreign as she contemplated her next steps, hot tears blinded her. Her faint hopes had been dashed against the rocks of the legal system like waves at high tide. A tear eased down each cheek, a reminder to make a plan, a path forward. Blinking the drops away, she squared her shoulders and started slowly toward home. At least she had time to decide what to take when she was forced from her home. After her parents fled, she'd be on her own. Her home was about to be snatched away. Panic glimmered in her soul as she contemplated the enormity of her predicament.

"Good day, Miss Samantha." Trent tipped his tricorne as he strolled up to pace beside her. "I cannot believe my good fortune. How are you on this fine afternoon?"

Could she not find peace anywhere in her life? Must he appear to vex her further? She stifled the urge to scream, aware the good people passing by might believe he'd come to accost her. Perhaps they wouldn't be far from the truth. She sighed as she turned to face him. "I'm afraid I'm not good company at the moment, Doctor."

"Anything amiss I can assist you with?" He settled his hat firmly in place and matched her quickened stride.

"It is none of your concern." She tugged her shawl tight about her shoulders, but it proved inadequate to protect her from the chill inside.

"Is it Benjamin?" He strolled casually alongside, intent on the street activity around them. Couples walked along the edge of the street, horse-drawn carriages leaving tracks down the center of the dirt road. "I'll admit that you're correct in one respect. We must work together, as he requested, to better his condition."

"We are doing so." Or at least she was, despite her misgivings of his abilities. Treating patients in her own way, in her own time, had proven the best approach in the past. Of course, circumstances would soon necessitate she work alone. Times did change and she tried to stay open to new possibilities.

"Indeed. Yet I sense a reluctance on your part, perhaps a misgiving?"

"I prefer to provide my own counsel, if you will." Being alone, though, had taken on new meaning with the looming departure of her parents. Her dark blue skirts dragged the dusty street with each step. "However, I do not begrudge your assistance with Benjamin's case. It is proving more challenging than first anticipated."

"Agreed. Say, looks like we have company." Trent stopped, bending down to greet a medium-sized white dog with caramel colored splotches that had trotted up and halted before them.

"I wonder where it came from." Samantha paused beside the pair, smiling at how friendly the young dog appeared. She offered it her hand to sniff and then patted its head. The soft fur slid easily through her fingers, and she rubbed its chin. "Whose is it? Do you know this dog?"

Trent shook his head, scouring the passersby for any one who may have missed the animal. "Appears to be a stray."

"Let us continue. Surely someone will come looking for him." Samantha started down the street, aware of the late hour and afraid she'd miss bidding her parents farewell. For the last time. She choked on tears and swallowed them. She'd not cry in front of Trent.

Trent caught her up in two long strides. "Her, if I'm not mistaken."

"Her who?"

He indicated the dog walking beside them. "I believe she is a female Water Spaniel, a good hunting dog by all accounts."

"Shoo, now." Samantha waved a hand at the dog, but it smiled up at her, tongue lolling out one side of its mouth. "I don't need a dog."

Trent chuckled as they turned onto her street. "Looks like she disagrees with you on that score."

"We shall see." Samantha suddenly spotted her father lugging a box out to the waiting wagon parked in front of her home, two bays stamping impatiently in the harness. "Oh no." She lifted her skirts far enough to prevent tripping on them and then practically trotted down the street, Trent and the dog trailing after her.

The vehicle sat ready to depart, trunks and baskets piled in the flat bed behind the single seat. Her mother hurried out the front door, a hamper heavy in her hands. She handed the woven basket to her husband and then spotted Samantha as she closed the distance between them.

"Mother, you're leaving so soon?" Skidding to a halt, long skirts kicking up a cloud of dust around them, she hugged Cynthia as though she'd never see her again. As well might be the case.

"The time has come for us to fly before the wrath of the patriots is inflicted upon us." Her mother's mouth pressed into a straight line, tears in her eyes. "Do not hate us, my dear. We love you and wish you good fortune. But we must go. You do understand, don't you?"

"I shall miss you both more than words can describe. When will I see you again? How will I contact you?" Questions and concerns crowded her mind as her father finished snugging the load into place and came around the wagon.

Trent and the dog stopped beside her, the pup sitting

down, her tongue still hanging out. He inclined his head to each of her parents, a question in his eyes. "Mr. McAlester, ma'am. What are you doing?"

"Leaving town for the final time." Aaron shook Trent's hand and then wrapped Samantha in a bear hug. "We'll send word as soon as we find a new place to settle. Do not worry, my dear. I trust you'll be fine after we've gone. You've always had good sense and are very capable." He regarded Trent for a breath. "Still, you'll need help. Watch over her for us, will you, young man?"

Trent nodded seriously, shaking Aaron's hand. His curious expression changed to one of happy determination. "Indeed, I will."

"Father, must you leave?" Samantha grasped her father's arm. "You've exhausted all other possible ways to avoid this irrevocable decision?"

Aaron shrugged and shook his head slowly. "These are amazing and confusing times in which we live, my dear. Amazing changes, therefore, will result as the world adjusts to the independence of the American colonies." He laid a hand on her cheek and studied her expression. "We'll miss you, but we'll always love you."

Samantha pressed her cheek against his hand, swallowing the sadness filling her throat, struggling to contain the fear mingled with despair in her chest.

Her father patted her cheek, a catch in his breath as he gave her a quick smile. "Time to go."

Samantha stepped back, stifling the gasp of pain at the imminent departure of the two people in all the world she loved beyond all else. Her head comprehended why they must board the wagon and depart town, but her heart rebelled at the need. A shout from behind her made her spin around and stare up the street she'd just traversed. A mob of men marched toward where her father prepared to abandon the town. A good sized pot rested in the hands of the man at the front of the crowd, another carrying an immense bag of feathers.

"Father, what is happening?" Samantha gaped at the mob as the men strode angrily closer with each passing second. "Why do they intend to tar and feather you? What have you done?"

"Nothing more than any other loyalist, my dear. Cynthia, my darling, climb aboard. The time has arrived when we must away. Good-bye, Samantha." Aaron helped her weeping mother to step up into the front seat, the wagon rocking with each movement. Cynthia sat huddled on the seat, soft sobs drifting on the afternoon air. He hugged Samantha again, then went around the wagon to climb up and take the reins. Without looking back as the men shouted and broke into a run, he slapped the reins on the horses' backs, urging them into a brisk trot, and quickly disappeared down the street.

Samantha stood without moving until the wagon, with its precious cargo, turned the corner, intent on maintaining her composure in front of the man beside her. The mob cursed him for several minutes after he'd left and then slowly dispersed. She glared at the men, refraining from chastising them with every ounce of self-control she possessed until they had left the street. Then, when the realization she'd never see her parents again lodged in the pit of her stomach, she started crying, wailing, then keening, and couldn't find a way to make herself stop. Gasping sobs wracked her shoulders, made it difficult to catch her breath, as she swayed in her grief and fear. What would become of her? What was she to do?

Trent enveloped her in his embrace, steely arms cradling her head against his coat which soon became soaked from her distress. His hand stroked her hair as she wailed. The dog whined, sidling to press against her skirts. Her only thought remained the solitary existence she faced as a result of the Americans winning the war for independence. She cried harder, gasping for air. She clung to Trent, grateful for his quiet strength and support as her world collapsed around her.

Chapter Six

The house echoed with each step Samantha took, pacing through rooms devoid of happy chatter. Dents evident in the oriental carpet in the parlor ached for the chairs and tables which once sat there. Each room reflected where some piece of furniture or decoration had been removed by her father, loaded into the wagon, and carted away. The empty spaces served as silent witness to the flight of her parents three days before. She paused at the door to what had been her father's office.

The dog who had adopted her despite Samantha's attempt to ignore it sat panting, content to remain at her side. After spending a day referring to the beast as "dog," she finally broke down and chose a name. A name that spoke to her Scottish heritage, a tie back to the proud and loyal ancestors her father had spoken of so warmly. No matter where she went, Thistle insisted on accompanying her. To the market, to the lawyer, to Benjamin's. The young dog remained at her side like a new appendage. Samantha reached down to run a hand over its curly haired head. Still, despite her protests, she had to admit the dog provided good company.

She perused the room, seeing its contents with a different perspective. So many books and maps left behind when her father fled the country. Shelves and one lone desk neatly held his collection, which had become hers as a result of his departure. Holding the lump in her throat at bay with an effort, she gripped the door frame with one hand. She'd cried enough over the past days to fill the urn by her bed. The memory of Trent's strong embrace supporting her as she cried made her cringe with mortification. She'd survived much worse without falling apart, so why had she done so then?

Loud rapping summoned her to the front door. With a long sigh, she headed toward the rapping. Thistle barked and raced ahead, her long curly hair dancing like a running mop. A rush of cold air chilled Samantha as she opened the door.

"Amy, what's the matter?" Samantha ushered her worried friend inside. "Is it Benjamin?"

"Oh, Samantha, you must do something for him." Amy wrung her hands. "He cannot continue in such a condition."

Thistle sniffed at Amy's black cloak and long burgundy skirts. Samantha waved the dog away, and Thistle returned to sit at her side. One thing for certain, the dog was smart and learned quickly.

"You've not located its owner?" Amy frowned at the animal, momentarily distracted from her pressing concern by the friendly face and lolling pink tongue. "I wonder if it ran away or if the owner might be dead?"

"I've wondered the same, but Thistle seems content to be with me and me with her. For now."

"You're content with the added responsibility of her care?" Amy shook her head. "With everything you're facing, I urge you to find someone to take the dog off your hands."

The house would stand empty and cold with only her rattling around within its walls to make any noise. No, better to have the dog to keep life in the homestead. "We're managing. Until the government steals my home from me. Then I do not know where I shall live."

Amy slowly shook her head. "I'm troubled on your behalf but have no means with which to help. Evelyn and Belinda along with the little one have taken the empty rooms at my house. Did your father not make any provisions for you?"

"He did." Samantha waved off the suggestion, wrinkling her nose at the idea of his partner choosing a husband for her. "None worth considering. But the time draws near when I shall be forced to move. I simply cannot bear the thought."

"In the event, you can always sleep on our couch if need be." Amy hugged Samantha, a brief embrace meant to bolster and comfort. "You're the strongest among us, my friend. We will do all we can for you."

Samantha folded her hands. "But tell me, what has brought you here with such urgency?"

"Ben's fever continues, though it's not increasing." Amy hugged herself, arms tight against the dark gray sash at her waist. "Mayhap Trent could do something? Please? You must help him."

Samantha clucked her tongue. "We are doing our best."

"I know, but he's no better." Amy stepped closer and gripped Samantha's arm, tears threatening. "As my friend, I'm begging you to find a solution. I can't bear to watch him die."

Neither could she. What more could she do, though? Benjamin's health and welfare occupied her thoughts to the point she'd put off dealing with her own situation. Without any certainty as to when her home would be snatched from her, she should have been making arrangements for a new living place, for deciding what she could carry with her and how she'd gain access to other medicinal sources. Instead, she'd spent her time combing through books and pamphlets with possible cures for his wound and fever. She scoured her commonplace book for any hints from the shamans, and finding the details of how Little Running Bear had broken fevers. The materials needed abounded this time of year. But would it work for Benjamin's case? The uncertainty held her back from suggesting the unorthodox treatment again. She'd focused on him to the exclusion of her other patients. She had no more ideas save one on how to proceed. She'd promised to consult with him, and she definitely meant to keep her word. In spite of how edgy and off kilter she became in his presence. She'd endure his proximity if it would aid her friend.

"Very well, fetch Dr. Trent to see what more he can do. I'll meet you at Benjamin's rooms in an hour."

Amy nodded and gave her a brief hug before spinning around and hurrying out of the house. The door closed behind her with a thud. Samantha sighed and started back down the hall to restock necessary items in her bag even as she pondered whether she should venture back into Trent's path. Would he lord it over her about her crying fit? Her fists clutching his coat as though she'd drown without his support? Or perhaps, if she were fortunate, he'd forgotten about the incident immediately after escorting her and Thistle through her own front door.

For two days, she had paced through the rooms and the garden, grieving openly at the impending loss of all she held dear. The books would go with her, along with her personal belongings. But other cherished items, such as the familiar kitchen goods and the heavy furniture her father crafted with his own hands, would of necessity be left behind. Booty for the next owner.

Each afternoon, Emily had stopped by to update her on Benjamin's condition. For that brief interlude, Samantha contained her grief behind a rigid comportment put on for the occasion. Her friends would not understand the depth and cutting sharpness of the pain she still nursed. How could they? Their fathers remained loyal to America and its ideals. Her father had abandoned those principles along with his daughter. Maybe he didn't mean to abandon her, but the bald fact remained that her parents had left her alone. She gulped back the rising emotion the memory evoked and then strode into the kitchen to continue her preparations.

An hour after Amy's urgent summons, Samantha and Thistle hurried into Benjamin's apartment, nearly running into Trent's broad chest. "Pardon me."

Trent grinned at her, eyes twinkling with repressed laughter. "Not at all. I did not expect to have you burst into the room, but I am pleased to see you."

She sucked in a breath, steeling herself against the awareness rushing through her. Best to keep to safe topics, to keep her emotions in check. "Have you discovered anything which would reduce our friend's temperature?"

"Perhaps." He inclined his head, and waggled his hand to indicate a level of uncertainty. "We'll know more tomorrow. Come, see for yourself." With a curious expression she could not decipher, he gently took her hand and led her into the patient's bedroom, Thistle padding behind her.

Dumbly, Samantha trailed after him, her senses chaotic from the press of his fingers wrapped around her hand. She ignored the unwanted reaction, focusing instead on the tableau before her. Surely, Trent felt no such electric pulse where their skin met, where the pressure of his tapered fingers heated her blood. If he could ignore the physical response, then so could she.

Benjamin sat propped against the headboard, Amy seated on the bed holding his hand. Ashen with sunken eyes, he nodded at her as she drew closer. How awful to see him in such condition. He'd been bursting with robust strength mere weeks earlier when he literally saved her and Amy's lives.

What did he receive in payment? A bullet to leave him ill and weak, mayhap on the threshold of death's door.

"Father insists the treatment I administered will work." Trent dropped her hand when they reached their patient. "You should be feeling better by morning, Benjamin."

His words removed the last fragments of distraction. Affronted by his tone, she folded her hands rather than retaliate. She'd suggested he try something new, so couldn't in good conscience rebuke him. But must he be so calm about his approach?

Amy regarded her for a long moment and then smiled. "Is there something you two have forgotten to tell us?"

Samantha frowned as Trent turned to her, one brow raised in question. She contemplated the humor in Amy's expression. "Not that I am aware of. Why?"

"Are you two courting?" Amy covered Benjamin's hand with both of hers. "Might you be following our lead for a change?"

Samantha gaped at Amy. Dismay and embarrassment contorted deep inside, beyond reach of any physical ability to assuage or smooth the sensation away. Could her friend perceive the physical reaction she experienced at Trent's touch? If so, who else detected it? She'd die of humiliation if any one else had noticed. "How absurd. Of course not."

Amy tilted her head, regarding Samantha for a moment before chuckling. "Have it your way."

Trent grinned and winked at Samantha as he addressed Amy. "I'm afraid you're mistaken, Miss Amy. Miss Samantha and I have not explored a personal relationship, only a professional one. Though I am open to such a venture if she might consider it."

She blinked at him as one brow lifted as though of its own accord. As tempting as his lips might be, a relationship of any kind was out of the question. "If we're quite finished, I have many tasks and other patients to attend. Come, Thistle." She didn't need to stay and be subjected to such a proposition. Especially when her visceral reaction attested to the desire for a closer acquaintance than accepted as proper. She clutched her medicine bag like a shield as the spaniel took up her position at her side. "Call for me if you should need further assistance."

"Wait, Samantha. Speaking of assistance, would you permit me to help you with your packing? If Benjamin doesn't mind, of course." Amy motioned to Benjamin, and then smiled at Samantha. "Unless you'd rather do it alone?"

"If your betrothed doesn't object, your assistance and companionship are most welcome, as long as your rumors are kept to a minimum." She squinted at Amy. "Perhaps Evelyn would sit with Benjamin for a while?"

"I shall ask her." Amy rose and bent over Benjamin to kiss his cheek. Slowly, she released his hand. "I'll see you later."

"I'll miss your sweet smile." Benjamin reached for her hand and she placed it in his again. He kissed the back of it and then winked at her. "I'll be here waiting for you to return."

With a last kiss, Amy strode to Samantha's side and clasped hands with her. "One day, you'll find someone to love and cherish as I do Benjamin. Do not fret."

"I beg to differ, my friend, since my vow remains intact." Samantha caught Trent smiling at her and focused on Amy's sincere expression. She meant well. If only she understood the reasons for why Samantha had sworn off marriage, perhaps Amy wouldn't be so quick to force the issue. "Come. There is much to do."

❦

The apartment door closed behind the ladies and the tan and white dog with a distant thud. Trent stared toward the common room door, imagining the threesome walking down the steps. As reluctant as Samantha had been to accept the dog's presence, the beast gave her a bit of protection while she lived alone in the huge house. He dragged a chair over to sit beside Benjamin, where he reclined against the headboard. The ailing man regarded him with amusement plain on his face.

"What diverts you so?" Trent lowered himself onto the hard seat, his tired legs grateful for the respite. He'd walked all over town, investigating possible locations for his hospital. Not that he'd found one, but he did have a great appreciation for the diversity of Charles Town.

"Your expression. Miss Amy is right, isn't she?" Benjamin shifted, wincing as he resettled against the pillows. "Regarding you and Samantha."

Trent perched on the chair, tension preventing him from relaxing against the wood frame. "Unfortunately, I'm afraid she is wrong, though perhaps in a different life, a different world as it were, our coming together might have been possible."

A weak grin worked onto Benjamin's face. "She's quite a woman. I believe she is your equal in many ways, if I'm not mistaken."

"How do you mean?" Trent tapped one fist into the other palm, considering his friend's observation. Should he be affronted by such a claim? Or dismiss it out of hand? Or be overjoyed at the endorsement of a relationship with the most tantalizing woman he'd ever met? His friend surely wouldn't jokingly slight him in such a manner without some foundation.

"She has a true gift for ascertaining the heart of an illness, for helping without harming." Benjamin rubbed the pads of three fingers across his forehead and frowned. "I trust her as much as I trust you. Between the two of you, I know you will help me."

Trent stiffened when Benjamin's meaning sunk into his brain, crossing his arms as he pondered the evident pain in his patient's countenance. "I dare say, with all due respect, I have more training than a midwife."

"She's more than a typical midwife or even healer." Benjamin rested his head against the headboard, peering at Trent through nearly closed eyes. "She's learned the ways of the Indians. Journeyed to the west, to the very frontier, and studied with the medicine men of the Creek and the Cherokee."

Idiotic. Intriguing. Impressive. What had she gleaned from such an experience? The bigger question remained: what was she thinking, exposing herself to the primitive savages on the edge of civilization? "I trust the education she received proved worth the risk she put her life in?"

"Her skills are without question among the best in the region. Though, admittedly, she's not infallible." Benjamin chuckled and coughed, making him cough even more for several minutes before he could continue. "Forgive me. As I was saying, everybody makes mistakes."

Poorly trained doctors could cause as much harm as ignorant midwives. Trent had witnessed the results of their kind before he elected to become a doctor in his own right. Mangled legs from disease eating away the flesh after a botched amputation by an untrained hand. Animal butchers who acted as though there was no difference between cutting up a side of hog and cutting off a limb. Women, like his mother, who endured one pregnancy after another for a score of years, ultimately dying from complications within their feminine organs. Having a large family was not worth the inherent risks. He sniffed back tears, waving a hand in front of his face to ward off an invisible fly as he did so. He could only hope Samantha wouldn't betray his trust in her, slim as it might be. He hoped for her trust in him to grow, and he planned to do whatever he could to see the eventuality occur sooner than later.

Trent tapped a hand on his elbow as he studied Benjamin's expression. "Fortunately, an end to the questionable abilities in town will arrive in due course. I shall build a better hospital as soon as possible. One where everyone may be treated with skill and respect and without fear of inadequate or unproven methods. I aim to surpass my father's capabilities as a physician."

"That's quite an ambition." Benjamin shifted his hips to a different position. "Will you include the accepted ways, or adhere to the newer techniques?"

Trent uncrossed his arms and leaned onto his elbows. "If I have my way, the old traditions will not be employed within my hospital. I have no interest in continuing such disproven practices."

"You wish to end Miss Samantha's practice then?" Benjamin stared at him for two beats then closed his eyes, folded his arms over his stomach, and sighed. "She'll fight you. She's a strong woman, which is a good thing given her present situation."

"You mean her parents' departure?" Trent recalled her sweet scent as he had comforted her while she sobbed. He'd never seen any one keen with so much grief and pain interwoven into each gasping wail, not even after a loving spouse or parent had died. But only for a short period of time did she permit herself to bawl before comporting herself. Though slender, he'd detected the strength of her body in his arms as well as the depth of her resolve. Thinking on it, he agreed with Benjamin. The woman had a strong character. "What will she do?"

"First, she'll need a new home." Benjamin rubbed his temple as he opened his eyes. "I cannot believe her father would abandon her, capable as she may be. He should have insisted on her accompanying them."

"From her reaction, she would not have gone with them. In the event, their departure left her in spasms of grief for no little time. She's fortunate to have Thistle as a companion to help ease her loneliness." Trent smoothed his hands down the thighs of his trousers. "I warrant the dog's presence helps relieve the anguish she felt at her parents' departure."

"Yes, it is happy the dog came along when it did." Benjamin blinked at Trent, as though to clear his vision.

"I found it curious her mother bore no trace of regret at leaving, though her tears appeared sincere enough." Trent peered at Benjamin, noticing increased tension on his face. "From the rumors I've heard, 'tis no loss to the town, either. Her practices were well enough feared by many."

"Samantha is more skilled than her mother. The older woman fast approaches the end of her midwifery days." Benjamin shifted to lay down in the bed, pulling the quilt up to cover his waist.

"What is amiss, my friend?" Trent leaned forward.

Benjamin screwed his eyes closed, gripping the edge of the quilt with both hands. "Bloody hell, but I ache all over. Have you anything?"

"Of course." Trent sprang to his feet and placed a hand on Benjamin's forehead. "I shall give you a strong enema to try one more time to balance the humors. I will help you. Don't worry."

Trent strode to his bag where it waited on the side table, and removed what he needed to prepare the medicine. He approached Benjamin, gritting his teeth with the hope the treatment would work. In order to prove his concepts superior to the old wives' tales, he must heal Benjamin.

A stray thought suggested he summon Samantha, inquire as to her opinion on the next course. But his desire to move the town forward with regard to the emerging techniques and practices kept him silent. In the process of making his point, however, he might also destroy Samantha's only means of support in the absence of her father's protection. He might also destroy the basis upon which she'd begin to trust him. Nevertheless, the enema must be applied. Benjamin must be cared for with every potential cure they could reasonably expect to work. The rest of the concerns drifting through his mind as he prepared the applicator to administer the enema would be untangled in due course. He had to believe as much, since he had no solution to offer her. For the present, he'd focus on the task before him and hope for a miracle to resolve Samantha's predicament.

Thistle wagged her way down the street in front of Samantha and Amy. The dog's friendship had also wiggled its way into Samantha's heart. She'd thought the beast would prove too much trouble to feed and care for, but in truth, taking care of Thistle created bright spots in her otherwise dreary days.

"I'm not prepared to move as of yet." Samantha strolled along beside her friend, enjoying the early winter sunshine warming her face. Thistle trotted off, nose to the ground, to investigate a scent. "In fact, I have not received notice to vacate the property. Your assistance, therefore, may be premature."

"I still find it hard to fathom the pickle you are in. I'm glad to see what I can do to help, though." Amy nodded to a passing townswoman. "Benjamin's condition is holding its own for the moment. I'll return to his side shortly, after I speak to my sister about helping me care for him. With all honesty, I cannot stay there all day and night and still meet my other obligations."

"With the war ending, has your smuggling ended as well?" Samantha chuckled at the wiggling dog, her head and shoulders buried in the base of a bush, tail wagging.

"For a time." Amy looked around her as though afraid she'd be overheard. "We shall see if that activity has come to a complete end within a few weeks."

Samantha flicked a glance at Amy and then noted her surroundings, relishing the crispness to the light breeze scuttling leaves down the street. The weather would change ere long, and leisurely strolls would be abandoned in lieu of brisk trots between buildings. "What do you know?"

"Nothing definite."

"Are the Britons leaving very soon?" Samantha kept her pace even, but her heart raced along with her thoughts. Thistle bounded back to trot at her side, content again to be Samantha's companion. At least until the next intriguing trail presented itself to Thistle's sensitive nose.

Amy remained silent as she nodded to the loyalist rector of St. Michael's as he strode past in a rush. Soon he'd be out of a post, and a patriotic rector would be reinstalled. After he'd moved out of earshot, Amy grinned at Samantha. "The next favorable tide, whenever such occurs."

"Welcome news, indeed."

The brutal, bloody British couldn't evacuate Charles Town soon enough to meet her desires. If only the loyalists did not fear such retaliation from the patriots, then her family would not have been ripped apart, scattered to different lands. She must look to her own future and determine a suitable place to live and continue her healing practice. The means to secure both were at her fingertips in the house, though she would need to transfer them to her new abode. She had refrained from descending upon her friends for succor, unwilling to take advantage of their friendship for an extended period of time. Perhaps she could find a family in town in need of a boarder. Buying her herbs might prove challenging, but she could locate many of the plants in the forests surrounding town. The apothecary carried most of the other items she needed. Yes, she had recourse to ways to provide for herself despite her parents' defection. She reached to pat Thistle and smiled at Amy.

"What's brought such a gorgeous smile to your face?" Amy aimed a questioning smile at Samantha. "You look happy."

"I believe I am." Samantha perused the street, noting the serious expressions and hurried steps. Everyone seemed to be intent on their own private missions, but with a new air of purpose and anticipation. "My future looks quite bright, in fact."

"Hallo!"

Samantha whirled about, her long skirts wrapping about her legs as she stopped, spotting Frank striding toward her, Emily on his arm. "Good morning."

Thistle edged in front of Samantha, tail wagging slowly as she watched the couple approach. The happy pair sported blond curly hair and similar eyes, hers blue and his gray. Even their attire complemented: he in dark trousers with a white shirt, gold waistcoat, and snowy cravat peeking out from beneath his dark gray cloak. Emily's ebony cloak covered a mourning dove gray dress visible as the heavy cloth shifted with her movements. They belonged together. If Samantha could read auras, she'd wager theirs would reveal a blend of contentment and delight. If only she possessed such an ability perhaps her efforts to heal Benjamin would be better informed.

"Good day, friends." Amy stepped forward to hug Emily and then moved back beside Samantha. "What brings you out this morning?"

Emily tapped a hand on Frank's arm. "We've been

searching out appropriate material for new drapes. Frank's connections have proven excellent resources."

"It's truly impressive how many people one meets when running a printing business." Frank tilted his head toward Emily, a pensive smile on his lips. "I may continue being a newsman even after the British leave. The pretense yields many wonderful connections."

"I pray you do." Emily grinned at him. "Your position makes my efforts worthwhile." Emily gasped and covered her mouth, eyes wide as her horrified gaze flitted from one person to another.

"You can forget the act, my dear cousin." Amy laughed, glancing to Frank and Samantha before sliding her laughing expression back to Emily. "You're the mysterious essayist Penny Marsh, aren't you?"

"Wh-what do you mean?" Emily's hesitant grin belied her stammered question.

"You can't fool your friends on such an important matter." Samantha chuckled and then hugged Emily. "I applaud your daring and your insights which you share in the marvelous essays we've all read in the broadside."

"Indeed. But why did you not share your secret with us?" Amy huffed, obviously pretending to be offended. "Do you not trust us to keep your activities in confidence?"

"Shhh!" Emily cast a frantic glance about her. "Do not speak so loudly. If Father learns of my scribbles, he'll disavow me immediately after he denounces my writing. You know he does not approve."

"Then you'll want to avoid my mother as well." Merriment danced in Amy's eyes. "She intends to dissuade you from opening a shop upon your next meeting."

Emily groaned, briefly rubbing two fingers across her furrowed brow. "Am I to have no assistance with my true desires?"

Frank drew her closer to his side, wrapping one arm around her slender shoulders. "I have begun making inquiries into your chosen location. Be patient, my sweet."

Thistle woofed at a black tom cat slinking along the foundations of the brick houses lining the street. Turning hopeful eyes to Samantha, she wagged her bushy tail. Samantha tapped her thigh and the dog reluctantly sidled into position by her side. Such a smart girl, learning hand signals as though she understood Samantha's intent. As the dog sat down to wait, Samantha noticed she'd put on some weight. Time to cut back on the table scraps. Musing on possible changes to the dog's diet, Samantha again focused on her friends.

Emily frowned and shook her head. "Patience is not one of my strengths."

"Yes, be aware of her inability to wait for events to come to pass." Amy pulled her cloak more snugly about her shoulders as the wind gusted around them. "I'm so cold."

Samantha nodded, aware the temperature of the air had dropped during their walk. "We should be on our way."

"Fare thee well, ladies." Frank made a half bow with a flourish of one hand.

Emily hugged her friends quickly and then took Frank's arm. Samantha smirked as she recalled how resistant Emily had once been to performing the simple courteous act. Seemed falling in love softened the most recalcitrant heart. Emily had avoided all contact with Frank, in a futile effort to protect her heart. Emily's vow to never marry verged on becoming a life forever with the man at her side.

Amy bent her head in acknowledgement of Frank's parting words. "We shall speak soon, Emily, about further wedding plans. Until then."

"Fare well." Samantha waved at Frank and Emily as they continued on their way down the street. She turned to Amy.

"I'll send word to you when your help will be of most benefit."

"Very well. I am going to speak to my sister and then return to Benjamin's." Amy started walking away, her steps hurried.

As Amy disappeared into the crowded streets, Samantha patted her leg once more, and then she and Thistle headed for home.

Chapter Seven

The next afternoon, Trent sauntered down King Street toward George Manning's residence. Low clouds obscured the sky, hinting at rain in the distance. The town suited him, with its neat houses lining the streets, the hustle and bustle of merchandise in and out of the harbor, and the acceptance he'd received from everyone. Well, except the intriguing and beautiful Miss Samantha, but then her reaction to his aims was understandable. Fortunately, his father had moved to Charles Town the year before the British succeeded in capturing the port city. Because the elder doctor agreed to remain neutral and the Britons needed physicians, the occupying force permitted him to continue his practice. Trent's years in Philadelphia studying medicine had prepared him for his profession, but not for how fond he'd become of the southern city upon his return a few months earlier. As much as he enjoyed the benefits of living with his father, he needed to establish his own place, his own path forward. Thus his plan to investigate available properties within the city limits suitable for his hospital and perhaps quarters for himself.

Increasing his pace with renewed determination, he turned to approach the elegant brick house. Three stories tall, the building hinted at the affluence of the owner. Much like the continual demand for doctors, legal matters plagued folks even during war. Bounding up the three brick steps, Trent knocked on the door, aware of the abundance of flowers and shrubs as well as the fresh paint on the black shutters. Subtle but clear signs of a well-tended home.

A whoosh announced the opening of the heavy wood door, drawing his attention to the dark haired man smiling at him. His first impression of George was of a man about his own age with an honest face and amiable features, standing a couples inches taller than Trent. He stood straighter as a result.

George greeted him with a welcoming smile. "May I help you?"

"Good morning, sir." Trent introduced himself as they shook hands. "I'd like to discuss acquiring a property, if you have a moment."

"I do have a few minutes." George opened the door wider and ushered Trent inside. "May I take your cloak?"

"Yes, thank you. I won't stay long."

"That's quite all right." George hung the garment on a peg by the door and then indicated for Trent to follow him. Trent trailed after his host as he led the way down the dimly lit hall.

Although sparsely furnished, the accoutrements and ornamentation of the furnishings in the Manning home impressed Trent. Elaborate gold framed oil paintings hung on the wall. An oriental vase stood on a small round table. Elegantly worked wainscoting and door frames subtly revealed the elevated sensibilities of the man leading him toward the back of the house. George's tastes mirrored Trent's, so much so being in the house felt as much like coming home as any place he'd ever lived. A desire to own such a home bloomed in his chest as he followed George along the carpeted hall and through the open door into his office.

"Please, sit down." George pointed to a chair as he walked around the desk and took his seat.

"You have a fine home." Trent moved in front of the chair, flipped his coat tails out of the way, and then sat down. "I hope one day to have a comfortable house to call my home."

"Is that why you've paid me a call today?" George slid open the drawer on the desk, placed a sharpened pencil into it, then closed it again.

"Not exactly." Trent started to say more, but Catherine eased into the room at that moment.

"Pardon me, gentlemen." Catherine approached the desk with a tray bearing a steaming tea pot, cups, and plates of biscuits and finger sandwiches. "I thought you might enjoy some refreshments."

While Catherine and George arranged the contents of the tray on the end of the desk, Trent perused the gleaming furniture and variety of furnishings. George's office space appeared tidy and organized, no doubt reflecting the same qualities as their owner.

The office housed quite a variety of books displayed on built-in floor-to-ceiling shelves. A quick look at the titles revealed George had several of the same titles as Trent. Many revealed they shared a deep curiosity about nature. An elaborate globe rested in a gold stand in the corner by one window. A highly polished mahogany desk stood in the middle of the room, two wing-backed chairs facing it. Behind the glossy surface, George occupied a high-backed chair, reminiscent of a king's throne. Haphazard stacks of papers flanked a clean stack of linen paper. An elegant silver inkstand and quill stood ready for his hand.

One day Trent planned to have fine furnishings such as those surrounding him. After he succeeded in establishing his hospital. Trent relaxed a bit at the thought and crossed his legs. George appeared to be a man who approached life with respect for others and integrity in his transactions. The kind of man he could do business with.

Catherine dipped into a brief curtsy before excusing herself from the room. George settled back against the chair, regarding Trent with curiosity in his eyes.

"I see you love to read as do I." Trent motioned to the collection of books. "Who is your favorite author?"

"Have you read Tobias Smollett's *The Expedition of Humphry Clinker*? He's extremely good fun to read." George chuckled, a brief snort of sound, before shaking his head.

Trent nodded and drummed the fingers of one hand on the armrest. "He has a fine way with the language and in giving the reader something to consider after he closes the book."

"Yes, such as how ineffectual over the long term the poor chap's effort proved to be to unite Britain across its national borders." George shuffled the pile of papers into a neat stack.

"Or between the Motherland and her colonies." Trent crossed one leg over the other and relaxed against the plush chair.

"Indeed. You make a good point." George studied him with a wry grin as he tapped the polished mahogany desk with one hand. "So tell me, as I know you didn't come to discuss literature or politics, what sort of property did you have in mind?"

"One large enough to be a hospital." Trent tugged his waistcoat into place. "Do you have such a building on the list of confiscated properties?"

George drummed his fingers on the desk, squinting in thought. "You'd want something rather big with plenty of rooms..."

Trent shifted in his seat. "I need a large space for an operating room, as well as room for beds for the invalids."

"The old McAlester place might be large enough for a small hospital." George stilled his incessant drumming. "It would be a good place to start, a temporary location while we search for more appropriate accommodations."

Trent swallowed. The image of the impressive home, with its picturesque garden and welcoming gazebo drifted into his mind's eye. From what he'd heard, the place was laid out in a satisfactory manner, though too small for the scale of operation he envisioned. He might eventually build on to it, make it more suited as the demand increased. He seemed to recall an empty lot beside the building, and of course he could build over the current garden if necessary. But Samantha's home? "I thought it was occupied."

George nodded. "Ere long it will be in the inventory, as soon as I can process the paperwork. Should be within the next week. I can give you a fair deal on it if you're interested. I wouldn't even need to put it up for auction, if so."

Curiosity piqued, he couldn't resist. "How much would you ask?"

George waggled a hand and shrugged, then quoted a price so low as to be an embarrassment to Aaron McAlester's good name. All he'd worked for over the years, essentially given away in disgrace. Still, purchasing the house at a low amount would enable him to finance better equipment. An idea worth considering... He pictured a steady stream of patients flowing through the wide front door. Perhaps convalescing among the beautiful flowers that would fill the garden in the spring and summer, the mingled scents creating a heaven on Earth for the injured and ill. He imagined doctors and nurses moving through the many interior rooms, checking on the well-being of the people lying on comfortable cots as they recuperated from surgery. On top of all the fine dreams, he saw again the scene when he stood on the street watching Samantha's parents drive away. Then the memory of Samantha sobbing in his arms brought him back to reality.

She'd kill him in his sleep. Stab him with a knife through the heart. Or mayhap something less violent but just as effective, like poisoning his ale. Maybe he should rethink the idea. "Do you have anything else, perhaps larger?"

"Hmmm…" George started flipping through the stack of papers on his right. He paused to read one, shook his head, turned the pages, and then stopped to read another. "This one might be a possibility. It's a three-story building on the north side of town, used to be a warehouse with private quarters on the first floor. It's available, but since it's not a confiscated property, it will cost a good deal more than the other. Several gentlemen have considered it but the amount we'd need for it was more than they could manage."

"Tell me more about it." Anything to keep Samantha from harming him in his sleep or worse. Although he didn't really believe they'd ever be more than colleagues, he'd rather have her good will toward him than the opposite. They may find themselves working together for another patient's benefit at some obscure time. And maybe one day they might even find a way to be something more on a personal level. "How much will it cost? When is it available?"

They discussed the particulars, including the fact the building would cost ten times Samantha's house. His burgeoning hope deflated. An astronomical price well beyond his meager means. If he sold everything he owned, he could not afford such a place. Perhaps his father could assist him in his endeavor or at minimum make a suggestion as to how the purchase might come to pass. Though it did rankle a touch to require his father's assistance in the matter, the end result outweighed his pride.

"If it meets with your approval, I'd like to visit the property.

Then I'll consider it and will inform you should I decide to buy the building."

"I have no problem with you inspecting the building for its suitability to your need." George rose and extended a hand. "Let me know when you'd like to visit the place, and I'll make the proper arrangements."

Trent pushed to his feet and shook George's hand. "Thank you for your time."

"My pleasure."

"We shall settle on a date and time in the near future. For now, I'll see myself out." Trent fingered the brim of his tricorne hat he held in his hands. "I'll send word of my decision."

"Very well. I'll do whatever I can to help. Charles Town needs a decent hospital." George sat back down at his desk, straightening the pile of papers with a series of sharp taps on the wood surface. "Good day, my friend."

"And to you." Trent strode back down the hall, slipped his cloak off the peg and onto his shoulders, and then went out into a lightly falling drizzle. He set his hat on his head, and hurried toward McCrady's Tavern to meet his father. He needed advice, and his father had always served as a sounding board for him. Even when he'd been away, they'd communicated by letter each week, sharing news and seeking guidance from one another in a host of situations. At the moment, the question in his mind focused on how to purchase the building he desired rather than the one he could afford. He'd dreamed of founding his own high-quality hospital since he'd been a boy, assisting his father in caring for patients. The more he learned, and the better ways of treating illness and injury he'd witnessed, the greater his desire to make his dream a reality. All of the study and research led him to the brink of the hospital becoming real. He thought of nothing else but how to achieve his dream, his contribution to the future of Charles Town, one of the friendliest and finest seaport cities in the newly independent nation of America.

The rain fell harder and he lengthened his stride, pulling his cloak about him as puddles formed on the dirt street. He strode down King, then turned onto Broad and marched briskly on toward Bay and the tavern, all the while thinking about his one concern in the matter of the hospital's location. Buying the less expensive property would simultaneously accomplish his plan and further antagonize Samantha, but he had limited options. He either went with the McAlester house or gave up on his mission. It was nothing personal against her or her family, just business. He clenched his jaw against the driving wind. Surely she would understand.

Half an hour later, he sat across a scarred round table from his father. The senior doctor nursed an ale, the bittersweet aroma of hops scenting the air of McCrady's. Mutterings and chatter surrounded them. A fire blazed in the massive fireplace, fighting the chill from the December rain outside. Trent sipped a mug of steaming coffee, grateful for the warmth in his gut after the long walk in the blowing rain. The blasted weather would only lead to more illness in town, perhaps even more cholera or yellow fever. He swallowed a hot mouthful of coffee and hoped his thought would prove incorrect. The cold and wet weather, though, often did lead to more complaints. At least Trent's trousers were no longer cold and clammy against his legs.

"You're being awfully quiet." Robert considered his son. "So, how fares your gunshot patient? Benjamin Hanson, isn't it? Is he any better?"

If only he had some progress to report, Trent wouldn't feel like such a disappointment in his father's eyes. "The enema has had no effect. His fever worries me. I'm concerned the wound is inflamed and spreading poison through him."

"You know how these things progress, and thus what will happen next." Robert swallowed a long gulp of beer, and then wiped the foam from his lips with a cloth napkin. "You'll need to cut off the arm if so."

His thought exactly, but he'd given his word. Trent tapped a finger against the clay mug. "He won't permit me to, and Miss Samantha plans to defend his position."

"Surely you jest." Robert studied him, his hands gripping the bottle. "You're the doctor. You alone must decide what is best for your patient."

"If it were solely my judgment, then I'd say amputate." He beat his fingers on the table. "However, I've given my word to Benjamin I'd consult with Samantha."

Robert snorted as he shook his head. "Then you must talk sense to the girl, make her see reason." He lifted the bottle to his mouth and took a long drink.

"A task easy to give to another, but not easy to complete." The vision of Samantha's serious eyes and determined set of her pretty mouth occupied his mind. "I shall try again, but I hold out little hope."

"At a minimum, you'll need to increase either the frequency or the amount of the bleeding to balance his humors." Robert wrapped strong fingers around the bottle. "If you cannot balance them, the poor man has no chance of surviving."

Trent frowned and pressed his hands onto the table top. "He will run dry if I bleed him too often. I think instead I'll increase the enema's potency."

"Sounds like a reasonable alternative for the time. If you had access to better facilities, perhaps you'd have more chance of success." His father nodded and then drank from the bottle. "What did Mr. Manning have to say?"

What indeed. He could speed the ousting of Samantha from her home or take on a monumental debt. Either way had its negatives. "The perfect place is available over on the north side of town. Space aplenty for beds and an operating room, and it has living quarters attached."

Robert peered at him. "I sense a hesitation?"

Trent nodded. "It costs more than I have any possibility of possessing. Which brings me to the second property."

"One you can afford?"

"Yes, but it's Aaron McAlester's place. George said he could sell it to me for next to nothing."

"I see." Robert tapped a finger against the glass bottle. "The house is in a decent location, but it's rather small for a hospital."

"Agreed. If I start there with a clinic, I can wait and allow its reputation to grow along with its client base. Then move when funds permit." He swallowed a gulp of coffee, the heat slowly working its way down his throat.

"A sound plan. I always say one should live within one's means."

"Indeed, it's the conservative approach. However, there is a major drawback I cannot ignore." He tapped the fingers of his right hand on the scarred surface. "Miss Samantha will not take kindly to the idea of me owning her father's house instead of her."

"Business is business." Robert waved off Trent's objections as easily as blowing away wisps of smoke from a candle. "Besides, she has no claim to the property. The state has decreed property owned by British sympathizers be confiscated and sold at auction to true citizens."

"Her head may agree with the concept in theory, but I believe her heart will disagree with the actuality." Trent leaned against the wood chair back and crossed his arms. The more he pondered the ramifications, the less he liked them.

He closed his eyes for two beats and then focused on his father. "Someone will buy it, but it won't be me."

"Be sensible, son." Robert stared at him for several moments. "Don't throw away your ambitions over a woman's sentiment."

Was he considering her feelings over his own? If so, why? It wasn't like she held any sway over him. Her jade green eyes and flowing black hair made her appear an exotic woman, one intriguing and beguiling and yet dismissive of him. Still, the anguish she demonstrated within the circle of his arms couldn't be ignored. Far be it for him to make her feel such grief again. He wouldn't allow it. But his father needn't be apprised of his ponderings on the matter.

"I'm considering the long term over the short term." Trent sipped his coffee, buying a few minutes to formulate his arguments. "The cost of relocating the enterprise once established could prove beyond my means, and thus I'd be confined in a building too small for what I intend to create."

"You've made up your mind, then?" Robert studied him, eyes searching Trent's.

"As of this moment." Trent gripped the mug in both hands. His dream verged on disintegrating if he couldn't finance the purchase of a suitable property. Yet he wouldn't cause Samantha more grief. "The McAlester place is out of the question."

"Then, tell me more about the other place." Robert twirled the bottle before grabbing it up and taking a swig. "Would it suffice for a longer span?"

"From what George said, it's the perfect location." Trent contemplated the steam rising from the mug before gulping down more of the liquid. "But I cannot conceive of such a quantity of money let alone squeeze it from my bank account."

"Do you know whether the townspeople believe in your idea as strongly as you?" Robert fiddled with the bottle, slowly angling the mouth one way and then the other.

Trent nodded vigorously, hope igniting as his father continued to swivel the bottle, a sign he had an idea. "Every person I've mentioned it to has agreed we need a better place more representative of our fine city. George himself said he would help any way he could."

Robert settled the bottle squarely on the table and studied Trent for several long moments. "Then do like the theater does when it wants to cover the expense of presenting a play. Seek out subscribers."

Trent stilled as he considered his father's suggestion. "Share the cost of establishing the property and the equipment with the townspeople?"

His father inclined his head in agreement. "Let them put their money in to make the hospital happen."

"That's a brilliant idea, Father. I'll put together the papers this evening." He tapped his mug to his father's bottle, relief at having another way to pursue his idea flooding his chest. A way which didn't include further upset to Samantha. If his father's idea worked as he envisioned, then his other plans might well come to fruition after all.

Chapter Eight

"What do you think, Thistle?" Samantha inspected the small marble statue of Athena, the Greek goddess of wisdom. Where had her father acquired it? So much of his business had been conducted without comment over her life she found herself confused as to what he actually did to earn his money. "Keep it or leave it for the new owners? Who needs her guidance more

Thistle thumped her fluffy tail on the floor, hope in her eyes, head on front paws.

"I agree." Samantha plunked the weighty item onto a shelf and turned to survey the remaining things in the room. "We're nearly finished going through my father's things. I suppose we should start on my mother's next."

She turned to Thistle and frowned. "I detest this. I shouldn't be forced from my home."

Thistle sat up in anticipation, her sides bowing outward. The idea to change the dog's meals had led to the ultimate realization Thistle was eating for more than merely herself. Samantha released a resigned sigh. She did not need the complications associated with being adopted by a determined dog. Samantha had finally conceded the point and fed her, and then allowed the beast into the house, into her life, into her heart. The long hair hanging from the dog's sides no longer concealed her condition. How long until her puppies arrived? Days? A week or two at most? For that matter, how many puppies?

Samantha considered her father's discarded possessions. So many memories associated with each book, each piece imported from a distant country, each sketch of a distant city. She gazed at a sketch of London's skyline, wondering how often her father studied it and wish he'd moved to the Motherland. When did he know he would have to leave America yet didn't share the knowledge with her? The whole situation made her wretched. He'd been forced to abandon everything which wouldn't fit in the wagon. They'd taken the essentials, leaving behind the luxuries. Tears pressed against her eyes. How could she give away his treasures? Her mother's heirlooms inherited from Samantha's grandparents?

The house served as a home for more than memories. It was a home for cherished possessions acquired with difficulty and dear expense over generations. She had no place to store them if the government succeeded in dispossessing her of her home. She couldn't reconcile the concept of losing everything despite her beloved country winning the war. Surely she could do something to prevent the disaster befalling her.

"I won't give up." Swiping a hand across wet eyes, she squared her shoulders. "Come, Thistle. We shall try again to salvage my home."

Thistle bounded to her feet, tail wagging, and followed Samantha down the hall. At the entrance hall, Samantha donned a long, dark gray cloak, tied on a matching bonnet with black lace edging, and then pulled on warm gloves before picking up her purse.

She closed the door behind them and paused on the front steps. The chill in the air confirmed Christmas would arrive in a mere twenty days and Twelfth Night in only one month. Winter had definitely arrived and brought icy blasts of wind to torment the town. Dark clouds hinted at snow, a rare occurrence. The few others who dared to face the cold, coats and cloaks held close, hurried past where Samantha stood with Thistle panting at her side. Samantha took a deep breath and pushed it out again. "Let's go, girl."

Striding down the street, the pair rushed along Queen, turned onto King, and soon arrived at the Manning residence. Samantha paused to catch her breath after their headlong pace. Hesitating, she surveyed the house and garden, bushes and plants bowed from the cold. Another blast of wind pushed her four steps toward the house. Taking Mother Nature's hint, she marched up to the door and rapped three times.

The door swung open a few moments later to reveal Catherine's concerned grin. "Samantha, my dear, what brings you here on such a foul day? Is that your dog?"

Samantha glanced at the white and caramel spotted animal. "Her name is Thistle. She found me and refuses to leave my side." Samantha pulled her cloak around her as she shivered in the biting wind.

"Oh, my, forgive me." Catherine opened the door wider and motioned her inside. "Come in, come in."

Despite the chill racing through her, Samantha hesitated to step through the door. "Thistle, too?"

"Of course. It's too cold out for the poor thing."

"Thank you." Standing inside the warm house, Samantha shivered. Thistle settled at her feet, sitting primly. "Mrs. Manning, my apologies for coming unannounced. But I'm here to speak to your husband on an urgent matter, one that cannot wait."

Catherine sighed and shook her head. "He told me of your situation. I'm so sorry to hear about your displacement."

Samantha bristled at the thought the entire town may well know of and condone her predicament. "Is Mr. Manning at home? May I speak with him, please?"

"Of course, but…" Catherine searched Samantha's face for a long moment and then sighed again. "I fear your pleas will not change the outcome. But follow me. I'll take you to him."

Samantha followed the woman down the hall, Thistle padding beside her. Catherine paused to tap on the closed door to George's office.

"George, dear, Miss McAlester is here to speak with you."

"Come," a masculine voice called out.

"If you need me, I'll be in the parlor." Catherine opened the door and indicated for Samantha to go in. Thistle stayed close to Samantha's long skirts as she approached the mahogany desk and George's serious face.

"Miss Samantha, what may I do for you?" He rose to greet her and then waved her into a chair. "Would you care for some tea?"

"No, thank you." She remained standing, kneading the soft cloth of her purse with both hands. "Mr. Manning, I've come to beg you to reconsider taking my home from me. My father built the house with his own hands, he planted the massive garden for my mother and I to use. I must have access to its contents for my midwife practice. I've supported the patriot cause all through the war. Please, isn't there some legal means for me to retain ownership?"

George, who had also stayed on his feet, started shaking his head before she stopped speaking. "My girl, as I said before, the matter is closed. Indeed, the paper work is complete."

She frowned and clutched her purse. "Pardon me? What do you mean?"

"Why, simply put, you have one week to remove your

possessions and your person from the house before the town assumes ownership." He picked up a document and looked over it before setting the sheet back on the desk. "As a matter of fact, someone has already inquired about purchasing the property. I anticipate a new owner for the place very soon."

One week? Shock and fear filled her. So it would happen. No matter what argument she could devise or plea she could compose, the house no longer belonged to her father. She had become, in effect, an intruder in her own house. She drew in a shaky breath. One miserable week. "Are you certain?"

He nodded, concern evident in his expression. "May I assist you in locating a family to stay with? Or in moving your things?"

"Thank you for the kind offer." She pushed words through stiff lips. How had this happened to her? How could her parents leave her in such a pickle? One thought echoed in her mind. Flee. Run. *Escape.* But to where? "I shall send word should I require such assistance."

"Very well." George walked around the desk and escorted her from the office. "Let me show you out."

As if she couldn't locate the front door on her own or, more likely, was not trusted to refrain from venting her anger and rage on the lovely furnishings they passed. Thistle padded close beside her, seeming to sense her distress. Samantha kept pace with George, her limp barely noticeable despite the ache caused by the cold weather. She'd take the good where she could find it.

After bidding the lawyer good day, she and Thistle stood on the street for several minutes while she tried to calm her racing heart, capture her chaotic thoughts, and ignore the primitive desire to howl her pain and grief like a lone wolf in the forest.

She needed a focus, a task, to determine a direction for her next steps. Something positive and hopeful. Searching her mind, she discarded several ideas before smiling. *Benjamin.* She'd visit him and make sure he was finally on the mend. She turned and hurried toward Bay Street and her patient. At least she still had her practice. The thought buoyed her steps. Nobody could take that away from her.

The wind howled, whipping her cloak about her ankles as Samantha scurried to Benjamin's with Thistle at her side. Reluctant happiness filled Samantha each time she looked at the dog. As a child, she'd begged her father for a pet, but he refused. The irony did not escape her that she found Thistle the same day her parents departed. She preferred to believe God or the universe sent Thistle to keep her company. She stroked the spaniel's head and then pushed through the door.

"Close the door before you let out the heat." Amy dried her hands on a towel and then dropped it on the table as she crossed the room to greet Samantha.

Samantha waited for Thistle to trot into the room before acting on her friend's request. "How is Benjamin? Please tell me his fever has broken. I need some good news."

"I'm afraid not. Trent is with him… Oh…" Amy clutched Samantha's hands, tears suddenly trailing down both cheeks. Anguish shone in her eyes. "I cannot tolerate seeing Ben in such distress and pain. I fear for his life. I beg of you, please do something. You must save him."

Samantha nodded, gripping her purse. "That's why I'm here. He has been fighting the inflammation for a very long time. Too long. Come here." She broke away from Amy's grip, dropped her purse on the table, and then hugged her friend while Amy sobbed against her shoulder.

Thoughts of Edward floated through her mind. His

compassionate ways, incredible strength, and patriotic fervor combined to make him an amazing person. Watching her husband killed, the shot robbing him of his last breath, remained the most horrible memory of the battle at Cowpens. Even her own injury paled in contrast. The physical pain could not match the emotional distress losing her husband had inflicted upon her. Now, comforting Amy, Samantha found herself in the unique position to truly understand the fears and hopes ricocheting within her friend.

After the sobs became sniffles, Samantha eased Amy away from her and peered into watery eyes. "Let me go to him."

"Yes, of course, I'm sorry to detain you."

"No, do not be sorry." Samantha flashed a smile before sobering. "I'm here to help you both in any way I can."

"Thank you for everything you're doing for him." Amy pulled her lace handkerchief from her bodice as she sniffed and turned away. Dabbing at her tears, she moved to where she'd been brewing a pot of tea. She arranged the tray with the pot and cups while Samantha, shaking off an enervating sense of foreboding, strode into the bedroom to check on the patient.

Trent pivoted to nod in her direction when she entered the room. Benjamin lay on the bed, his right arm hanging over the side to permit blood to flow into the bowl below. A quick sweep of her gaze revealed his condition had not improved over the last few days. They'd tried most of the usual cures for his complaint. What were they doing wrong?

She joined Trent at the side of the bed, ignoring the buzzing under her skin at his proximity. Thistle took up her normal position, laying under the window, watching Samantha's every movement. "How is he?"

The young doctor shrugged. "No better, nor worse. I've given him something stronger along with the increased bleeding."

"Must you take so much of his blood?" She leaned closer to inspect the site of the scarification. The incisions appeared cleanly made and the blood flowed freely as desired. Yet the act worried her, given the diverse results the method yielded.

Trent nodded, applying pressure to encourage the flow. "It is the only way to bring balance back to the body's humors."

"Such a practice gives doctors a bad name." She flicked a glance at his face and then focused on their patient since her pulse raced by simply gazing on his gorgeous eyes. She drew in a calming breath and released it on a huff. The scent of him, the combination of his cologne with the leather of his boots and a tantalizing mint, did nothing to quell the reaction. "There must be a better way."

He snorted, then addressed her. "Your mother had a bad name, and she was no doctor."

Samantha straightened and propped her hands on both hips. Handsome or not, she'd defend her mother against his accusations. "She had her challenges, I admit, but she also helped many others. My aim has always been to improve on her success, or lack thereof, by studying with other more capable healers."

"Like the Cherokee?" His gaze bored into hers. "Or the Creeks? Is that who you consider better?"

She resented his tone. He had no idea of the generosity and experience of the Indian healers. "They've used the same methods for centuries, methods doctors have never heard of let alone employed. I follow their advice in order to be the best healer possible."

"I, too, wish to be the best doctor possible by studying with those who have stellar reputations for their physic." He grinned at her as he shrugged. "We do have something in common, after all."

Samantha met his gaze without permitting a smile to

emerge onto her lips. "I'm sure the only commonality is trying to heal this poor man's shoulder and restore him to health."

Trent glanced at Benjamin and then back to study Samantha. "If we work more closely together, we can achieve both aims."

"Indeed. Since you are averse to me employing the Cherokee way of breaking a fever, I thought I'd try a bread and milk poultice to draw out the heat." She peered at him, noting the smile beginning in his eyes and on his mouth, and then merriment in his gaze. A flutter in her stomach made her blink. She must attend to the matter at hand. "What do you think?"

"Give me a moment." He pulled out a wad of lint and pressed it against the incisions to staunch the blood flowing into the pot. After a minute, he tossed the bloody mass into the crackling fire before straightening to answer her question. He regarded her for several moments before shaking his head. "I agree with you that poultices are good for some injuries. I'll even admit you have impressive training, from what Benjamin has told me. With both in mind, what if we try using plain old rum mixed with honey to keep it open rather than using an ointment? Let the poison drain out on its own."

Try as she might the poultices and ointments had done nothing toward curing the wound. Perhaps Trent's idea would make the difference. "I've had some success with the combination in the past."

Trent clasped her fingers in his, pressing his lips to the back of one hand. "Thank you, Miss Samantha, for deigning to trust my judgment."

Over the rush of her pulse in her ears she heard the gentle sarcasm hanging on each syllable. Trent's endearing features and impressive strength couldn't undermine her composure.

She wouldn't allow it. "You flatter yourself, Doctor Trent. Although I agree the rum salve can work, we need not make such a rash change immediately."

Thistle moved to press between them, pushing them apart. Samantha glanced down, pondering whether the dog knew more about Trent than she ever would have guessed. The dog remained standing between them until Trent dropped Samantha's hands.

"Ah, so you wish to wait still longer, give your impotent potions more time." He tilted his head with a wry smile, revealing intriguing dimples. "Well, I daresay you would not have done so for me."

"Indeed not. Your ideas do not deserve more time." She grinned up at him, enjoying the twinkle in his sapphire eyes. He'd pulled his sandy blond hair, usually left hanging loose and soft, into a queue. How disappointing. "Besides, it is not my place to swell your opinion of yourself further by lauding your talents."

He guffawed and stepped closer to her, pushing the dog from between them as he recaptured her hands. He lifted them to rest against his broad chest, his grin sobering into a smile. "My dear, you delight me."

The change in his demeanor occurred in a flash. So fast she barely had chance to assimilate the shift from sarcasm to sincere, from trifling to tempting. He couldn't be considering what he was apparently contemplating. Such behavior was improper as a minimum, and possibly even immoral. She gasped when he leaned toward her, closing the dwindling distance in a single beat of her heart. His breath carried spearmint when he exhaled before pressing his lips to hers.

Lightning flowed through her, igniting wave after wave of illicit sensation. When he slid his tongue inside her mouth, she moaned and opened to his passionate exploration. She'd never experienced such an intense reaction to what would appear to be a simple act, a buss between a man and a woman. Not even poor Edward, God rest his soul, had drawn such a passionate response from her when they'd kissed. A voice whispered about the impropriety, the scandal of the depth to which she savored and returned the buss. She—who rebuked Trent for his position on midwives and healers, for denigrating her mother, for denouncing her treatments—clung to him, seeking support as her knees trembled.

After long moments, he pulled back, gifting her with a bemused smile. "Your response to my kiss is all the flattery I need from you."

She blinked away the lusty fog clouding her thoughts. His startlingly blue eyes reflected his pleasure. *Her* pleasure as well. *Gramercy.* How could she have permitted herself to indulge in him? Knowing his opinion of her? She pressed her lips together, recalling the pressure of his firm mouth on hers. Heat coursed over her skin, warming her neck, then her cheeks. Still, the man certainly could kiss. Her mind cleared by degrees with each passing moment until stellar clarity revealed the extent of her feelings for the young doctor. The attraction she'd denied betrayed her and became something more, a desire craving his touch. His kiss and caress tempted every fiber of her being, summoned her as surely as night evoked the stars.

A slow knowing smile spread on Trent's face. "My dear, what is the matter?"

"I do not know what you mean. I—" She drew in a sharp breath when the truth of the situation shimmered in her mind. Love? She loved him? Dear Lord, what had she done?

Chapter Nine

The following afternoon, Samantha ambled through the bleak house with Thistle at her side. Only the sound of their footsteps echoed within the walls. Thanks to Amy's quick hands and determination earlier in the morning, crates and barrels held every item of value. Samantha's efforts to locate a place to live on her own terms, however, had failed. No self-respecting female would dare to live on her own, or so she'd been informed. No one would allow her to rent a room, let alone a house. As a result, all her things stood packed and ready, waiting for a miracle.

The kitchen fire burned brightly, warding off the chilly winter morning. She stopped to stir the rabbit stew she'd started earlier. Tasting the concoction, she wrinkled her nose. It needed something. She tasted it again. Pinching off a quantity of dried savory, she stirred the herb into the simmering pot. Another taste and then, satisfied, she replaced the wooden spoon in the kettle. In another half hour, her dinner would be ready.

In the meantime, what should she do to occupy her idle hands? With everything of importance packed up, she had nothing demanding of her time. She drifted through the door and into the hall, meandering from room to room ensuring she'd included all her belongings. After dinner, she'd venture out in one final attempt to locate a new home. Even if it ended up being temporary. She might even resort to seeking assistance from Mr. Manning. No, not that. How humiliating to seek help from the very man who took her house away.

She paused at the rear window in the parlor, holding back the heavy drape in order to appreciate the vast garden surrounding the house. While the winter garden appeared barren and asleep, below the cold surface of the ground the seeds worked to create the next generation of plants. Just how they did so remained a mystery, but every spring tiny shoots poked up and reached for the sky and the sunlight. Eventually, Mother Nature presented a new batch of herbs and flowers for her table and simples recipes. She stood on her tiptoes, gripping the heavy brocade for balance. She glimpsed the gazebo in the back corner through the trees and bushes, only its peaked roof lit by the early afternoon sunshine.

Tears threatened as she gazed on her favorite place in all the world. How she'd miss working among the herbs and flowers. Digging and working the dirt yielded more than plants, but peace and a unique sense of achievement. Where would she find a replacement?

Dropping the drape back into place, she turned and sauntered through the mostly empty rooms. Only three days until someone else would possess the property. Three days until she'd be homeless and on the street. She stopped and swallowed the blubbering threatening her composure. *Enough.* Crying served no purpose. Resigned to her fate, she regarded Thistle, who sat beside her, fluffy tail wagging slowly.

"We shall be fine. We must keep the faith."

Thistle yipped and rose to her feet, moving closer to Samantha. Judging by the bulge of the dog's belly, puppies would be arriving before long. Where would they be born? On the street? No, not on the street. Samantha sighed. She needed a plan and fast. Reaching down, Samantha stroked the soft fur, grateful for the loyal companionship.

A knock sounded at the front door. She straightened, looking in the direction of the sound. She wasn't expecting any one. Samantha hurried to answer the summons, Thistle trotting ahead.

"Emily, what a pleasant surprise." She opened the door wider to permit her friend entrance.

Emily strode into the front hall, her heavy black cloak pulled close against the cold air accompanying her. She grinned at Samantha as she clasped both her hands. "I bear good news, my friend."

"And what might that be?" Samantha pushed the door closed with a foot, hope swelling inside as she perceived excitement emanating from Emily. "Pray tell me before you come apart."

"Father has invited you to live with us. We have the room and would welcome you to be part of our household for as long as you'd care to stay." She squeezed Samantha's hands and performed a tiny bunny hop. "You must say yes. I'll accept no other answer. Please?"

"Are you certain?" Had her miracle arrived? Samantha searched for any drawbacks to the idea. The Sullivan home was larger than her own, with a fair sized garden.

Emily bobbed her head in time with a series of hops. "We are agreed you'd be a most wonderful addition to our family. My garden will be at your disposal to claim as yours, if you wish."

Hope turned to joy inside Samantha's chest. "How could I refuse such a pretty offer?"

"Then you'll come?" Emily pulled Samantha into a dancing embrace, spinning and skipping down the hallway. She sang a ditty out of sheer happiness, finally stumbling to a laughing halt. "I'm so pleased you've accepted."

Samantha's composure was rattled by the exuberant celebration, and she settled her skirts with trembling hands. "You're too kind, my friend. I thank you most gratefully for proving to be my salvation."

Emily tilted her head, one brow lifted in question. "Come now, I am no miracle. But I am your friend and am here to tell you Father's big wagon shall arrive to move your belongings to your new home within the hour."

"You were that sure I'd say yes?" Samantha shook her head, aware of the relief and calm easing through her. But an hour? "Am I so predictable?"

"Perhaps, but I also had vowed to not take no for your final answer." Emily nodded twice with a grin. "You needed a home and we have one for you. So, yes, I knew you'd agree. Tell me, what assistance might I be?"

"I'm ready to move my things, as you can see." Samantha led Emily through the house, indicating the clusters of wooden barrels and crates scattered throughout. "I plan to leave the furniture behind as it has no use for me. Although, it pains me to relinquish my father's fine craftsmanship to strangers. I do hope all the tables and chairs and carpets suit the next owner."

"Very well. Father permitted me to bring the light carriage to welcome you in style." Emily spotted an open trunk of dresses and another of bonnets and gloves. "Shall we load your clothing and be on our way? Solomon and Richard can handle the rest later."

"I must douse the cook fire first." Samantha led the way into the kitchen. Grabbing a napkin, she removed the kettle from the hook over the fire and placed it on the hearth.

She glanced up at Emily. "May I bring my stew along for supper at your house?"

"Our house now, and yes, of course." Emily snagged a few heavy cloths and laid them on the table. "Let's wrap the kettle in these for the trip."

Samantha moved the pot onto the napkins and Emily folded the cloth about the hot metal. Samantha turned to douse the fire using the urn of water on the sideboard. Steam rose up the chimney as the first drops hit the flames.

"Now for the trunks." Samantha carried the swaddled pot and placed it on the floor by the front door.

"Between the two of us, they should be no problem." Emily hurried down the hall to the open door leading into Samantha's bedroom.

They made short work of securing the trunks on the back shelf of the conveyance. Samantha noted its gleaming metal wheels and black wooden sides with the Sullivan family crest announcing the respected owner. Two black horses stood patiently while the ladies and Thistle mounted the two steps and settled on the front seat. Emily lifted the reins, clucked to the pair, and the carriage rolled down the street. Thistle's heft wedged between the women, tongue lolling from her open mouth.

It all happened so fast, Samantha didn't have chance to consider the importance of the event. As the horses walked along the dirt road, gusts of icy wind lifting their manes, reality sank in. She'd left the house for the last time.

Leaving her family's home proved bittersweet with the opportunity to move into a nicer dwelling in a better part of town. As the carriage bounced along on the uneven dirt surface, Samantha viewed Charles Town with a new view to the people and their aims. From the start, the first shots fired in anger, the people had become divided between those loyal to the Crown and those seeking an independent existence.

For years, the fabric of the community they lived in had been torn by the differing opinions. Might peace mend the tear? Might she find a means to fix a path for her future? Perchance the respect the town held for Captain Sullivan might lend itself to her reputation as well. With all the questions surrounding her talents, she wouldn't mind the positive boost.

Emily drove behind the Sullivan home and stopped the carriage in front of the small stable. Richard appeared to handle the horses in time for the ladies to climb down. As Richard tied the reins to the hitching post, Thistle bounded to the ground and began exploring the area. The dog sniffed the bushes edging the cobblestone drive, then disappeared into the stable while following a mysterious scent trail. *Curious.* The loyal and protective dog typically stayed close to Samantha's side, especially as her time to have her puppies neared.

Samantha regarded her new home with a fresh appreciation for the tidy barn and separate building for the kitchen. The tall brick house boasted three stories with wide piazzas on the southern exposure. She'd visited many times, but this visit felt different. In truth, she had no idea how long this stay would extend. She spun slowly in place, taking in each detail of the backyard. The small family garden included an adequate herb section near the brick kitchen, and a neighboring flower garden with winding crushed seashell paths. The flowers and herbs sparsely dotted the soil, leaving plenty of space for additions of other plants. A smile emerged on her lips. With some time and effort, she'd create a smaller version of her former collection of plants.

Solomon, his dark hair trimmed close to his head, grabbed up one trunk at Emily's request, and carried it toward the back door of the three-story brick house. Richard lifted the second trunk with strong black hands and followed. Slaves. A thrill of unease drifted across her shoulders, making her shiver. She recalled the horrific tales of the slave uprising in Haiti and the resulting drastic changes to America's laws associated with owning and catching runaways. Brutal beatings, whippings, and even hangings comprised the allowed punishments. Freeing the poor slaves became ever more difficult under the restrictions imposed by law. The number of blacks, both free and enslaved, in South Carolina was far greater than whites. An uprising would put every citizen of the state in jeopardy. Samantha had forgotten the Sullivans' owned them. Everyone knew they treated their slaves with dignity and kindness, but her family had never needed extra hands, so the reality left her disconcerted and unnerved. In fact, the only time they'd had a slave in their house was while Evelyn stayed with them and had Belinda with her. She may have to find another place to live after all, depending on how everyone got along. Samantha turned to Emily when she walked up.

"You'll stay in the room next to mine." Emily led her inside, the two men trailing behind. "It's empty now that Frank has regained his own home."

"Do you miss having him stay with you?" Samantha followed Emily down the short hall and then trudged up the wooden stairs behind her. "Seeing him daily?"

Emily chuckled as she turned the knob on the door. "I still see him daily, he merely has to make more of an effort. Here we are." She pushed open the door and ushered Samantha and the men inside.

Samantha had not been in this room before so she paused to take stock of her new quarters. The hardwood floor, probably made from cypress, was covered by a colorful braided rug. A single bed stood against the far wall, draped with an elaborately stitched quilt. Even from the door, she could tell the quality of the stitching involved for sewing the blanket. Heavy curtains hung at the lone window. A sampler, stitched by a child's learning hand, hung on the wall above the headboard. To the left, the writing desk and a spindly chair waited. Samantha smiled when she noticed the plain silver inkstand. Her notes on birthing could continue as she worked to unravel the reasons why so many women and children perished in the aftermath of childbirth. With luck, she'd unravel the reasons for the frequent deaths of women in her mother's care.

"Will this suffice?" Emily swooshed past Samantha to open the window. "A little fresh air will help, I dare say."

"The room is lovely. Thank you." Samantha crossed to the desk and dropped her purse on its surface. "I am most grateful for your father's hospitality."

"Pshaw. He knows I'll be moving out shortly, once Frank and I marry next month. I fear he's afraid of being lonely." Emily crossed her arms and regarded Samantha. "I wonder whatever he'll do without me to run the place."

"He'll discover how important an asset you've been for his peace of mind." Samantha untied her cloak in preparation to remove it.

Footfalls echoed on the stairs. "Miss Emily!"

Samantha spun at the urgent tone. "Something is amiss."

"Jasmine?" Emily strode to the open door, her boot heels hard on the floor. "What is the matter?"

The young black woman stopped, panting, in front of Emily. "Miss Samantha's dog…" She gasped in another breath and let it out in a rush. "She's in the stable…"

"What about Thistle?" Samantha hurried to stand by Emily. "Is she causing mischief?"

"No, miss." Jasmine gulped another breath, placing one hand to her throat as her breathing slowed. "She be having her pups. Solomon noticed as the third came out."

"Gramercy, I knew she was due to drop them soon. I must go to her." Samantha retied her cloak and then lifted her skirts a bit off the floor with shaky fingers, hurrying from the room and down the stairs. Emily and Jasmine trotted behind, their footsteps echoing in the narrow confines of the stairway. "She's so young to be having puppies."

"It's a natural occurrence," Emily said. "I'm sure she'll do fine. She's strong."

"I must be there to assist. I owe her healthy pups." Samantha pushed out the back door and strode across the stone drive to the barn.

Inside, she paused for a brief moment to let her eyes adjust. Spying Thistle lying on a pile of straw in the far corner of the small building, she hurried past four horses tied by their halters in narrow stalls. Thistle gazed at her with distracted eyes, her attention turned inward. Beside her, four tiny pups crawled in the sweet straw. Thistle panted harder, and then another puppy emerged. Samantha smiled as the tiny creature received licks from its mother, drying and cleaning the newest arrival. After a moment, concern replaced the joy in Samantha's heart. The puppy lay still. Thistle licked it more vigorously, nudging the wee pup, until finally laying back down to push another puppy into the world.

Emily stopped beside her, a smile on her lips. "She looks so content, doesn't she?"

Samantha watched numbly. Not every pup born would thrive or survive, but seeing the struggling puppy still increased her anguish. What could she do to help the little puppy? With all her training and experience, surely something would revive it. Of course, she must wait for the time being as she couldn't do anything while Thistle labored to bring all her pups into the daylight. Samantha sifted through possibilities in her mind but nothing seemed even possibly effective.

"What's wrong with that one?" Jasmine smoothed her apron after her hurried steps to keep up with Emily.

"I fear it was a stillbirth." Samantha stared at the lifeless form, wishing with all her being the wee creature had lived. Thistle panted and gazed up at her. Trusting her, the poor wretched dog. "I'm sorry, girl. I don't know what to do to help."

The dog nosed one of the older puppies, tentatively licking its face before ignoring the white and tan body. Samantha peered closer, crushing dismay filling her when she detected the puppy's struggle to breathe. Its sides barely moved as its little mouth opened, gasping for air. Not another one. She couldn't bear it.

"I must try to save the wee one." She kneeled beside the mass of puppies and carefully lifted the struggling pup. Holding the little body, she sensed a heartbeat more than felt one. Perhaps the warmth of her hands would help revive it. Cuddling the little creature to her, she cleaned its nostrils hoping to increase its ability to breathe. Massaging its side, she tried to stimulate the tiny heart to keep beating, to pump life into the ever more limp body. After several minutes, she checked again for signs of life.

"I've failed." Samantha held the dead puppy close as tears dripped onto its still shoulder. "The poor thing."

"What have we here?" Trent stood framed by the afternoon light in the door of the stable. "Thistle with pups?"

Gramercy. She hadn't seen Trent since the sensational kiss and the disastrous realization she loved him, craved him, and he chose this particular moment to make an appearance? To witness her failure in caring for her own dog's tiny pups? Providence would not give her a break no matter how hard she strove.

"You're just in time." Emily motioned for him to join the

trio attending the dog. "Thistle has delivered six puppies, but unfortunately two did not survive."

"There is nothing to be done now." Samantha flicked a glance between Emily and Trent.

"May I?" After Samantha's reluctant nod, Trent took the dead puppy from Samantha's trembling hands to examine the body. "I trust you did everything possible to save this little creature."

Shudders rippled across her shoulders, shaking loose the self-doubt and anguish she'd locked inside. "It made no difference. Two of her offspring died in front of me." She focused on Trent, a frown on her face. "I could not save them."

"We each have limits to our abilities, my dear." Trent bent to lay the pup alongside the other still body. Then he turned to address Samantha. "God or Mother Nature determined they were not strong enough to survive in this world of ours, and so took them home to heaven. It's not your fault. Do not cry."

When his thumb brushed away a tear from her cheek, she sucked in a breath at the touch of his calloused skin over sensitive flesh. Fighting the urge to lean into his hand, she sniffled and pulled a handkerchief from where she'd tucked it up her sleeve. She wiped her damp cheeks and contemplated the sincerity on his face. "Mayhap you were right to suggest I give up my practice. After seeing my failure, I'm beginning to agree with your conclusion."

"I did not come to argue with you. Amy told me she'd helped you pack this morning, and Frank mentioned that Emily planned to fetch you. He said I might find you here, so I came to seek your opinion on a possible treatment for our friend." Trent captured her hand and raised it to plant a kiss on the back. "You're distraught and out of sorts. No one can blame you for feeling that way, what with the need to vacate your house posthaste in addition to the loss of the pups. We can discuss the matter at another time."

She withdrew her hand from his grasp and shrugged. Everything she thought she knew had been wrong. With the loss of her garden and the loss of the puppies, her ability to heal any creature of any illness stood in question. "Do what you will. My attempts have failed in that regard as much as in this."

"Tomorrow you'll feel differently." Emily wrapped an arm about Samantha's waist, a bracing comfort. "Jasmine, will you please see to Thistle and her brood's comfort, while I escort my friend inside for a pot of tea?"

"Yes, Miss." Jasmine bobbed her head and began tidying up the area.

Forlorn, Samantha watched the dark-haired slip of a woman sweep up the scattered straw into a pile. Her inner resolve to be strong and stoic wavered in the face of repeated deaths on her watch. The two tiny white-and-tan spotted bodies lay side by side, as though merely asleep. Knowing not all animals lived did nothing to lessen the feeling of failure, a dead weight in the pit of her stomach.

"I'll take care of the…" Trent motioned for Samantha to do as Emily suggested. "Go ahead, but save me some tea if you've a mind. That wind slices right through a body. I'll be along in due course."

Samantha nodded, grateful for his consideration in not baldly stating what he'd do with the two dead puppies. She hoped he'd bury them under a lovely shady tree. Burying her disgrace at the same time. A part of her desired to shake off the doubt, put behind her the instances leading to the chasm of uncertainty in her heart. Then again, when a person cannot succeed in their chosen endeavors, it behooves them to admit as much and then pursue a different objective. Benjamin's situation lingered in her mind, a cankerous reminder of her failure. Another disgrace. On top of losing her home and garden. All leading to the biggest question in her mind. What would she do if forced by circumstances to not be a midwife and healer?

Early the next morning, Samantha forced herself from the comfort of a warm bed and donned a dark green wool dress. Goodness but she'd rather stay abed than face yet another round of challenges and ultimate failure. Green was her favorite color, reminding her of the deep coolness of the forest and the promise held in the tiny plants poking their first shoots through the spring earth. Green bolstered her mood. She buttoned her dress and overlaid it with a fresh apron. Despite her misgivings, obligations beckoned to her. Wallowing in her own doubt could not continue if she had any hope of tending to other ills and needs. Indeed, visiting Benjamin to judge his condition was at the top of her list of tasks. Immediately after checking on Thistle and her little ones. Wrapping her cloak about her shoulders, she slipped out of the cool house into the cold December morning sunlight.

She shivered in spite of the heavy fabric hanging from shoulders to ankles. Briskly striding to the barn, she tugged open the heavy door far enough to fit through. She made her way down the clean swept aisle to stand and grin at the happy family. Thistle thumped her tail in greeting, while four little bodies lined up at her belly with mouths sucking noisily. The cute little ears hugged the small heads, stubs of tails rigid in their earnest feeding. Each of the puppies appeared robust. Fortunately. She didn't believe she could accept yet another difficult illness or, worse, death. At least Thistle's family continued to thrive. Satisfied, Samantha turned and hurried back out of the building.

She strode down the street, the brisk pace helping warm her. Few others ventured out on the street so early in the morning. The sun had barely cleared the horizon when she climbed the steps to Benjamin's quarters. Knocking three times, she let herself in. Amy rose from a chair by the fire where she'd been stirring something in a steaming kettle, porridge from the scent wafting to meet Samantha at the door.

"What brings you here so early this morning?" Amy wiped her hands on the well-used apron tied about her waist.

"You seem surprised." Samantha untied her cloak and then removed it, draping it over one arm.

"The sun is barely shining through the windows and here you are. Come, I've made a fresh pot of tea. Have some to ward off the chilly morning."

"After I look in on Benjamin." Samantha dropped the cloak over the back of a chair, received a nod of agreement from Amy, and then strode into the patient's bedroom.

Standing by the bed, she examined Benjamin's sleeping features. His brow showed signs of distress, while his thin lips wore a blue tinge. The cuts on his right arm from the frequent bleedings stood in stark contrast to the pallid flesh. Her latest application of ointment had been almost entirely absorbed, leaving a faint glistening over the recalcitrant bullet hole which refused to heal.

She stood there for a long time, thinking and considering the wound and the various treatments she and Trent had tried over the past several weeks. All to no avail. They'd kept the wound open, not even covered with a cloth, in order to allow for the flesh to heal. The ointments she'd applied had healed so many others, why did it not do so for Benjamin? Peering closer at the remnants of the ointment, she prayed for its success as she pondered her next daring move. How would Trent react to her intended effort to break Benjamin's fever once and for all?

The kitchen door opened and closed, and then a familiar male voice spoke quietly in the other room. She couldn't make out his words, but the tenor of his voice carried into where Samantha stood. The voice hushed and then footsteps approached. She squared her shoulders, anticipating Trent's arrival. Dreading the moment he'd open his mouth, begin asking questions she couldn't answer, even as his footsteps drew closer and then stopped. Sighing, she glanced at him and then focused on Benjamin, who opened his eyes when Trent cleared his throat.

"How do you feel today?" Trent laid a hand on Benjamin's forehead and frowned. "Something has been preventing our treatment from doing its job. Let us try another purge and see if it will finally augment balancing your humors into alignment so you'll improve."

"I'd prefer to delay switching to a different approach until after he is no longer feverish. That will enable us to see what is working and what is not, rather than changing more than one element of his treatment at the same time. Something is impeding his healing."

"That's a good point." Trent put his medical bag on a side table and crossed his arms, a typical smile on his face. "Do you have any idea as to what it might be based on the condition of his wound?"

What could be blocking the effectiveness of the ointment? She went over the various ingredients she'd used in her salves, but no one item could have worked against the intended purpose. But what if some combination of them or sequential application might have blocked the healing properties from working? What if… Samantha froze, a sudden realization making her queasy. Why hadn't she seen it sooner? She crossed her arms to stop the tremors of despair starting as ripples and then rocking her to the core. With all her heart, she wished she didn't have to say the next words. "It's likely my ointment."

Trent looked at her with worried eyes. "Your ointment? The one you've insisted must be applied twice a day?"

Mute in the face of his annoyance, she nodded. "I'm sorry, I—"

"Do not say anything more." Trent shook his head, chagrin mingling with the disappointment in his expression. He paced away from the bed, one hand repeatedly dragging across his chin. "This is my fault. I cannot believe you managed to persuade me for so long to go against my better judgment."

"I believe it may be the combinations of ointments working against us. But I've never seen such a response before. I'll clean it off and we'll most likely see improvement." Turning away from his censure but unable to ignore her own, Samantha ran to the pitcher resting on the side table and poured water in the basin. Grabbing a cloth from a pile at hand, she hurried back to Benjamin and began to bathe the ointment from his arm. Benjamin gazed past her while she worked, then suddenly his eyes rolled up and his lids descended. *Oh no!* "Trent! Hurry."

Samantha retreated several steps, clinging to the linen square like it could save her life. Or Benjamin's.

Trent appeared at her side in a flash. "Ben? Can you hear me?" He gently jostled Benjamin, and then repeated the motion harder when he received no response. "Ben?"

After several more attempts, Trent lifted one of Benjamin's eyelids to peer at his eye. Pinning her with a hard stare, Trent shook his head as his frown deepened. "Now see what you've caused? He's unconscious and nonresponsive."

Amy bounded into the room, eyes wild and frightened. "What? What has happened?"

Trent stepped aside so Amy could kneel at Benjamin's side. She clutched one of his hands to her chest, peering closely at her betrothed. "Ben? Honey? Do not leave me!" Her words blurred into stabbing sobs, great gulps so painful as to threaten to tear the woman in two.

Samantha wrapped her arms around her waist, crying along with Amy. What had she done? Her pride had prevented her from facing facts. She had no business being a healer. No business trying to cure any one of anything. No business calling herself a friend to any one. She sobbed quietly, the death of her practice as frightening as losing her parents, her house, and her friend. Samantha tried, but failed, to stem the wave of anguish combined with grief battering its way through her.

Amy raised tear-drenched eyes to stare at her. "Is he going to be all right? What's going on?"

"I-I'm sorry." Samantha blinked and swiped at her own tears coursing down her cheeks. What more could she say? "I was wrong."

Trent opened his large black bag and rummaged inside. "Yet another reason why my hospital is needed. Everyone knows not to trust the potions and powders of old women like your mother."

"My mother had nothing to do with this." No, Samantha was the one to blame. Benjamin would die all because of her pride. Her obstinacy. She'd hindered Trent's better methods. She'd insisted on her ways as the right answer. She'd followed in her mother's footsteps and killed someone. Or almost. Same thing. Her mother had been suspected of permitting several women to succumb to illness during or after the delivery of their child. Samantha proved no better.

"But your mother may have had a hand in Emily's mother's death?" Amy struggled to her feet and propped fists on each hip. "And of Elizabeth's? Quite a coincidence she attended both of them and they both died." Fear lurked in Amy's eyes. Her reaction was entirely understandable as she faced the distinct possibility of losing the man she loved.

"I do not know the particulars of either of those ladies' deaths." Samantha folded her arms as much to hold her composure together as to provide a protective barrier to the onslaught of anger and grief aimed in her direction. "I suspected my mother may have complicated the situation in some way, but I could never prove her involvement."

Trent raised both eyebrows and crossed his arms over his chest. "Indeed? And you claim to follow her ways?"

His declaration confirmed in her mind that no matter what else happened, no matter how hard she tried to correct her error, to improve her education, she could never be close to Trent. He would never trust her judgment. All the outstanding kisses or gentlest of caresses could never make him believe in her abilities again. Despite her newly discovered love of the man regarding her with serious eyes, she must do what she'd longed to do before. Flee. Run. *Escape.* After all that had transpired, no one would stop her.

"I understand. I'll be going then." Silently, she prepared to vacate the room, intent on retrieving her cloak and letting herself out. Avoiding those judgmental eyes. She gathered her bag and hugged it to her as she raised her eyes to peek at Amy bending over Benjamin and then slid her gaze to Trent's stern expression.

"Yes, that's the best thing you can do." He shook his head slowly as he crossed his arms over his chest. "Go."

The command, delivered in a deep baritone shaking with disappointment, shattered her confidence. She gulped back the sob pressing against her throat. She turned and made her escape, trotting from the bedroom into the common room.

She glanced back at the empty doorway, a sob slipping through her defenses. He'd not followed her, not attempted to comfort her. She was left to fend for herself, alone on yet another level of her existence. Grabbing her cloak, she bolted through the door into the cold winter day.

Chapter Ten

*L*aughter and chatter greeted Samantha as she reluctantly followed Emily up the stairs to the upper parlor of Amy's home later in the afternoon. Keeping her balance proved challenging as she held her skirt with one hand and clutched a large bag stuffed with unfinished shirts and sewing materials in the other. She had almost refused to venture out of her new home after the events at Benjamin's earlier in the morning. Her mood did not bode well for her to be fitting company. Nevertheless, during a light noon meal, Emily had convinced her to accompany her to the weekly sewing circle. Stitching shirts posed no threat to any one's welfare and may even benefit someone, so she'd agreed.

Easing onto her usual seat by the fireplace, she laid out pins, needles, scissors, and thread on a small square table. Emily made her way across to her waiting loom, set up earlier through the efforts of Richard and Solomon under the direction of Jasmine. The three servants had perfected the routine over the past year, quickly and efficiently assembling and breaking down the heavy apparatus and carting it to and from the Sullivan home. The amiable strength of the two men served the needs of the family well, and from what she'd witnessed, they seemed happy enough in their situation. Still, she prayed for the day they'd realize freedom.

Samantha threaded a needle with bleached thread. Around her, ladies discussed the approaching withdrawal of the British troops. Amy ambled among the spinning wheels, loom, and long skirts, finally settling on a chair near Emily. Let them converse without her. Evelyn must be relieving Amy from sitting by Benjamin, or surely Amy wouldn't have left his side. Guilt washed across her back making her shiver. She'd been unsuccessful in her endeavor to help the man. Pressing her lips together to prevent any sound or cry from escaping, Samantha focused on her stitches, precise and even. Best to keep her thoughts to herself and her eyes on the task at hand.

"Did you hear about Tabitha Cook's revelation?"

Surprised by the conspiratorial tone in the woman's voice, Samantha looked up to determine who spoke. Catherine Manning sat in a whitewashed wooden rocking chair, keeping the seat in motion with the slow flexing of a satin-slippered foot. Elegantly yet simply dressed in a canary day dress with a dark green apron and matching kerchief about her neck, Catherine waited for a reply with mirth in her eyes.

"Nicholas Cook's daughter?" Emily tossed the shuttle back and forth on the loom without pause. "What of her?"

"She's been racing his horses behind his back." Catherine lifted a brow and then sniffed. "Seems he disapproved of her riding astride, as well he should. Proper young ladies would not disgrace themselves in such a fashion."

Amy laughed out loud, and then sobered as the other ladies regarded her with slight frowns drawing their brows together. "My apologies, but my father taught me to ride astride as well."

"My dear girl, surely you do not indulge in so crude an activity?" Darlene Walters leveled a disapproving stare at Amy, who gazed steadily back.

"On occasion." Amy clasped the spinning wheel with tense hands.

"What sort of 'occasion' warranted such indecorous behavior, pray tell?" Darlene appeared affronted by the mere idea.

For goodness sake, how pedantic of the women to take such a tone. Samantha laid the sewing in her lap as she took a deep breath. "Saving my life."

A collective gasp preceded excited chit chat among the women. Amy caught Samantha's eye and inclined her head in silent appreciation for her statement. Although Samantha had pushed the memory aside, she'd never forget how courageous and strong Amy had been the day they escaped the renegade loyalists. Richard Abernathy's powerful stallion, Icarus, had carried them to safety under Amy's sure hands. Indeed, Samantha had ridden astride behind her and thought nothing of it. When one's life is in danger, the niceties become a secondary consideration.

"Nevertheless, while I'm sure it was necessary, what Amy did was an exception." Darlene sniffed and shook her head. "Young Tabitha had no reason for her actions. Keeping secrets is never an appropriate course of action as they tend to lead to indignities and fester into cancerous sores within the household."

"Yet every family has their share, I dare say." Fanny Norris, the petite, vivacious brunette who spoke her mind to any one who'd listen, winked at Darlene. "I wonder what skeletons are in your family's closet?"

Darlene waved away the idea. "Mr. Walters and I foreswore secrets when we married."

Fanny chuckled. "So you believe."

"Ladies, please." Lucille Abernathy glided into the room and raised both hands. "Enough of the bickering. I think we can all agree secrets should be kept to a minimum in order to live an honest and forthright life."

Emily's hands froze in her throw of the shuttle. Samantha peered at her friend, detecting a fluttering pulse at her throat as she swept the group of women with her agitated gaze. She'd not seen her friend so distressed in a long while.

Emily cleared her throat and then rested her hands on the batten, letting her gaze touch on each woman in the room. "In the name of honesty, I have a confession to make."

Silence settled on the crowd, an expectant hush. Samantha tensed, her fingers clutching the silver needle. Knowing her friend's confession beforehand increased her own anticipation. How might the ladies react to what Emily prepared to reveal?

"I am Penny Marsh." A weak smile graced Emily's lips. "I wrote the controversial essays you all have been talking about over the last few months."

"Oh, my dear, tell me you'd not sink to such depraved amusements?" Darlene stopped the rocking chair to lean forward, her eyes hard with disapproval.

Emily nodded mutely. The other ladies slowly absorbed the truth behind the identity of the mysterious author. Some smiled and nodded, while others regarded Emily with open disdain. The opinions of the women of Charles Town were important to Emily as well as to Samantha. The women influenced their husbands' decisions as surely as the sun rose every morning. However, Samantha would not let those very same opinions direct how she'd live her life. Not any longer.

"There is more." Emily wet her lips and folded her hands in her lap. She glanced at Lucille's frown and pursed lips before taking a deep breath and letting it out slowly. "I intend to lease the Widow Murray's old bakery and open my own accessories business."

"Oh, Emily…" Lucille shook her head, disapproval in her eyes.

"What? How?" Catherine angled her head and blinked at Emily. "Legally, you cannot sign the lease, let alone operate an establishment."

"My betrothed, Frank Thomson, agrees with my aim and has pledged his support." Emily smiled openly for the first time since her revelation. "Shortly after we marry, we shall open the doors for customers. Is it not exciting?"

Darlene snorted a laugh. "No one will dare spend their money in your shop. Captain Sullivan should not allow you to fool yourself as to believe you'll find success in your ill-advised venture."

"Father's opinion will not carry as much weight after I'm married." Emily's smile drooped but clung to her face. She inclined her head in a slow nod. "Your estimation is noted, Mrs. Walters. I shall not expect you to cross the threshold."

"I, for one, applaud your spunk." Fanny clapped her hands and several others joined in. "We need creative and stalwart women to support our town. Well done. I'll be happy to frequent your shop."

Emily blushed and bowed her head in gratitude. Samantha dropped her needle onto the fabric in her lap and added to the echoing applause. Although not everyone approved, the ladies of the sewing circle once again stepped up to support one of their own. With such an air of support pervading, the time had come to reveal her own burdensome secret. Keeping mum on her important underground activities, as though they were something to be ashamed of, weighed on her conscience. She'd never even told her friends, let alone her disapproving parents, about her marriage and dressing as a man to fight alongside her husband. If she were to start over with a new means of providing for herself, she'd prefer to do so with the ladies' blessing. And with a clear conscience. She squared her shoulders. No better time than the present moment.

"I, too, have a confession." She waited for quiet before continuing. All eyes aimed her direction, curiosity and concern an equal mix. "I misled everyone when I left town last year. I do not have a grandmother in Savannah."

Emily cocked her head, one brow arched. "Then where did you go?"

"And how did you sustain the injury to your leg?" Amy asked.

Samantha drew a steadying breath. "My husband and I fought side by side at the pitched battle at Cowpens. He died protecting me, but I suffered a bayonet stab to my thigh."

"Hold. You had a husband?" Emily's mouth fell open. "Why didn't you tell us?"

Guilt flooded Samantha at her friends' shocked expressions. She should have told them, trusted them to keep her secret. They would have shared the burden, thus lightening her own. She saw the truth now, but the damage was done. She sighed. "I could not, as my parents refused their blessing." Samantha clutched her hands together to still their trembling. "I wanted to, but feared they'd hear. And after Edward died, there seemed no good reason to reveal the truth."

"And he is the reason you joined in our vow to remain unmarried?" Emily gripped the shuttle in both hands as she blinked slowly at Samantha. "The hurt you never wished to experience again?"

Samantha nodded, remaining mute. What more could she say to make them understand?

"And you fought?" Amy gaped at her, astonishment painted on her face. "How?"

"Pulled my hair up under a wool hat and bound my

breasts flat." Samantha looked at each startled woman's face, slowly changing to disgust or pride depending upon their views of a woman's role in society. Despite feeling shunned, she pressed on. "Everyone called me 'Sam' and praised my shooting and knife skills."

"I do not believe my ears." Darlene humphed and shook her head. "Pretending to be a man so you could fight. Serves you right to have been injured. Women should stay home and tend the hearth, not gallivant around like a wisp of a real man."

"I still cannot fathom that you were married. And widowed." Emily crossed her arms and studied Samantha. "You did not warrant your closest friends should know?"

"We kept our wedding a secret from my parents as they did not approve the match." Samantha lifted her shoulders in apology. "After his death, there seemed no purpose in sharing with any one what we'd done."

"Until now." Lucille strolled over to lay a hand on Samantha's quivering shoulder. "What purpose does telling us serve?"

Samantha endured the disapproving scowls from the ladies, the disappointed looks from her friends. She inspected Lucille's countenance, discerning the woman deplored her revelation, and then bowed her head. "In the event, none worth mentioning."

Lucille patted her shoulder. "You've endured quite an ordeal, both physically and emotionally. Perhaps the act of sharing will allow your true healing to commence."

"Perhaps." Then again, sharing the past may have simply relegated her to being the outcast and town pariah she'd hoped to avoid becoming. She bit her lip as she noted each woman's speculative expression. What did they expect from her? She couldn't undo her past any more than she could retain possession of her home. Her entire life had unraveled with the approach of the war ending. With the arrival of the young handsome doctor. With her abilities and techniques called into question every day because of ill or dying patients.

She gathered her sewing materials and shoved them into her bag. Time to go home after this long, hellish day. "If you'll excuse me, ladies, I believe I've outstayed my welcome." Everywhere. She rose and strode out of the room, refraining from meeting any one's judging look and seeing even more censure or derision in their eyes. She'd seen enough.

Samantha kneeled in the straw pile, playing with Thistle's puppies. At least something positive had happened over the last few days. Four tiny wriggling lives to bring a smile to her face. Thistle licked one pup with long, slow lavishes of her pink tongue. Samantha lifted another, a nearly identical color as its mother, and stroked its downy fur. The motion soothed the tormented thoughts tumbling in her mind.

For as long as she could remember, she'd wanted nothing more than to be useful to others. Following her mother's lead into healing satisfied the desire to help, a deep seated need akin to mothering. Becoming a mother had not been necessary in order for her to look for ways to provide assistance or to look out for others. Caring for the sick and injured made her feel needed.

With the events over the last weeks, could she say the same? Did any one need her any longer? And even if they did, could she actually help them, or had she been fooling herself into believing she possessed the skills to heal, to help? Questions spun and twisted in her mind, questions with no good answers.

The pup in her hands wriggled and squirmed, anxious to return to his mother. Samantha placed him on the ground and laughed as he stumbled over his paws in his hurry to reach Thistle to nurse. She sat back on her heels, resting her empty hands on her thighs. The family appeared healthy and happy. She'd have to ask Captain Sullivan about the future of each of them, given she depended upon his generosity. He may not wish to have so many dogs on the property, which would mean deciding on new homes. A rush of sadness passed through her at the thought of giving away the dogs. Another pup wiggled its way toward her, curiosity lighting its tawny eyes. She scooped up the warm body and hugged it to her, chuckling when its tiny pink tongue licked her finger.

The censure of the sewing circle ladies crashed through her memory. Her decision to share about Edward, about Cowpens, about everything, had seemed the right one at the time. Thinking on it in the aftermath of their reactions, however, how could they not have been full of approbation toward her previous activities? Lying about having a sick grandmother in need of her assistance. Masquerading as a man. Living with the militia on the cold, hard ground or in tents, sharing their living quarters such as they were. Even though she and Edward married against her parents' wishes, witnessing the various stages of undress of the other men that such close proximity lent itself to, turned out to be unacceptable in the extreme. The memory brought warmth to her face and she pressed the puppy's wriggling body to her cheek. Closing her eyes, she stroked the soft fur.

So many queries about her past but even more about her future. Opening her eyes, she set the puppy down and watched it mingle with its brother and sisters. As an only child, she envied the friendship and camaraderie of big families. Observing Emily and her much larger family intrigued her imagination. Emily and her sister Elizabeth had been very close, sharing and confiding everything with each other. If Samantha could have had a sibling, she'd have enjoyed such a sister. When Emily's three brothers returned to town, after the fighting ended and the militia could disband, the house would resound with their booming voices and barks of laughter as it surely had before the war. What would a full household be like, having the three men living in the same house?

The tap of light footsteps sounded in the barn, apparently coming from someone running on the cobblestone drive. Mary, the young slave who served as assistant cook and wet nurse, trotted into the stable, heading straight for Samantha. She wore no cloak or shawl over her black dress with a red apron. Samantha's heart sank when she detected the worry etched across the woman's face. What now?

"Miss Samantha, Lydia be needing you." Mary came to a stop, towering above Samantha where she kneeled, surrounded by puppies.

The baby. She could redeem herself and her reputation by successfully delivering the wee one to its new family. Maybe she'd even manage to make amends for all her recent failures in the process. Careful to avoid stepping on tiny paws, she lurched to her feet, her right thigh aching with the motion. "It is her time?"

"Yes, Miss." Mary chuckled at the playful pups surrounding her, curious about the smells clinging to her shoes. "You'll need to hurry, from the sound of the urgent summons."

A ripple of concern slid across her shoulders. "Please have a carriage ready in ten minutes. I'll grab my bag and then be on my way." She rushed inside to her room, checked the contents of the red bag, lamenting the fact she'd overlooked visiting the apothecary, and then swung her cloak about her shoulders. Nothing for it but to work with what she had until she determined Lydia's condition. If necessary, she could send someone to fetch what she needed from the good apothecary. With good fortune, however, all would be well with Lydia and the babe so she would not be called upon to use her contingency plan.

While she gathered the necessary items, she prayed for a healthy baby and strong mother. Both would be required for all to be well. She strode out the back door and climbed into the waiting carriage. Clucking to the bay mare, she kept a steady grip on the reins while struggling to steady her emotions. She'd be absolutely no help to Lydia if she couldn't rein in the rampant feelings filling her chest.

All the way through Charles Town, and as she presented her papers to the sentry at the picket line posted at the edge of town, she fretted about the possible complications inherent in an early birthing. Lydia's physical strength could mean the difference when considering the baby's chances. Yet strength alone did not equate to a thriving child even if successfully delivered without rips or tears to the mother or stress on the newborn. Still, other times, despite all indications of a healthy baby, within a short span the wee one or the mother, or both, succumbed and left their earthly existence. Her work to make note of the individual situations might yield important connections not previously detected. Her mother's successes and failures had drawn a great deal of attention from the townspeople. For Lydia's case, Cynthia had no connection and thus could not be blamed should anything go awry. She'd pay careful attention to Lydia's condition and add the particulars to her commonplace upon her return home. Samantha didn't need the approbation of the town for her midwifery or she'd have no practice left to rely upon.

Half an hour after leaving the Sullivans', she pulled up in front of the little cottage. Angel raced out of the house before the dust had settled. Samantha pushed aside the worry stemming from the young girl's rush to greet her as she tied the reins to the brake and stepped down from the vehicle. The lack of a smile on Angel's face hinted at the situation inside. Concern washed through her, tensing her shoulders until they burned from the strain.

"Oh, Miss Samantha, please hurry!" The girl took hold of Samantha's hand and tugged her toward the house.

Samantha grabbed her bag before Angel dragged her inside the dimly lit interior. Lydia moaned from where she lay on her bed by the hearth. The air crackled with an electric mix of tension, fear, and pain. The assault to her senses made her stumble. Catching her balance, she paused and steeled herself against the rising dread swelling in her chest. Lydia's powerful husband, George, stood with the boys by the table, eyeing her as she hesitated. She nodded at him, spotting the fear simmering in his eyes. She strode across the small room, relieved her legs continued to support her despite her concern, and then dropped her bag on the floor beside the woman.

"Let me examine you." Samantha didn't wait for Lydia's nod but immediately peeled back the threadbare blanket and then lifted the damp shift out of the way.

She inspected the vaginal opening. What she saw made her breath catch in her chest. A dark haired head pushed against red extended folds restricting its entry into the world. Slipping a finger around the part of the skull she could reach, Samantha worked to widen the birth canal enough to enable an easier birth. Lydia cried out as another birthing pain struck. Samantha focused on the emerging circle of hair that slowly revealed tiny ears on either side of the head. As Lydia pushed again, her wail stilling all other sound in the small house, Samantha prepared to catch the babe. With a rush of fluid, the little one slipped into Samantha's waiting hands. Only, the umbilical cord tightened around the soft neck. Samantha noted the tiny lips were blue, eyes closed, and then she sucked in a breath. It couldn't be. She'd ensure the baby arrived safely if it were the last thing she did in this life. The child couldn't breathe with the cord constricting his airway. The solution was simple, then all would be fine. Pushing aside the panic threatening to incapacitate her, she snatched the birthing shears out of her bag, and cut through the cord with one decisive movement. She swallowed as she dropped the tool to the floor, willing away the tears pressing at the back of her eyes.

"Heavens above…" Samantha cradled the tiny infant with trembling arms, aware of the lack of movement, the silence, surrounding the stillborn babe. She pressed fingertips to its chest, detecting no movement under the light pressure. Tears trickled down her cheeks. The wee one had perfect features, its bitty fingers and toes, its slender legs and arms lying limp in Samantha's trembling arms. Lying still and silent, like the puppies the day before. Her tears flowed unchecked at the senseless death of the baby in her hands.

"What's…What?" Lydia struggled to sit up far enough to see the baby, and then she cried out and fell back onto the mattress. She moaned and gripped her abdomen, eyes wide and panicked.

"George, take your son." She gently transferred the lifeless form to its father's shaking hands. Peering into his stricken eyes, she shook her head slowly. "I'm so very sorry."

"Help my wife." His eyes pleaded with Samantha to save the woman writhing on the bed. He hugged the child to his chest while the boys fixed wide eyes on their father. The child would have had a loving father to defend it against the inequalities of the world. If he had lived.

Samantha nodded at the stoic man before rushing to Lydia. She had no idea as to what possible problem or ailment caused the distress evident on her patient's face. The pregnancy had progressed normally by every indication. Cord accidents were rare, but would not threaten the mother's life. The random feeling Lydia had of things not being right had been the only concern which cast a shadow on her condition. Reviewing the signs and symptoms she'd witnessed on previous visits, Samantha performed another examination, searching for any possible cause. Lydia presented normal response to childbirth, other than the pain. Could it be associated with the failure of the afterbirth to emerge?

She scrambled in her bag for a strong simple to both kill the pain and to encourage the expelling of the placenta. Time slipped away as she searched for what she needed. She must hurry. Fumbling the tiny bottle into her still trembling hand, she pulled the cork with a faint pop. She placed the mouth of the bottle to Lydia's lips. "Drink this."

Lydia groaned but obediently opened her mouth for Samantha to administer half the volume. Lydia's eyes watered as she swallowed. She coughed on the bitter taste, dropping her head back onto the pillow.

"What did you give her?" George edged closer to stand beside her, peering down from his towering height.

Samantha glanced at him and then the baby in his arms. "Something to kill the pain."

"What's wrong?" George hugged the tiny body as though afraid it might break. "Why is she in such pain?"

"I don't know." All her fears joined into one massive failure. All her training ended up for naught. All her experience providing no insight as to even what to try. A woman's life hung in the balance. "I-I simply don't... I don't know."

"Who does?" George pinned her with a fearful gaze. The tall brawny black loomed above her, muscles bulging beneath his tattered shirt. His voice shook nearly as much as his hands. "Fetch someone who can help her. Please."

Samantha took a deep breath as she studied George's severe expression. One swat of the back of his hand would send her careering across the room. But she relied upon the fact that he needed her help to keep her safe from his anger and grief. "My mother was the only other midwife in town."

"Get her, then." George shifted the tiny body in his arms, not relinquishing his hold for a moment. "And be quick. Lydia needs help now."

Samantha shook her head. "Mother left town and won't be back."

"Then who else can you get?"

"There's no one else. No midwives, at least."

"You talking about one of them docs?" George frowned down at her. "Do they help slaves?"

Samantha shrugged. "I believe so. If I were to summon Dr. Trent Cunningham, I feel certain he'd attend posthaste." Just to make her failed efforts look worse. But he'd come and maybe he'd have a better idea as to what to do to help her friend.

"Do it." George moved to Lydia's side, taking hold of her hand with his massive fist. "I won't lose my wife."

Dr. Trent to the rescue. Yet again. Samantha sighed and shook off the impending dread inching across her shoulders. She could do no more for the poor woman. Other than seek help from the same man who wished her methods to go away.

"Very well. Send one of your boys for the doctor, Dr. Trent. You know him?" How she hated to need his help, but she must do whatever she could for Lydia.

Without a word to Samantha, he yelled for his oldest son and dispatched him on flying feet to retrieve Trent. Samantha turned back to Lydia, noting the pain had subsided along with some of her distress. A small sense of victory, of hope, edged into her heart. *Please, let her live.*

"Is the pain less?" Samantha asked.

Lydia nodded, her expression reflecting the easing of the discomfort. "I'm feeling a touch dizzy, but otherwise not so bad as before but still not right. Can you do somethin' about the pain? Please?"

"I suppose." Samantha retrieved the little bottle and uncorked it, sifting in her mind the dosage limitations of the potion. She placed the bottle to Lydia's mouth, propping her head up with her other hand. "Take a tiny sip. That's all you should need."

Lydia obliged and Samantha eased the woman's head back onto the thin pillow. "Try to get some rest. Relaxing may help you overcome the soreness."

Rubbing her belly in slow circles, Lydia moaned and closed her eyes. Samantha used a kerchief to dry the perspiration from Lydia's brow and cheeks. All the while, she prayed for Trent's arrival with each passing minute. She'd done all she knew how. Lydia's fate rested in Trent's hands. An hour flowed by like molasses on a winter's day, cold and dark and bittersweet.

Samantha moved away to refill the tea kettle with water and hang it over the fire, As she returned to Lydia's side several minutes later, she inspected her condition. She didn't like what she saw. "Lydia, are you feeling any better?" She smoothed a hand over the woman's damp black hair, away from eyes squeezed shut in response to the pain. "Lydia? Did you hear me?"

Lydia cried out, hands pressing onto her stomach. Then a low sigh preceded silence as her hands fell from her abdomen to drop onto the cot at her sides.

"Lydia!" Samantha grabbed the woman's shoulders and gently rocked her. "Lydia! Please. Don't do this."

She pressed frantic fingers on the side of the woman's still neck. No pulse. Lydia's chest didn't rise and fall. Samantha positioned her cheek over the open mouth but no air brushed her skin. The pain induced tension around her eyes and mouth had relaxed into a peaceful expression. *Oh dear God.*

Lydia, no! She stepped back from the bed, one hand covering her mouth. Turning to George, she shook her head, unable to say the dreadful words.

George blinked several times and then belted out an angry grief-filled string of curses. He placed his dead son on the cot at Lydia's feet, and pushed Samantha out of the way. He kneeled beside the bed, a deep rumbling moan filling the air. He lifted Lydia's body into a bear hug, rocking to and fro as he repeatedly sobbed her name.

Samantha sank to the floor, her legs not capable of supporting her shock. What had happened? George's sobs hammered her senses. The other son and Angel stood by the table, adding their cries to the grief in the room as they witnessed and responded to their father's anguish.

The front door burst open and Trent rushed inside on a blast of cold air, followed by the older boy. Trent took in the situation in one sweep of his gaze. The question in his eyes shifted to understanding as quickly. He rushed to where she sat on the dirt floor, her dark blue skirts a puddle around her. He held out a hand to help her stand. She reluctantly accepted his offer, and rose to her feet all in the space of a minute.

"What has happened here?" His tone suggested he knew the answer. "Why have you sent for me?"

Oh, how she wished she didn't have to say it out loud, with the family hanging on every word they exchanged. "Her baby was a stillborn after the cord suffocated the poor thing. But then Lydia suffered from some pain. I tried to help her. She d-died despite no other known problems, nothing apparent to my eye." Her voice quavered as her gaze drifted to where George continued to rock with Lydia in his embrace. The woman had hoped to be free after her baby was born. Not like this, though. Samantha choked back a sob. "I don't understand."

"Following your mother's ways again. I thought we'd moved passed such nonsense." Trent headed toward George, making a shooing motion toward Samantha. "You've been through enough. Why don't you go home? I'll take care of things here."

She bristled at the implied insult until she realized he spoke the truth. Bowing her head, she sucked in a fortifying breath. Let it out while counting to five. She must face the reality, the true meaning of the situation. Her involvement had led to misery and death. The only thing any one needed from her was to step aside and let others heal. Quelling the emotion threatening to choke her, she grabbed her bag and fled the house.

She mounted the steps into the front seat of the carriage and picked up the reins. She wouldn't think about it. Wouldn't permit herself to feel the grief stabbing her like sewing needles to the heart. Better to do something without thinking or feeling. Slapping the reins on the horse's rump, the vehicle jolted forward.

She made her way back along the bumpy road toward town, through the obligatory check at the sentry, and then on to the Sullivans' home. All without being able to stop seeing Lydia's still body, or that of her tiny baby's. If only she could stop hearing George's sobbing. Stop hearing the weeping of the three motherless children. Stop hearing Trent's disappointment when he confronted her failure. Parking at the stable, she handed off the reins to Richard. Numbly, she descended to the cobblestones, dragged her bag out of the vehicle, and stumbled toward the house.

"Pardon me, Miss."

Now what? She couldn't withstand any more surprises. The man limping toward her appeared to have stepped off a ship. He was dressed like a sailor in dark blue wool shirt and tan pants, a knitted cap on his head. He had an agreeable countenance and easy manner. He didn't appear threatening, so Samantha lingered until he stopped in front of her.

"How may I help you?" Samantha stayed still with an effort. She longed to escape to the privacy of her room, away from any chance of additional turmoil and tragedy.

"My name's Mack Hanrahan. I understand you took in a stray dog, a white-and-tan Water Spaniel to be specific."

Gramercy. What did he want? The truth dawned slowly in her mind. No, not Thistle. She needed her dog. Yet something in his expression conveyed his sincerity as he awaited her response. "How is my dog any concern of yours?"

Mack slipped his knit hat from his balding head and clutched it at his belt buckle. "Rose is my best hunting dog. She ran off a few weeks back. I'm hoping to find her afore she has her pups."

Gramercy. He wanted Thistle and the puppies? She must think, get her brain working. She couldn't lose the dogs on top of everything else. Who was he to take her friend away? "How do I know she's your dog?"

"If'n you don't mind, I'll just whistle for her and we can answer the question." Hope sparked in his eyes as he twirled his hat between his hands.

What could it hurt? One more tragedy to pile on top of the others. If Thistle wasn't his, she'd ignore the sound. If she had run away, then the thing for Samantha to do was to return the dog to her rightful owner. But if she had her choice, she didn't want to do the right thing. She wanted to keep Thistle, the loving, smart dog that had made a place in Samantha's heart no other being could ever fill. The hope in Mack's eyes decided the matter. On a sigh, she nodded.

He put first and fourth fingers in his mouth and blew three short high notes. Before the last note died on the breeze, Thistle bounded out of the stable and ran straight to Mack.

He rubbed her head and she leapt up to put her paws on his chest. Close behind, four pups wiggled and waggled their way to her side. Samantha's hope deflated as she witnessed the elation on Thistle's face and in her furiously wagging tail.

"Ah, she's had them, then." Mack squatted and extended a hand for the puppies to sniff and lick. After a few minutes, he stood and withdrew a leather purse from his pocket. He removed several coins and offered them to Samantha. "Them pups are valuable to me, and I'm much obliged for your help. Thank ye for caring for Rose and her pups so well for me. I'll be taking them home now."

Automatically, she held out her hand to take the coins. As they clinked onto her palm, her heart shattered into sharp-edged pieces. She didn't want his money. She wanted Thistle and the pups. She closed her hand over the coins, feeling their cold weight. Sobs she'd held at bay erupted from her, startling Mack into silence. She shook her head, unable to speak, unable to put words to the grief engulfing her, unable to stay one more moment with the man destroying the last shred of hope in her life. Flinging the money to the ground, she raced for the back door, afraid she'd never have the courage to emerge from the safety of the house again. No one would care, of that she could be certain.

Closing the door behind her, she leaned against it to catch her breath, calm her thundering heart. She thumped her head against the hard wood, eyes closed, tears scalding her cheeks.

"Samantha? What is troubling you?"

Samantha cut off a sob and opened her eyes. She scrubbed a hand across her wet face. Emily stood at the entrance to the dining room, an arm wrapped around a porcelain bowl brimming with apples resting on her hip. Samantha pushed away from the door, her legs wobbly but managing to barely support her.

"What is troubling me?" She cackled, surprised by the harsh sound, and then sobered abruptly. She sniffled as she shook her head. "A woman died, along with her baby. Benjamin is unconscious. The town abhors me for my lies and my secrets. Thistle and her pups have been claimed by their true owner and taken from me. Need I continue?"

"Oh, my dear friend." Emily placed the bowl on a hall table and hurried to envelop Samantha in a sturdy hug, intended to bolster and comfort. "You have endured a very trying day, and I beg your forgiveness for bringing even more unwelcome tidings."

Samantha stepped from the embrace and sighed until all her breath had departed her lungs. Bracing herself for the next revelation, she crossed her arms. "What do you know?"

"Father dined with Mr. Manning today and discovered that your father's house has been purchased."

The last straw landed with the force of a shooting star, exploding inside her heart. She could only stare at Emily as the truth struck home. She'd lost everything. Every being and possession she cherished. Her legs crumpled and she collapsed to the floor, keening as she hunched over and rocked back and forth, certain she'd never recover.

Chapter Eleven

After visiting Amy as she tended to the still insensible Benjamin, Trent hurried to meet with his father and Frank at the proposed location for the new hospital. The streets thronged with people and conveyances as the day approached for the British to evacuate Charles Town. Men worked day and night to load supplies onto the vessels. Loyalists flocked from the city or to the quartermasters to arrange passage on one of the three hundred ships anxious to carry Britons to their homeland. The weather at long last had cleared sufficiently for the ships to safely hoist anchor and sail for England. Trent's spirits soared with anticipation of both the freedom of the town and of his long held dream becoming a reality.

He strode along King Street, anxious to investigate the property. Finally, after walking for blocks, he spotted the three-story warehouse at the corner of King and Jacob's Alley. The red brick building dominated the street. Dark green trim at the window sashes and door frames added to the overall effect. He lengthened his stride, excitement building in his chest so that breathing became difficult. He waved to Frank, who waited at the base of the three steps leading to double crimson doors. The location held a place of prominence and easy access, two features valuable to the future success of the enterprise.

"Hallo!" Trent halted beside the other man. "What do you think? Impressive, isn't it?"

Frank inclined his head, glanced down the street, and then back to Trent. "Where's your father? I thought he'd be with you."

"He should arrive momentarily." Trent searched the crowded street for a hint of his father's distinctive gray hair and beard, wearing his stylish black tricorne hat. "Ah, there he is now."

The elderly doctor soon wove his way through the passersby to join Trent and Frank. He craned his neck to perform a brief sweeping inspection of the exterior and then shook hands with Frank. He turned, eyes serious, to contemplate his son. "I believe this place may prove ideal for your purposes."

"Shall we go in?" Trent retrieved a key from his coat pocket. "Mr. Manning entrusted me, given the financial assurances I was able to present."

He bounded up the steps and soon had the door unlocked and swung open. His first impression of the interior was of a grand ballroom, light flooding the space from the banks of windows set into the whitewashed walls. The closed door to the right probably led into the area used by the previous owner as living quarters. Depending on its design, he envisioned using the space as locked storage for the medicines and apparatus. He strolled farther into the room, stopping to slowly pivot and dwell on every detail.

"This place would make a wonderful hospital." Frank stopped beside him and motioned to the left. "You could set up a primary clinic over there, under the windows by the door. You'll want a place where you can determine how ill or injured a patient is before admitting them."

Trent surveyed the open area, envisioning patients resting on cots with nurses working over them, ensuring their comfort as well as their care. Doctors moving between the beds, making recommendations and performing seeming miracles with their skill and expertise. "The other floors could be bed space and the surgery, from what George told me. Let's go have a look." He led the way to the narrow staircase along the far right wall.

The second floor had been subdivided into smaller rooms than the first floor, but large enough Trent could imagine each containing seven or eight beds. Nurses would be occupied with providing the necessary care and feeding of the patients. In his mind's eye, every bed held a patient on the road to recovery.

The third floor matched the second floor in number of rooms and how they connected. Trent planned on leasing out a few of the smaller rooms to highly competent doctors to use for their individual practices. The combination of capabilities of each man would contribute to the overall success of the hospital.

He gripped his hips as he noted the reactions of his companions. "I plan to invite world renowned physicians to work here to give the best care possible to our citizens. I'd invest in the latest equipment in order to conduct experiments on possible cures."

"I applaud your intent. We need to better understand the causes of so many ailments. Medicine is still more mystery than not." Frank moved past and paused at a window overlooking the alley. He stood motionless for a few moments and then turned back to Trent. "Have you spoken to Miss Samantha about that slave woman?"

"Not yet, but I expect to see her ere long." Trent looked at his father. "Based on the symptoms, Father, have you discovered a possible cause or at least a cure we missed? In order to prevent another similar tragedy, I'd like to know what happened."

"As Frank said, we have much to learn about what makes people sick and die." Robert grimaced and slowly rotated his head side to side. "It's a shame, but from what you've shared, nobody could have saved the poor thing."

"So Samantha couldn't have hoped to save her. That is good news." Frank strode back to stand in front of Trent. "The news will be quite a relief. Emily told me Samantha collapsed in her distress."

"I'm sorry to hear that." Trent frowned as the vision of Samantha crying over her parents' defection rose yet again to his mind. In the event, despite her grief, she'd soon composed herself. To think his strong, courageous woman had buckled under the pressures of losing a patient. Surely she understood not every patient could be saved. It was good to commiserate with clients, to fathom their emotions and reactions, but not to fall apart when one died. The accusing words he'd uttered upon his arrival at the slave quarters echoed in his mind, berating him for assuming the worst of Samantha. She couldn't have saved Lydia; no one could. Yet he'd not given her the benefit of the doubt, merely sent her away. He needed to make amends. "I will speak with her. Come, the day is wasting."

They descended back to the first floor. Ideas and plans spun in Trent's mind. First order of business included making a list of repairs and replacements needed. Locks, hinges, even some floor planks required attention. New doors would need to be made and hung. The whole place cried out for a good scrubbing, too. The windows barely let any light through, what with the dirt clinging to the outside of them. Where would he find the men to do the work? Perhaps Frank might know, or Father.

"You have enough subscribers to afford this place?" Robert surveyed the spacious room on the first floor with his jaw slackened. "The building is much larger than I thought."

"Nearly have adequate numbers of interested businessmen." Trent's financial status worried him, truth be told. How could he fund all of his desired properties? Perhaps he should not have dipped into his funds prior to investigating the current location. But he considered his acquisition an investment in his future. If everything worked out the way he hoped, the latest addition to his growing list of properties would be put to very good use. Still, possibly he should have delayed the unexpected expenditure. He eyed his father. "Would you know of any one else I might ask?"

"I may. Let me think on it." Robert strolled across to open the door and went inside the apartment. Trent and Frank trailed after him, exchanging questioning looks as they moved through the door.

The apartment included two rooms, a spare kitchen and an equally barren bedroom, neither graced with furniture or furnishings of any kind. The walls had no decoration except for the requisite wood chair rail. Above the fireplace, a simple mantel with carved scrolls attached to the wall. From the entrance, Trent could see through the open door connecting the two rooms that each had two windows overlooking King. They sauntered across the first room to peek into the bedroom and then turned back to the larger common room. The end setup for the kitchen consisted of a small fireplace with one metal hook along the wall shared by the bedroom. Living in the bleak apartment would prove a grim existence indeed.

"This would suit my purposes." Robert paced through the rooms, pausing frequently to eye a loose board or inspect a stain. He muttered to himself as he drifted from one area to another.

What purpose did his father have in mind? Trent sifted through their previous discussions, searching for hints but nothing surfaced. "What do you mean, Father?"

"A minute." Robert inspected every corner of the quarters, before halting in front of Trent. "If you'll allow me, I would be interested in contributing the difference in what you require in exchange for these quarters for my practice as well as access to the surgery."

Had he heard him aright? Trent gaped at his father before grinning and pumping his hand. The last barrier overcome, he could proceed to make his hospital a reality. Joy and immense satisfaction filled his chest with pride. His plans for his professional future were falling into place in such a way as to make hope for his personal future swell in his heart. If only the foundation he'd laid for the intimate side of his prospects worked out as desired, then he'd feel confident of his ultimate success in both arenas. The next step would begin the process. "Thank you, Father. I shall inform George forthwith."

Samantha stayed in bed late, unwilling to face yet another disastrous day. If only she could snuggle under the quilt instead of emerging from the warmth and comfort and safety of her bedroom. The call of a mourning dove filtered into the stillness surrounding her, a lonesome, haunting sound in the comfortably furnished room. A knock at the door made her throw the covers over her head, hoping whoever was there would leave her alone.

"Samantha? Are you awake?"

"No."

A soft chuckle came from the other side of the closed door. "Are you talking in your sleep, then?"

Samantha grinned as she stared at the door, immediately recognizing the voice. The day might be worth facing after all. "Yes."

"I'm coming in to witness this phenomenon for myself."

The door opened to admit Evelyn, dressed in a charcoal gray dress. Her mourning garb. Was it sacrilege to wish she did not grieve for her husband?

"What brings you here?" Samantha sat up, pushed the quilt to one side, and swung her feet to the floor.

"Emily told Amy how upset you've been, and I thought you could use a friend."

Samantha sighed and shook her head, rising to stand facing Evelyn. "I'd rather talk to my new sister, if that's okay with her."

Evelyn hugged Samantha, a tentative yet comforting embrace. Surprised at the unexpected sign of affection, Samantha hesitated a moment before returning the hug. Evelyn stepped back to peruse Samantha's face. "I like that idea, too. I'll put on some tea while you dress."

"Do you know where everything is?"

"No, but I'm sure Emily's girl can help me put things together. Now hurry up so we don't get interrupted."

"I'll be down in a few minutes."

Samantha rushed through her morning routine, inwardly grimacing at the late hour, and then slipped on a cornflower blue dress with purple stripes radiating from the waist to the hem. Grabbing a pair of hair combs, she swept her thick curls up to the crown of her head and let the ends dangle down her back. She looked in the mirror one last time before straightening her shoulders and walking out the door.

Evelyn met her in the downstairs hall, Jasmine behind her with a tray. "Come, we'll sit in the parlor and indulge in some quiet conversation."

After they settled in their chosen seats, and Evelyn poured tea for them both, Samantha found she couldn't relax. She needed to do something, something that succeeded, but for the first time in her life she doubted her ability nearly as much as Trent. She half-heartedly engaged in some feminine gossip and other chit chat, all the while stewing on questions regarding her future.

"What will you do now?" Evelyn held her porcelain cup gracefully as she studied Samantha, waiting for a response.

Was Evelyn reading her mind? "I'm not sure what I can do. I've lost everything over the past several weeks." Samantha sipped her tea, delaying the need to speak further about her plans.

"Amy asked me to tell you she's waiting for you to come see Benjamin, to help him." Evelyn peered at Samantha over the flowered cup she held poised before her mouth. "I know walking away from the responsibility is tempting. But you're not that kind of woman. You mustn't give up trying, or you'll never forgive yourself."

"You have a point." She stared at Evelyn for the span of four slow breaths. She was a fighter, not a person who quit when the job became difficult. She placed her cup and saucer on the table, flowed to her feet, and then paced the oriental carpet, thinking about what her move should be. Then inspiration struck. Little Running Bear's remedy may be the answer they sought. "Will you help me?"

Evelyn nodded, mischief lighting in her eyes. "What do I need to do?"

"Go to the market and buy ten ears of corn and then meet me at Benjamin's."

"Corn?" Evelyn gaped at her. "What for?"

Samantha grinned. "You'll see. Now hurry. We're wasting daylight. I'll meet you there."

An hour later, Samantha swept into the common room of Benjamin's quarters. Amy greeted her with surprise and delight.

"How is he?" Samantha removed her cloak and draped it over a chair. "Any change?"

Amy shook her head. "Please tell me you have struck upon a course to help him."

Samantha grimaced. "I hope so. I'll need your help, though. Are you up for it?"

"Of course. What do I need to do?"

"You'll think I'm crazy." Samantha slipped her gloves off and laid them with her cloak. She met Amy's curious gaze. "Find a pot big enough to boil ten ears of corn and get the water boiling. Evelyn will be here any minute."

"Corn?"

Samantha grinned. "That's what Evelyn said as well. Please, hurry. While you do that, I'll put the rest of my plan in place."

Amy pivoted, her long skirts belling around her slim figure, and scurried to do as asked. Samantha slipped into the bedroom, careful to not disturb Benjamin. He appeared asleep, yet his pallor and damp shirt spoke volumes about his condition. She searched the room, locating a stack of blankets on a shelf. Pulling them down, she placed them near her patient. A pang of guilt swept through her when she realized she'd not consulted Trent as promised, but she simply couldn't bear to see censure or disappointment in his gaze again. She heard the outside door open and close and hoped it was Evelyn arriving and not Trent. She needed time to make this last attempt to redeem herself.

Before long, Amy poked her head into the room. "Evelyn is here with the corn. Do you want me to husk it first?"

Samantha grinned at her. "There's no need. Just boil them in their wrapping until they're hot. Then bring them in here."

Amy spun around and moved out of view toward the fireplace. Samantha unfolded each blanket and carefully covered Benjamin with the five warm layers. What else had the medicine man done? She snapped her fingers. She crossed to the windows and closed them. Keeping all the warmth inside aided the process. With any luck, Benjamin's fever would be over very soon.

Scuffling drew her attention to the door. Amy and Evelyn carried a large wooden bowl between them, the ears of corn steaming.

"Bring them here." Samantha indicated the table beside the bed. Using a fold of her skirt, she grabbed each ear of corn and placed them under the blankets so they surrounded Benjamin.

"What are you doing?" Amy's surprise made her voice squeak.

"The Cherokee use corn or rocks to sweat a person with a fever." Samantha tucked the edge of the blanket pile under the ears of corn to be sure the steam heated Benjamin's body. "Now we wait for the corn to cool and his body right along with it."

"How does that work?" Evelyn stood near at hand, within easy distance to assist if necessary. "I don't understand."

Samantha shrugged. "Little Running Bear used this technique many times while I was staying with him. He never explained how it works, but it certainly does."

"I hope you have success." Amy stood at the head of the bed, lightly caressing Benjamin's good shoulder. She sniffled and glanced at Samantha. "I want to see him laugh and smile and tease me again."

"He will, my friend." Samantha studied Benjamin. "This will work."

An hour later, the corn was cool but Benjamin was not. What had she done wrong? Perhaps she should have used stones instead, but the corn was available, more so than rocks. She'd do it again and hope the next time would work.

"Gather up the corn and let's reheat them." Samantha plucked two ears from under the blankets and dropped them into the waiting bowl. Amy and Evelyn followed suit, and Amy carried them all back to the boiling pot.

Samantha laid a hand on Benjamin's brow, feeling the heat

on her skin. "I'll make all this up to you, Benjamin. I will."

"Of course, you will." Evelyn moved to stand at her side, looking down on the unconscious man. "Do not let a few setbacks devastate your confidence. I've seen you in action, remember? You helped me overcome the stomach pains and safely delivered my son."

"Thanks for the kind words." Samantha glanced out the window while she thought about Evelyn's sentiment and waited for Amy to return with the corn. After what seemed an eternity, Amy called to Evelyn to help her.

Again, they placed the ears under the blankets, tucking in the edges, and then stepped back to wait. Samantha thought about sitting down, but didn't want to relinquish oversight of the sweat to Amy and Evelyn. She swayed on her feet, reaching out to brace herself against the wall.

"What's wrong?" Amy wrapped an arm around Samantha's waist. "You need to sit down."

"No, I must tend to Benjamin." Samantha's head was spinning, starting to ache, and her limbs trembled even though she was not cold.

"Are you sick?" Evelyn moved to help Amy guide Samantha to a chair. "When did you eat last?"

Samantha weakly shook her head. I…I don't know." The hard wood supporting her as she sat down made her legs stop feeling like earthworms trying to keep her standing. "Yesterday, maybe?"

Amy frowned and peered closer. "You need to go home, eat, and then get some rest. You're exhausted, and no good to any of your patients in such a condition."

"I'll walk with her back to the Sullivans' house," Evelyn said. "Do you wish for me to return once I see her home, Amy?"

Amy shook her head. "I'll cover things here. If anything happens, good or bad, believe me I'll send for you.

"Let me know of any change, Amy, and I'll come back." Samantha peered at her friend, wishing the room would hold still and the dark spots before her eyes would go away. Yet again she'd attempted to provide aid and comfort, and her efforts failed to produce the desired result. Maybe some rest would do her good. With Evelyn's help, she gained her feet, lurching to and fro as she tried to keep her balance while they walked toward the door. "If this doesn't work, then I'll have at least a partial answer to the question of my future."

The next afternoon, Trent lifted the knocker on the Sullivans' front door and let it fall with a resounding thud. He'd considered coming to visit Samantha the day before, but he'd elected instead to put the wheels in motion for the purchase of the building. He'd considered his next steps with utmost care, thinking through every angle and nuance. The process had taken time, but time well spent. Besides, he had to determine what to say to restore her faith in herself. Since his longtime aim neared success, he realized he didn't want to miss the chance to continue to work with her. But if she stopped believing in her abilities because of a misunderstanding, then he'd never convince her to accept his offer. He'd used the time to compose his thoughts, all the while longing to see her, be with her, and maybe steal another kiss or two. He smiled, recalling the last buss they shared. Maybe working together would lead to a more permanent arrangement. With his professional path determined, he could begin to seek the appropriate woman to be his wife and helpmate. After a few moments, Samantha opened the door with a slight frown marring her pretty face and then started closing the heavy door when she spied him. Her surprise equaled his, as he'd expected Jasmine to answer his knock.

"Hold, Miss Samantha." He stepped forward to block the swing of the door and then removed his tricorne and held it in nervous hands. He'd practiced his speech for the past several hours, but the words suddenly seemed trite and stilted. Unworthy for the effort to share them with her. Yet he'd walked over to do that very thing. "Will you permit me to speak with you?"

"Have you come to belittle my abilities again?" She clung to the door, blocking his entrance. "If so, you have wasted your time as I have no patience for more abuse."

She appeared drawn and pale, her face ashen against her coal black locks. Even her lips had lost some of their rosy color. An erratic pulse beat at her throat, from dread or excitement? Maybe she felt something for him after all. Her eyes narrowed as he stood studying her, and he cleared his throat to give himself time to summon his courage to begin the conversation.

"Trent, I do not have time to stand here with the door open to the chill while you gape at me." Samantha made to close the door. "Good day."

He blocked the door with one hand. "Wait. I beg your indulgence. May I come in off the street?"

On a sigh, she stepped aside. "Very well, but know I am not afraid to physically remove you from these premises if your behavior warrants."

The image of her carrying him through the door made him smile. It might be well worthwhile to aggravate her enough to have her make the attempt. Another day, though. "I shall do all in my power to avoid the necessity."

She closed the door behind him. "I cannot understand why you should venture here today."

"I promise to only take a short amount of time." He fingered the soft brim of his hat. "I have an urgent matter I wish to discuss with you."

"We've just sat down to tea. Would you care for a cup?"

"I'd enjoy some to take the cold from my bones. Thank you."

She led him into the front parlor with its wall of books and a softly blazing fire to welcome him. Emily rested on a chair to the right of the fireplace. A silver tea service sat on the low table situated between the matching chairs and settee, a plate of biscuits and a bowl of what appeared to be apricot preserves nearby.

"Why Trent, what brings you here?" Emily set her china cup and saucer on the round table at her elbow.

"Miss Emily, I bring happy news to Miss Samantha."

"Please, have a seat." She waved him into the other chair. "Tea?"

He nodded at Emily and then smiled at Samantha. "Where is Thistle and the puppies?"

Emily shot him a look that shut his mouth with a snap of front teeth. Samantha closed her eyes and slowly shook her head, a tear sliding down her cheek. There he went, putting his foot in his mouth again. He must have hit a mighty big sore topic.

"As I was saying, after you left the slave hut, I investigated further into the woman's symptoms and those of her child. Then I shared my findings with my father, a consult if you will for another view of the circumstances of her death."

Samantha speared him with an intense gaze but remained silent, considering him.

He accepted the cup and saucer from Emily and added sugar, stirring quickly with a silver spoon provided for the purpose. Resting the spoon on the saucer, he returned his attention to Samantha.

Hope flared in Samantha's eyes as she raised her chin. "And what pray tell did you discover?"

"As far as we can determine, the ailment she contracted

has no known cure." He sipped the fragrant tea. "And of course, her child died due to an unhappy cord accident. Both sad occasions, but I'm here to tell you, my dear, neither died as a result of your actions."

"How can you say that?" Samantha picked up her cup and saucer, the china clattering delicately in her fingers. "I should have seen the cord was tied about the neck and removed it sooner. I should have recognized Lydia had signs of a serious illness. She had told me she didn't feel right, but I dismissed her complaint as having no consequence."

"You did all you could. Of that I am certain. I spoke with Lydia's husband and he bears no grudge about any of your actions." Trent leaned forward, driven to relieve the unwarranted guilt lingering in Samantha's expression. Her green eyes should shine with hope and strength, not be dimmed with uncertainty. "You are not at fault. You must believe me."

Samantha shook her head, gripping the saucer with one hand, the cup tinkling in its place. "You were not there, Trent. You do not know."

Trent set his cup on the table and moved to stand by Samantha's chair. He removed the saucer from her hand and placed it on the table. Then he clasped both her hands in his, drawing her attention. Her delicate yet strong fingers chilled his hands. "You must hear me. I've investigated Lydia's death and her baby's. There was absolutely nothing any one could have done to change the sad outcome. You did everything possible, and even tried a few unusual remedies which likely eased her passing."

"You are certain?" Samantha gazed at him, the hint of tears making her eyes shimmer in the firelight. "I have felt such a failure on top of losing everything else of import in my life. Please do not jest with me."

Unsure as to what she meant about losing everything of

consequence, Trent frowned but squeezed her hands. He knew she'd lost her parents, of course, and the house, but she retained much more. What else had happened in his absence? He'd inquire later, but for the moment, he could reassure her on one score as a minimum. "I am positive you did not cause either death. We do not always fathom why one treatment works and then does not on a different occasion. All we can do, my dear, is our best. Which is what you did."

"Thank you for saying so, Trent. And speaking of unusual, you remind me of an idea for helping Benjamin. It's rather uncommon as well, but after much consideration I can think of no other reason for his decline." Samantha pinned Emily with her gaze as she slipped her fingers free from Trent's grasp. "Please have Frank return the little silver box to Benjamin as soon as he can."

"The one with the pendant? But what purpose might the gem serve?" Emily regarded Samantha with a puzzled expression. "Frank planned to return it to the governor upon his return to town."

Samantha nodded. "In the meantime, let us see whether the legends are true about smoky quartz having healing powers."

"A piece of rock has some kind of ability to heal?" Trent gawped at Samantha and then closed his mouth when she raised a brow at his tone. The look told him to hold his tongue. She needed to rebuild her confidence if he would ever convince her to work with him. Instead of interrogating her further, he shrugged off his disbelief. It was time to put his faith in her experience and opinions without requiring proof before-hand. "I suppose it's worth the attempt."

"It shall be my last attempt at healing any one." She smiled weakly and then relaxed against the back of the settee, her hands folded in her lap. "I've been thinking about my future. I've decided to find another occupation for my time and talents."

Trent scowled at her. She couldn't stop being a healer if it was her calling. He'd been wrong to not trust her, to equate her with her mother. He had to make up for his error. "Why? You've demonstrated you have significantly more training than one might expect of a woman. You needn't forego practicing as a midwife solely due to your patient's dying from an unknown ailment you couldn't cure."

She contemplated him, her mouth opening and closing several times before finally choosing her words. "I've given the matter considerable thought. There is nothing more to say."

He splayed his hands across his hips as he regarded her. He had more to say, if he could convince her to listen. "I was hoping you'd consider working with me at my new hospital. Our town needs the compassionate touch and approach you have shown to each of your patients, no matter whether they have recovered or not. Your caring is important." He enclosed her hands in his again, their slender strength pleasant in his grip.

Samantha huffed a laugh and tried to withdraw her hands. He held on, grasping for words to convince her of his earnestness. He needed her by his side. He'd realized exactly how much she meant to him when he saw the angst on her face the day Lydia and the baby had passed on. After that day, he'd wrestled with the depth of emotion her situation caused within him. Why did her reaction hold such consequence? Finally, he understood.

"Do not joke about such serious affairs." She tugged on her hands. "Release me if you're going to make fun of my grief."

He shook his head, his short queue rubbing the collar of his coat. He must make her believe his sincerity. "I am serious. Your happiness and well-being are my first and utmost concern."

She frowned, a delicate drawing together of dark brows. "And why might you say such a thing?"

"You've bewitched me, my dear." He grinned at her and then kissed the back of her hand. Focusing once more on her startled eyes, he squeezed her fingers. "You may not believe me, after my prior grievous behavior. Sorting out exactly why your actions and reactions have meant so much to me took a great deal of consideration to resolve. But now I can say with all honesty that I love you, Samantha McAlester. I wish to court you in order to prove the depth of my feelings for you."

Samantha laughed, a throaty bark of sound. She tugged on her hands again and this time he let them slide from his surprised grip. "Now I know you're in jest."

"I've never been more serious in all my twenty-five years."

Emily coughed lightly as she flowed to her feet. "I believe that's my cue to exit for a brief while. I'll see about supper." She pinned her gaze on Trent. "I shall return in five minutes."

He nodded, waited for Emily to leave the room, and then recaptured Samantha's hands. Gazing into her mirthful expression, he knew what he must do. He pulled her up with him, standing toe to toe in the confined space between table and settee. Without considering the myriad possible reactions to his next inappropriate but necessary move, he kissed her. After her sweet cry of surprise, he stifled any further attempt at speech. Explored her lush lips and tempting mouth, their tongues dancing to an ancient rhythm. She resisted for a second and then leaned into him. He released her hands to wrap his arms around her, pleased when she pressed her fingers against his back.

Ending the buss, he lifted his head to examine each lovely feature including the dazed expression in her eyes. "We make a good team, both in healing others and in private matters. Please permit me to call on you, to convince you of my sincerity." He waited, searching her eyes for the answer he desired.

She blinked, a happy grin easing onto her face, and then moistened swollen lips with the tip of her tongue. "I shall consider your offer."

"Do not force me to wait, my dear." Trent winked at her, squeezing her fingers at the same time. "Your answer is of extreme importance to my peace of mind."

She searched his face. Her eyes widened as she let her gaze move from his eyes to his nose to his mouth and back to meet his gaze. "Pardon me for mistaking your intent. Why, you are serious?"

He nodded, not taking his eyes from her. "With all my being."

"I daresay you do not know what you are getting yourself into." Her somber expression lightened as a brilliant smile emerged on her lips. "I appear to draw trouble to my person."

"Then call me 'trouble' from here on." He whooped with glee and a sense of victory. "You shall never regret putting your faith in me, my love. We can do anything as long as we're together."

He pressed his lips to hers again, sweet happiness filling his heart and soul.

Samantha's smile left her face. "Except perhaps help Benjamin."

Damnation. They'd tried so many possibilities with no positive result. Why did she have to spoil the moment with the reality they both may fail their friend?

Chapter Twelve

Samantha quick-stepped down Bay from the Sullivans' house to Benjamin's apartment. Amy's urgent summons so early in the morning shot fear deep inside, shredding her composure. After all she and Trent had attempted to help the man improve, nothing seemed to make any difference. Trent's insistence on bleeding their patient so frequently weakened him ever more, but they knew not what else to attempt. Emily had ensured that Frank returned the gem, and it hung about Benjamin's neck, with no evident change. Now this. The imperative to attend Benjamin immediately, delivered by a breathless, young slave minutes before, left her shaken. Racing up the back steps, she burst into the dimly lit kitchen. Gasping to a stop, she let her eyes adjust, ascertained the room stood empty, and then ran into the bedroom.

The sight that greeted her made her stumble to a halt even as she smiled.

Benjamin sat up in bed, grinning at her. The mass of blankets and ears of corn had been replaced with a lone quilt. The beautiful smoky quartz heart reflected the morning light from where it hung about his neck. "Good morning, Miss Samantha."

She chuckled at his formality. "After all we've been through, please, call me Samantha." Relief swept into her heart. She strode to check his temperature, peer into his eyes searching for any symptom of ill health. She inspected the bullet wound, detecting only pink edges instead of red or black, an amazing sight after the weeks of worry. No signs of ill health were visible. She found clear eyes and relaxed features. No pain. No stress. She would never know exactly which change evoked the miraculous healing, because they'd made two at the same time. Was it the Cherokee sweating or the mysterious gem that had worked magic to heal Benjamin? She couldn't explain it, but she could celebrate the results. "I'm happy to find you feeling so much better."

Amy crossed the room from the window and grabbed Samantha into a bone-bending hug. After a long moment, she broke it off, grinning giddily. "I'm sorry I doubted you, my friend. Without you and Trent working together to cure this awful ailment, I know not what I'd have done."

Pounding footfalls warned of Trent's sudden appearance beside them. "Benjamin, what a relief." He repeated Samantha's movements, checking for any signs of illness. His expression shifted from concern to relief, mirroring her own emotional progression upon seeing Benjamin. His impressive shoulders impeded her view of Benjamin while Trent performed his lightning fast examination. He'd not even taken time to fashion a queue before answering Amy's summons. As a result, his sandy blond hair hung loose between his shoulder blades. Enticing her to touch the silky strands. She tucked her hands into her apron pockets to control the impulse.

After a minute, Trent straightened and patted Benjamin on the shoulder. "I'm pleased to see you looking yourself."

Benjamin threw off the quilt and swung out of bed. "As am I." He stood on shaky legs, one hand braced on Amy's shoulder. "I have lain here far too long. There is much to be accomplished ere the Britons embark."

"Samantha's idea to use the gem has turned the tide in your favor. I never would have guessed some truth might actually exist to the legends we hear." Trent swiped a hand through his hair.

Must he tease her so blatantly? Should she tell him about the sweat? She didn't know whether it had done any good, in the event, so she stayed mum. She withdrew her hands from the pockets and clasped them together, interlocking her fingers to deny the temptation to feel the silky textures. His words brought a swell of pleasure to her heart. Crystal blue eyes darted a look her way, his smile broadening to fill every aspect of his face. Could he be any more alluring if he tried? Imagine his lips touching hers, his hands exploring her in ways she'd not experienced in years. The thought sparked a sudden urge she quickly forced back. Benjamin's quarters were not the place for such a reaction.

Samantha tore her gaze away from Trent to focus on Benjamin. "Captain Sullivan believes they sail tomorrow with the tide."

"So my timing is perfect for finding my feet again." Benjamin tugged his nightgown into place, a sheepish look marring his washed out countenance. "Where are my garments?"

"Do not rush so." Amy grabbed him about the waist, attempting to detain him from jumping into his clothes. "You've only begun to recover."

Benjamin shook his head in denial but the motion threw him off balance, and he flopped back onto the bed, dragging Amy onto his lap in an unladylike sprawl.

Samantha helped Amy to her feet. "Benjamin, behave. Sit there and think about your next actions. You've been ill far too long to spring up like a jack in the box."

Trent offered Benjamin a hand. "Slow and easy now…"

"Very well." Benjamin had the good grace to heed the advice as he stood up and steadied himself by placing one hand on Amy's shoulder. "But I shall stand on the street to bid adieu to the British and welcome our new governor and our valiant and victorious men."

"We shall all turn out for such a glorious event." Samantha crossed her arms. "I must say, though, how happy I am you'll be able to attend after all of your efforts for the cause."

Amy shifted under the weight of Benjamin's hand but held firm. "I imagine the entire town will bid the Britons be gone and welcome our boys upon their return."

"It's been a long and arduous journey to arrive at the brink of true freedom." Trent folded his arms and aimed a smile at Samantha. "We've had our travails arriving at our own victory with regard to Benjamin's health, have we not, Miss Samantha?"

"My goodness, we certainly have." She shook a finger at Benjamin and then grinned. "It may have taken two of us, but we managed to save your life. My debt to you is now repaid."

Benjamin laughed. "You owed me no debt, Samantha."

"Indeed I did, for saving my life from the renegades." She gave Benjamin a quick hug, aware his ordeal had left him smelling of stale sweat. "Thank you."

"We must always watch out for our friends and family, especially as we forge our country." Benjamin squeezed her upper arms and then stepped back. "It's powerful good to be on my feet again."

"Powerful indeed." Amy cleared her throat and caught Samantha's eye. "I believe I'll fetch some hot water so Ben may freshen up."

Taking the hint, Samantha turned to Trent. "Shall we

leave them so Benjamin may prepare for emerging into public again?"

Trent offered her an arm. "I'd be honored if you'd permit me to escort you home."

They strolled along the bustling street, avoiding the growing crowds of people who dared to venture out of their homes during daylight for the first time in months. An air of celebration overhung the beleaguered town. The scars after six years of fighting and deprivation would take time to fade. Burned buildings, broken roads, and skeletal people only touched the surface of the mars and wounds left behind by the British.

When they arrived at the Sullivans', the house sat silent in the early morning sunlight. Once safely inside, Trent gazed down at Samantha, his expression soft and open. "The place is very quiet this morning."

She nodded. "Emily planned to be at Frank's at first light, and the Captain said he had urgent business to attend prior to the British embarkation."

"We're alone?" The crystal depths of his eyes snared her attention and refused to relent. Her pulse throbbed in her ears loud enough to distance all other sound.

"For a little while. I'm sure Emily will return before long." She blinked and his lips seemed closer, parted ever so slightly, as he watched her moisten her suddenly parched lips.

"Samantha, my dear, I cannot thank you enough for all you did for our friends." The bright blue of his eyes deepened to the color of a twilight sky. "My relief proved great upon seeing him this morning."

"As Amy said, our working together enabled the positive outcome." His nearness, so close she could feel his breath upon her cheek, muddled her brain. She permitted him to take her hands and hold them gently, as though he held quail eggs in a nest. Her fingers appeared fragile compared to his. "I should tell you that I set up a fever sweat yesterday, one I learned from the Cherokee. I hope you will not be upset, but it was urgent to do something before he grew worse."

Trent inclined his head, looking directly into her eyes as he did. "I'm certain you did what was in the best interest of our patient. My respect for you and your expertise is exceeded only by my feelings for you." He pressed a kiss to each palm. Then he gazed at her, not a swift survey but a slow consideration of each element of her face, ending by searching her eyes. "I no longer have any doubt whatsoever."

She moistened her bottom lip, aware of a growing desire awakening deep in the center of her being, spreading lower as he continued to smile at her. "Doubt about what, pray tell?"

His gaze flashed to her mouth and then up to her eyes. "I love you, Samantha McAlester."

She inhaled and let it out slowly while she explored her feelings for the handsome man standing before her, holding her hands while a sensation much like a mild jellyfish sting sizzled through her entire body. As a result, she lost the ability to string together coherent thoughts. Somewhere among the foggy remnants, as she peered up at him, she rediscovered her answer. One she'd dismissed as too fearful and sudden when she first discovered it, but now fit like a doeskin glove. She grinned at him. "I love you, Trent Cunningham."

He continued to study her, exploring her expression for a long moment. The silence stretched like a cat after its nap. A little boy grin eased onto his lips. "Will you forgive me for my errant opinion of your talent and training?"

If he continued to regard her with those enchanting eyes and devilish grin, she'd forgive him any trespass. "Only if you'll forgive my tendency to stubbornness."

He inclined his head. "I have something I'd like to give you, with your permission?"

"That depends upon what you wish to give me." Goodness, whatever could he mean?

He squeezed both of her hands, closing the distance between them in one fluid motion. "An understandable request. Miss Samantha, I wish to bestow upon you my hand in marriage. Will you accept?"

Shock swept through her like the vibration of a walking stick struck upon bedrock. Marriage? Such a sudden idea, unexpected but surprisingly not unwanted. "Are you teasing me?"

Trent's smile sobered. "Indeed not, my dear. I am in earnest. Will you marry me?"

The fog in her brain descended, and she shook her head to try to clear it to no avail. "I cannot answer you. 'Tis too sudden a question."

His grip tightened then relaxed. "I did not mean to offend you. I shall withdraw my question."

This beautiful man wanted to marry her? After all they'd been through? *Despite* all they'd been through over the past month? His proposition held merit. Not only did she find him attractive, but more important he had the means to provide for her and the ambition to make a life for them. Marriage meant relying upon each other to forge a working household, a place to raise children and make a life together. Love was not the primary consideration, but it came with a deepening of respect and trust between two people. The fact they shared such a love at the outset of their relationship boded well. She could continue to work alongside him, but if she were to be with child, then she'd have the luxury of caring for herself first to ensure a safe delivery of the babe. Until then, she'd have a partner as well as an intelligent and enticing companion. But what of her desire to remain unwed? Her vow to be true to Edward and their love?

"No, do not withdraw your question, unless you desire to do so." She squeezed his hands. "I'm honored by your proposal, Trent. I simply require time to consider your offer. Will you grant me a day to deliberate?"

Trent inclined his head in a half bow. "In that case, please allow me to give you one thing with which to make your contemplation more productive." A flicker of something wicked flashed in his expression.

Gramercy but he took her breath. She swallowed and then raised an eyebrow and slanted her gaze at him. "What sort of thing?"

"This." Wrapping his arms around her waist, he lowered his mouth to hers.

It was a natural response to circle his neck with her arms, clasping one hand onto her other wrist and pulling him closer. Despite the fact decorum dictated her hands should stay primly on his arms. Very muscular arms, but abandoned for the welcome feel of his hair beneath her fingers. *Finally*. Desperate to enjoy the luxurious softness, she slid one hand through his hair before clinging to him for stability. Trent slipped his tongue between her lips and teeth, exploring and tasting, first tentatively and then with more assurance. She let her eyelids fall while she savored the sensations exploding in her mouth. Sensations unlike any she'd felt in her life, not even with her first husband.

His arms became bindings, lashing her body against his chest. His kiss devoured, leaving her breathless and hungry for more. She pressed against him, their tongues playing and cavorting, desiring nothing more than to become one with him. A low moan began in the back of her throat and worked its way up and into his mouth, where he swallowed the sound. Still, they stood locked in an embrace neither wanted to break, locked in a kiss neither wanted to end, locked in a moment neither wanted to forget.

Samantha finally had to come up for air, gasping and disoriented by her wanton demand for his touch and his kiss. Forcing herself to step back so her breasts no longer pressed into his hard chest, she chose to strive for poise despite the churning inside. Besides, she should never have allowed him such an improper act. Gift or not. Heat flushed up her neck and into her cheeks. Words, however, did not come to mind as she stared at the luscious man, one who could be her man if she so chose. Did she?

"I'm afraid I must leave you for the time as I have an urgent errand to run." He released her and half bowed from the waist. "I shall come for you on the morrow to watch the spectacle, if you'll permit me?"

Yes, he should leave. At the moment, she'd permit him most anything he desired. Her body still trembled from his assault on her senses, her heart still raced, and her lips still buzzed like a swarm of bees. She needed time to think, to consider, to recover. She drew in a shaky breath. "'Tis very kind of you. I shall look forward to it."

Crowds of Charles Town's citizens lined Broad Street the next afternoon, watching the British troops slowly trudge past on their way to the ships in the harbor. Their faces displayed misery and relief. Misery at their defeat by the ragtag Americans. Relief at finally putting their backs to the newborn country once and for all.

Samantha stood between Trent and Emily. Joy filled her heart with each passing row of Britons marching down to the docks and then boarding the vessels bound for distant lands such as England, Florida, St. Lucia, and Jamaica. Not that she cared where they went as long as they left.

She sneaked a glance at Trent, his beautiful face wreathed in a happy smile as he chatted to Benjamin on his other side.

She'd thought long and hard throughout the night about his unanticipated question. Pacing the wood floor, afraid she'd wear the boards thin, she had considered the ramifications of his proposal. While the short-term result would be a place to call her own, the long term meant tending and caring for another husband. Did the foundation exist for them to love, to trust, and ultimately to take the fearsome step of joining their lives together as long as they lived? Life had become pleasant with only herself to consider. Did she want to have someone else to think about and look after?

Thistle came to mind along with the thought. What had happened to the dog and her puppies? Were they being well cared for? She imagined the pups had grown, become more agile and sturdy over the past days since she last watched them play. She sighed. She missed their furry, plump bodies squirming to secure a spot to nurse from their mother. She missed their sweet smell when they licked her hands and her cheek. Caring for someone else brought a feeling of joy and of being useful.

The soldiers continued to stream past, so many men with harsh, determined faces. All of them no doubt harboring grudges against the Americans as well as looking forward to reunions with their loved ones on the other side of the ocean. So much had occurred over the last few days that her head spun. Which direction should she journey next? Down the single path or take the branch leading to matrimony?

Then she must also answer the question as to her midwifery and healing endeavors. Her failure to adequately help Lydia and her child festered and stung. Despite Trent's reassurances, her abilities and reputation had been tested and found wanting. Benjamin's recovery stemmed from the unknown qualities of an ancient fever reducing sweat and the smoky quartz, a mysteriously powerful stone. Should she even contemplate continuing her practice? So few successes to her name led her to lean toward foregoing the effort and search for something else to do with her time. Like making food stuffs to sell in the market. Or perhaps she could join with Emily in her shop, stitching shirts and dresses which Emily would embroider for others to wear.

A movement beside Trent caught her attention. She smiled at the woman approaching, carrying a child swaddled against the coolness. A step behind, Belinda strolled along with a faraway look in her eyes. Samantha moved to offer her greetings. "Evelyn, how are you?"

"Very well, and very glad to watch the bloody British depart our fair shores." Evelyn waved a hand at the backs of the men marching down King toward the wharfs and then faced Samantha. "And how fare you?"

How indeed? Confused and scared and hopeful. "The Sullivans' have been very kind to me while I sort my options."

"We should chat as we have much in common, at least given what Amy has told me."

Samantha tilted her head and raised a brow as she regarded Evelyn. "Like both being widows?"

Evelyn grinned and nodded. "And we're both without a home of our own."

"Mayhap we *should* visit and discuss possibilities." Samantha lifted the soft blanket from where it snugged around the baby's face. "Including little Jim's future. Will you return to the manor house?"

"Rebuild?" Evelyn's gaze drifted to the British soldiers marching slowly away. "I hadn't considered doing so, but now that you mention it, I might. Though I'd want a friendlier dwelling if I have my way."

"It would entail quite a few helping hands, I dare say, to make a go of living so far from town." Amy stepped up to stand with the women. "I doubt you and Belinda would prove enough to manage."

"The property is a fair piece from town." Emily joined the cluster of women. "You'd be better served finding a place closer to town, or even within its boundaries."

"Definitely something to consider." Evelyn bobbed her head several times and shifted Jim to a more comfortable position. "I know my limitations. I'll need a good man, a better man than Walter, to become my husband and provide a safe and sufficient home for my little one and myself."

Amy laid a gentle hand on Evelyn's shoulder. "You'll always have a home with me, no matter what else happens."

Tears sprang to Samantha's eyes at the love openly shared between the sisters. Family willing to nurture and shelter their own. She suddenly wanted nothing more than to have a family of her own to love and provide for, to comfort and celebrate with through the upcoming years.

Benjamin huffed, a poor substitute for a chuckle. "You ladies should not bother your pretty heads with details such as building an appropriate dwelling or locating a proper house." He sniggered from where he stood nearby, though he made no move to further interrupt the women's conversation.

Amy shooed him with one hand. "Ignore us, Benjamin, as our talk may well be over your head."

"Very humorous, my dear." He sobered but aimed a knowing grin her way. "Your meaning is well taken." He briefly bowed his head and then turned to continue watching the parade.

"Men." Amy snorted and individually looked at the women's faces waiting for her reaction to her betrothed's statement. "At least he's learned when his opinion is desired."

"And when it is not." Emily laughed and crossed her arms inside her cloak.

Samantha observed each of the women circled around her, their skirts and cloaks crushed together as they chatted.

Amy's bright smile and sparkling eyes after verbally sparring with Benjamin. Emily's grin as she glanced at Frank's profile. Evelyn's contented perusal of Jim in her arms. Each happy in her own way. Samantha flicked a glance to Trent, where he stood conversing with Frank. Trent's open and engaging expression attracted her toward him as surely as the night attracted the stars. Gramercy, what a handsome, intelligent, compassionate man. His first thought had always been for the welfare of his patient, the good of the town, and even her sensibilities after the death of her patients. And he loved her. He said as much. A smile lifted the corners of her mouth.

As if she'd spoken his name, Trent turned toward her. Her smile widened as his eyes changed from curious to twinkling the longer they gazed at each other.

"Samantha, you're making a spectacle of yourself." Emily lightly swatted Samantha's arm. "You'll have the entire town gossiping about you and Trent if you're not careful."

"What would they have to gossip about?" Samantha brought her gaze to rest on the circle of friends again. "We're merely sharing a private moment."

Amy clapped her gloved hands, a muted thud repeated against the fife and drum corps marching past, the din increasing as the musicians marched by. "All the more fodder for inventive minds to work with. If you want the town to talk, pray continue. I shall be most amused to hear their stories."

The ladies laughed in chorus, the merry sound a consonance against the steady marching tune. From the corner of her eye, Samantha spotted a cluster of people standing nearby, watching the cheerful clutch of women. Samantha didn't care. She was happy for the first time in many weeks. Soon the occupied town would be free just like her heart. Free to move forward and love anew. Time to focus on the future and not dwell on the past. To plan for tomorrow and the next week, next month, next year.

She pivoted and sidled over to Trent. With each step, her confidence grew. She had her answer to his question.

"I've been hoping you'd come stand by me. The Americans will be arriving soon, and I wanted to share this historic transition with you." Trent turned to her as she neared and took her hand in his with easy familiarity. Drums beat the rhythm of the withdrawal as he held her attention.

"I cannot think of anything I'd rather do than share with you the momentous day when our town takes control of its future once more." She squeezed his hand as best she could with her smaller one. His clear blue eyes searched her face while she stared up at him. "Like the rest of the town's residents, today is the first time in years I can seriously plan for my own future as well."

"Are you saying…?"

She moved her head up, then down, keeping her eyes focused on his loving expression. "I believe you asked me a question yesterday."

"And?"

A shuffle behind Samantha alerted her to the straining ears of her friends. They were about to learn about the meaning of the previous shared moment between her and Trent. She could almost feel their breath being held in suspense the longer she studied Trent's questioning smile.

"I'm afraid I'm not quite certain I recall your precise question." After her previous secretive engagement and marriage she wanted everyone to witness this one. "Would you repeat it, to make sure I can answer with the appropriate response?"

Trent smiled at her, then glanced over her head to note their audience. Understanding brought a twinkle to his eyes. He placed a kiss on the back of one gloved hand, and then raised both of her hands to hold in front of his chest.

"Miss Samantha, would you please put me out of my misery and answer my plea from yesterday. Will you marry me?"

The commotion of the men marching by, the cheers of the crowd, the fife and drum marching tune played by the retreating British, and the rush of wind fell away. Samantha pressed her lips together, remembered the intensity of his kiss the day before, the intensity of his gaze when he'd asked her to marry him.

"I am honored by your request, and I accept on one condition." She waited until she received his agreement. "We shall work together in your new hospital to provide the best care possible."

"Together?"

"As equals."

"Agreed." He whooped and lifted her into the air on a whirl of wind.

The women clapped and cheered and rushed to crush around the newly betrothed couple.

"What's happened?" Frank asked. "What did I miss?"

"Here I thought you were so observant." Trent grinned as wide as the Cooper River. "Samantha has agreed to become my betrothed."

Congratulations came from all of their friends who surrounded Samantha where she stood in the circle of Trent's arm. She accepted them with a happy smile of her own.

"Oh, Samantha, you must plan to marry this gorgeous man on the fifth of January along with Emily and me." Amy clapped her hands together and performed a little hop, her skirts flouncing and stirring up the sandy soil. "Say you will."

"A triple wedding, how wonderful!" Emily hugged Samantha. "I can't think of a better day."

"There will be a lot of plans to put into place to plan an event of that magnitude in such a short period of time."

Evelyn jostled Jim in her arms, a huge smile lighting her face. "I'll help any way you need."

"Thank you, Evelyn. I fear I'll need all the assistance my friends can provide." Samantha touched Trent's arm. "What say you?"

He gazed down at her, grinning, and shrugged. "I'd marry you today if you'd agree. But if you wish to wait until Twelfth Night, so be it."

Squeals met his pronouncement. Samantha reached up and kissed him square on the lips to the delight of her observers. Her life with him would begin in less than four weeks. Sweet joy spread through her chest, warming her.

Trent hushed the excited chatter with a motion of his hand. "Anon, I have a surprise. One I cannot contain a moment longer." He took both of Samantha's hands in his and peered into her eyes. "As a wedding gift to my exquisite bride, I am pleased to share that I have purchased the old McAlester place."

Samantha froze, blinking back tears as the meaning of his words sank into her befuddled brain. "You bought my father's house?"

Trent bowed and then grinned at her. "Do you approve?"

"Oh yes! I'd heard it had been sold, and I thought all was lost." She threw herself into his waiting arms and kissed him soundly. Tears of joy cascaded down her cheeks. "You're wonderful. Thank you seems impotent in the face of such generosity."

Benjamin slapped Trent on the back and guffawed. "You sure know how to impress. How am I to live up to such a high standard of wedding gift for my own wife?"

"Yes, Trent, you've definitely set the mark. It shan't be easy, in the event, to equal your effort." Frank shook his head. "I'll need to ponder on the situation for quite some time."

Amy chuckled. "I did not know wedding gifts were a competition."

"Apparently among these three." Emily tucked a hand in the crook of Frank's arm.

A cannon blast announced the arrival of the war weary American army. By the angle of the sun, Samantha calculated the time as about three in the afternoon. Leading the tattered men, General Greene rode into view and passed down the sandy King Street. The army's martial tune provided a merry atmosphere as the happy crowd cheered and welcomed the victorious men home. The two armies were separated by mere yards. The men, in fact, marched close enough for the last ranks of the British troops to exchange greetings with the first troops of the American forces.

Suddenly Emily stilled and stared at the patriots returning to town. "Is that…? Could it be?"

"What, dear?" Frank glanced at her and then back to the throng of shabby, malnourished, and limping men marching proudly past the small group.

"It is! Luke!" Emily tore her hand from Frank's arm and, lifting her skirts enough to not drag in the dirt, ran to greet three men in pieced together uniforms. "Ethan! Bill!"

Emily's brothers had arrived home safe and sound after three years fighting across the southern states. Samantha's happiness for her friend buoyed her already happy thoughts. They looked the worse for their time in the field, but smiles countered the shabby attire and limping strides. They were indeed fortunate to have survived the ordeal relatively unharmed. Putting their lives back on track after the battle dust settled would take some time.

The future looked bright for everyone as the sun shone on the victors as well as the group of friends. Samantha couldn't stop the silly grin on her face. Twelfth Night loomed only weeks away, and the three couples would be married. Despite the three women's initial vow to remain unmarried, each had found a man worth breaking their promise. They had each made a choice to spend their lives with men who more than respected them, but loved them. The secret to a contented life rested in discovering a person to love and cherish as well as respect and trust. Her future indeed sparkled like the stars in the heavens, full of points of light, hope, and love.

Epilogue

The first floor of Frank's house fairly bulged with people, the many guests repeatedly glancing to the wide staircase. Evelyn spotted a cluster of the sewing circle ladies Amy had introduced her to over the past several weeks, including the loquacious Darlene Walters and her meek husband, Louis. Catherine and George Manning chatted with the dashing Luke Sullivan, probably interrogating him about his adventures with the militia. Candles flickered throughout the newly redecorated house, illuminating bouquets of flowers tied with long curling ribbon secured to the banister and resting on tables. In the parlor, a string quartet played softly while Captain Sullivan conversed with her parents, Lucille and Richard Abernathy. To Evelyn, it seemed the entire town had crammed inside the house to witness the event of the season.

Evelyn envisioned Emily, Amy, and Samantha helping each other with the final touches to their wedding dresses. Planning the event had proved easier than she'd expected as they'd simply expanded upon the usual Twelfth Night festivities. With the end of the occupation came more trade and thus access to sugar, and spices, and finer materials to add to the plainer dresses they'd made over. With so many guests for the triple wedding, no fire had been lit and the windows and doors thrown open to ensure everyone's comfort. The chilly January evening stood silent witness to the happy throngs, both inside the house and outside in the streets. The holidays had been made even merrier by the absence of enemy soldiers and the relief of the citizens. Topping off the holiday season with a triple wedding excited every person in town.

The quartet struck up a processional piece, announcing the brides' arrival down the stairs. Evelyn smiled through tears as Emily appeared on the steps in a pale yellow gown. She admired the embroidered white roses edging the scooped neckline and extending in rays to the bottom hem. Emily had fashioned her blonde curls into an intricate bun beneath a matching pale yellow hat made from lace and decorated with real white roses.

After Emily reached the bottom of the stairs, Amy appeared at the top. Delighted gasps came from the ladies in the gathering at the base of the staircase. Evelyn exchanged a quick smile with her before Amy focused on navigating the treads. She'd chosen a midnight blue dress overlaid with lavender netting. Amy's eyes sparkled with happiness as she descended toward the crowd. Her dark locks had been tamed into an intricate hairdo, a few curls left to hang beside her rosy cheeks. Amy accepted Catherine's well wishes before turning to saunter into the parlor where the newly elected patriotic rector from St. Michael's waited to perform the ceremony. The grooms lined up to his side, dressed in dark suits as they awaited the arrival of each bride.

Evelyn watched Samantha take the first step and flashed an approving smile in her direction. The emerald velvet gown, with its deep neckline and smattering of rhinestones across the bodice, suited her coloring, emphasizing the luster of her ebony hair and green eyes. She'd had Emily fashion her hair into an elegant braid for the occasion, with wisps of curls left to dance about her face. Gold bobs hung on her earlobes and a matching gold chain glinted at her neck. She flowed toward the guests with grace and poise, radiant in her joy.

Jim squirmed in her arms as Evelyn followed Samantha into the parlor. The furniture had been removed to permit the crush of friends and family to witness the wedding. Evelyn slipped among the throng until she found a spot by the cold fireplace. The three couples took their places in a half circle standing before Reverend Henry Purcell, his bible in hand. The former chaplain of the American army had taken control of St. Michael's pulpit upon the departure of the enemy the previous month.

A handsome young man—tall, intriguing dark gray eyes with black rims, brown hair pulled into a queue—sidled up to stand in the gap beside her, exchanging a quick glance as Reverend Purcell began the ceremony with a prayer. The man seemed familiar, but she could not place where she may have seen him. She closed her eyes for the prayer, joggling the baby to keep him quiet while the minister spoke. She tried to focus on the words, but the image of the man standing to her right encroached on her thoughts. He was a stranger in town. At least, she didn't think she'd seen him before. Then why did he look familiar? The room grew warm with the many bodies crammed inside. She heard feet shuffle, and then the man's arm bumped against hers and her eyes popped open. She glanced at him and then at George Manning, who wore a conspiratorial smile. What was he up to? She shared a hesitant grin with him and then the tall man and closed her eyes again. *Lord, give me strength while standing beside the handsome man.*

The minister ended the prayer and read the vows each bride and groom must make to wed the other. Evelyn noticed the three women kept their eyes on their soon to be husband's face. She prayed for each of them to have a better marriage than she'd had, one filled with esteem and love equally. For herself, her next husband would need to be kind and ambitious. Love was a secondary consideration to finding someone to be a good provider for her child. Jim would grow up with everything necessary for him to have a chance at a decent life with a capable and caring wife and sturdy intelligent children. She'd see to it.

After the couples exchanged their vows, Reverend Purcell pronounced them man and wife and the guests cheered. Evelyn cheered right along until she noticed the stranger watching her instead of the new-married couples.

"What is the matter, sir?" She hugged little Jim tighter until he squirmed. "You appear distracted from the happy occasion."

"My apologies if I've startled you, Madam." He half bowed with a smile. "I came looking for Major Hanson, but it seems he's a might busy at the moment."

"Why do you seek him out?" She turned her attention back to where the new husbands were taking advantage of the freedom to kiss their wives. "On his wedding day, no less."

"He suggested I look him up after the war." He faced front again, watching the happy couples make their way through the throng of people toward the hall. "Unfortunately, I see my timing is poor."

"How do you know him?" She sauntered down the hall, trailing the happy throng of brides and grooms and parents into the festooned dining room.

"We met at camp in October, right near the end of the fighting." The man looked at her, a soft smile edging his lips. "Back when I thought I still had a family to go home to."

She frowned and peered up at him. "What happened to your family?"

His open expression shuttered in the blink of an eye. "A British scavenging party raided my homestead, took what they wanted, and then set it afire. My family died in the blaze."

"How horrible." Jim snuggled closer to her, as though sensing her distress as she imagined the conflagration and the lives lost. She didn't even know the man's name, but sorrow flooded her heart as she stared at the carefully stoic expression. "My husband died at the hands of loyalist renegades, so I understand. My gracious, where are my manners? My name is Evelyn Hamilton. And you are?"

He inclined his head with a smile. "Nathaniel Williams, at your service."

"Pleased to make your acquaintance." Evelyn returned the smile. "I believe Benjamin may be free should you wish to offer your congratulations to the bride and groom."

"An excellent idea." Nathaniel swept a hand in the direction of the couple in question. "After you."

Evelyn wended her way through the throng of guests, protecting Jim from the gesticulating hands and shifting bodies. She slipped around a table burdened with clear glass tiered plates holding containers of colorful jellies and fruits. At the other end of the room, the three couples greeted the multitude of guests. Slowly, she managed to make her way, Nathaniel following in her wake, until she stood before Amy and Benjamin.

"Congratulations to you both, my friends." Evelyn hugged Amy with one arm, gripping Jim against her with the other. "I bring an acquaintance of yours, Benjamin." She nodded toward Nathaniel, who stepped up to her side.

"The cook! How are you, my man?" Benjamin clasped the Nathaniel on the upper arm in greeting. "What brings you here on this day of days?"

Nathaniel returned the greeting with a sheepish grin. "It

is of no matter on your wedding day, sir. We can speak later, once things settle."

"Very well, if you insist." Benjamin beamed at Evelyn. "My gratitude to you for taking him under your wing, Mrs. Hamilton. I'm sure he appreciates your kindness."

Amy stepped forward and addressed Nathaniel. "But pray tell us why you've come? My curiosity is quite excited by your mysterious mission."

Nathaniel glanced at Benjamin and then Evelyn. He shrugged as he smiled into her eyes before turning back to regard the major. "I come seeking assistance in rebuilding my life. The one the British have stolen away. Might I speak with you at your first opportunity, Major?"

Benjamin's smile sobered but stayed on his lips. "Of course. Tomorrow we will meet at McCrady's for supper, say one o'clock?"

"I shall be there." Nathaniel reached out to shake hands with Benjamin.

"In the meantime," Benjamin said, glancing at Evelyn, "perhaps Mrs. Hamilton would be so kind as to entertain you?"

Evelyn hugged Jim tighter to her chest as she gazed at the lanky man, his height and breadth impressive to behold. "I'd be pleased to introduce him around and make him feel welcome."

Nathaniel smiled at her, a puzzled look settling into his eyes. "Have we met? Your face looks vaguely familiar."

"You look familiar, as well, but I do not know where we might have met." She gazed at him, studying each feature and searching her memory.

He returned the study, his gaze flitting from eyes to nose to mouth and back. Then he peered at the infant in her arms. Finally, he lifted both brows and let out a low whistle. "I know where I saw you."

"Indeed?" She racked her memory but could not dredge up the occasion. "Where? When?"

"When my commander had us search your home for provisions."

She blinked as the memory of the fearsome day played in her mind. Gasped as the image of a youthful American army soldier took almost all of her fresh vegetables. "How dare you show your face in this house?"

"My apologies for upsetting you." Nathaniel bowed to emphasize his chagrin. "I was under orders, or I would not have ventured inside."

Benjamin watched the exchange with a light frown on his face. "I thought you'd spoken of the Hamilton manor when you spoke of the raid. What a coincidence you'd meet here on this day."

Nathaniel smiled at Evelyn, eyes sparkling with his suppressed laughter. "Or is it fate?"

Evelyn stared at him, silent and uncertain. She remembered he'd refrained from scavenging all of their produce because he noticed she was with child. The baby she carried in her arms. He had a duty to the soldiers, to provide sustenance so they could achieve the desired outcome of the war. Indeed, the handsome, kind man watching her with expectation plain in his expression asked a very good question. But did she want to know the answer?

The End

Thanks so much for reading *Samantha's Secret*! I hope you enjoyed Samantha and Trent's story. Turn the page for a sneak peek at the next story in the series, *Evelyn's Promise*!

To find out about new releases and upcoming appearances, please sign up for my newsletter via my website at www.bettybolte.com. I send out a monthly newsletter with book news to share with my readers, upcoming events and signings, and even a few favorite recipes, puzzles, and other doings!

I'd love to hear from you! Feel free to send me an email at betty@bettybolte.com, find me on Facebook at AuthorBettyBolte, follow me on BookBub, or connect with me on Twitter @BettyBolte.

You can always find an updated list of the titles in this series, as well as all of my other books on my website, at www.bettybolte.com/books/.

Thanks again for reading!

Evelyn's Promise

A More Perfect Union Series Book 4

Betty Bolté

Charles Town, South Carolina – 1783

Pleasure and grief battled in Evelyn Hamilton's chest. She cast a sidelong glance at the lean man standing beside her.

"Looks like the entire town turned out for the triple wedding and the festivities afterward." He glanced at her and then returned his gaze to the room at large.

"Yes, food tends to lure people out of their homes." She kept a smile on her face as she observed the multitude of people milling about in the candlelit and lavishly decorated home.

Her pulse throbbed in her ears at Nathaniel Williams' proximity, a sensation she'd only experienced when in fear of her late husband's next actions. She held still, though actively attempting to calm the alarm inside her chest. Not only had Nathaniel stolen food from her pantry but his height and breadth rivaled that of her dead husband. She'd learned to mask her inner strength, what she possessed, by bowing her head, studying her hands or even her feet if necessary. In her experience, men could be cruel without a second thought, and she wouldn't give them a reason to inflict said cruelty upon her person.

She surveyed the happy gathering, the friendly mood of the group working its magic as she held her murmuring infant son. She relaxed a bit, though having the tall, powerful man standing so close caused a fine tremor in her gut. He wouldn't harm her, not in the present situation. Nathaniel's attention lingered on the three happy couples as they received congratulations from the guests snaking past the newly married. She was exhausted and longed for a quiet room, but remained amidst the jocular gathering. "I understand you are to thank for the handsome decorations?" He lifted a brow and folded his arms across his chest, shifting his weight to rest on the hip closer to her.

"Thank you." She'd enjoyed applying her talents to making the house reflect the importance of the day's event. In truth, the triple wedding made Twelfth Night a livelier and more joyful occasion than in previous years, especially those under British occupation. "I enjoyed dressing the house for the happy occasion."

Nathaniel regarded her with a gentle smile. "After all the horrors of war, the opportunity to enjoy such merriments is a delight to the senses."

She shifted the bundle in her arms. "Even during the war, life has a way of pushing through to keep hope alive."

She looked down as her son squirmed in her embrace. A white cap, made with her own hands from fine linen, covered his wispy red-brown hair. His eyelashes fanned on his cheeks as the little mouth pursed in his sleep. The white dress he wore had been handed down from his cousin when he'd outgrown the garment. Even Walter, her deceased husband, had expressed pride in Jim. She'd promised herself that she'd do all in her power to ensure Master James Christopher Hamilton grew up to honor his name. No matter what she must do, she'd prepare Jim for whatever opportunities life brought his way.

She and Nathaniel, a virtual stranger to her up until the reverend performed the weddings a few minutes ago, had already paid their compliments to the three pairs of smiling husbands and wives. Her new friends and her sister stood together. Each bride shone with happiness, their smiles vying with the candles for lighting the room. The happy couples made a striking and impressive group.

Candles flickered throughout the newly redecorated house, illuminating bouquets of flowers tied with long curling ribbon secured to the banister and resting on tables. In the parlor, a string quartet played softly. The feeling in the home seemed magical and dreamy, like something out of a play. Even her old gown of silk and taffeta, with its embroidered stomacher and flowing cerulean skirts, appeared revitalized and beautiful. She'd been relieved when the dress fit upon her matronly figure after birthing the baby a mere two months previous.

Nathaniel caught her attention with a tilt of his head and wave of his hand. "Do you know all of these people?"

"On Twelfth Night, everyone is invited. I hope we don't run out of the rum punch and egg nog."

"Would you care for a cup of either, before such a tragic event occurs?" He winked at her, an impish grin teasing her. "I'm happy to oblige, if so."

"No, but thank you. My hands are already full." She tucked the light blanket around her son's sleeping face.

"I imagine they will remain so until your child is grown." He stepped closer to her as guests pushed behind him on their way to the virtually groaning table of refreshments. "It appears the party is just beginning."

"Yes, it should last for several days as long as the food and drink hold out."

Nathaniel towered over her petite frame, a giant dressed in fine clothes. She lifted her chin, despite her unease, and studied the stranger's scarred yet striking features. His luxurious chestnut brown hair, shot through with gold, tempted her touch, but she resisted the urge. His earlier brief conversation with Benjamin, her sister's new husband, revealed he had fought in the state militia. He had come to town at Benjamin's express invitation. What kind of business could he possibly have with the major? And, more urgent, why did he need to stand so close?

His steel gray eyes searched her face, his gaze flitting from mouth to nose and finally resting upon her eyes. "Unfortunately, I don't expect to stay for the duration."

"You'll miss the celebration of the end of the holidays." She drew a slow, unsteady breath as he continued to study her with the ghost of a smile. She lowered her eyes, smoothing the baby blanket as an excuse for looking away.

"I'll miss more than that, I imagine." He lifted the edge of Jim's blanket, peered at the sleeping infant before he speared her with his black-rimmed eyes. "He has your nose."

She giggled, then sobered, annoyed with her school girl reaction to the man. What was it about him that provoked such a reflex? She pressed her lips together but a smile forced its way through. "Perhaps he should give it back to me, do you suppose?"

Nathaniel's smile widened to reveal his teeth. "Mayhap you can share it."

Laughter bubbled out of her mouth and she quickly stopped it. "That would prove unsatisfactory."

He chuckled, eyes twinkling. He glanced away and then back. "Looks like we're about to have some company."

Evelyn followed his gaze. Her sister Amy and Benjamin led the others to where Evelyn stood with Nathaniel by the cold fireplace, its firebox laid with kindling and tinder for